Oceans of Love

II

A Twentieth Century Love Story
Of Ruth, the Love of My Life, and I

Gilbert R. Smith

GILBERT R. SMITH

PAGE PUBLISHING, INC.
New York, NY

First originally published by Page Publishing, Inc. 2017

ISBN 978-1-63568-333-2 (Paperback)
ISBN 978-1-63568-334-9 (Digital)

Printed in the United States of America

This story is dedicated to
my two marvelous children,
Tom and Judy;
my terrific grandsons,
Ruhley and Chase;
my good son-in-law Frank
and in memory of
my wonderful wife, Ruth,
and her twin sister, Ann.

Acknowledgments

The author wished to acknowledge the editing assistance
of the Page Publishing Inc. editorial staff.

Contents

My Life and Ruth's Life
Were Not at All Typical

I t was a very warm, typical mid-August day in 1931 for the city of Baltimore, Maryland, when Effie Moore unexpectedly gave birth to identical twin girls. She had no clue, no idea that she was carrying twins. They were six minutes apart, and it was a harrowing experience for her. It was a double breech birth, and they were both full term! She claimed that she barely survived the experience. At that time, there was no way to predict the characteristics of an unborn child.

In those days, twins were so rare and unusual that they were the talk of the hospital. In fact, they were the first set of twins born at that hospital in ten years! Just about everyone that worked at the hospital came by to see them. This event was almost newsworthy!

The Moore twins were given the names Ann and Ruth. The parents, Effie and John Moore, were justly proud of their new offspring. Or should that be offsprings? Twins! What do you do with twins? Well, you work twice as hard, and you spend twice as much money! And oh yes, you spend twice as much time attending to them! On the upside, they are twice the pleasure. On the downside, they are twice the trouble and worry.

Personally, I had no idea what a profound effect these twin girls were to have on my life. It was nearly sixteen years later that I met them. The Moore twins lived in the western side of the town in a two-story row house. I lived in the south-central, downtown area in a fourth-floor walk-up. Baltimore is relatively large, and as children and youths, our paths never crossed.

This story is an account of the never-ending romance and great love between my wife, Ruth, and I, as seen through my eyes. Before we met, we were wandering through life unaware of the existence of the other. I suppose that, in general, this is typical of people. However, my life and Ruth's life were not at all typical. I was not your typical guy, and she was not your typical girl. Ruth was an identical twin. In that, she was not the average person. My reaction to the fact that she was a twin was not the usual "negative." This set me apart from the average person. The average person has serious difficulty in dealing with the idiosyncrasies of twins. Because Ruth was a twin, this story is also a treatise on the subject of twins.

Ruth was unique. She was a most extraordinary person. She exuded love. She loved life, people, nature, and music. In addition to being blessed with beauty, she had a cheerful, outgoing, adventurous, and upbeat personality.

Before she passed away, I was married to Ruth for forty-eight years, and at that time, I had known her for fifty-eight years. Ruth was one of those rare people that was made of love. Her love of life and people was boundless. Ruth and I loved each other deeply. We were always trying to make each other's life better and trying to be sensitive to each other's needs. It has been said that if you have love and happiness, your other needs will come easily. My life with my wife has been a story of chapter after chapter of unfolding love.

Memories of past moments, occasions, or time periods are sometimes tainted with inaccuracies that are common to the human mind. On this subject, there is the *experiencing self* and the *remembering self*. The remembering self is always subject to some degree of error or bias, be it large or small. For example, if an otherwise good marriage of twenty years ended in divorce in the last year, we tend to remember the marriage in the context of the last bad year rather than the good nineteen years.

Storytelling is our natural response to remembering. We remember significant changes or milestones more vividly than the commonplace events of our everyday lives. There are many facets of my life and Ruth's life that are an uncommon departure from the usual, and this is the incentive for writing this book.

In life, controversy seems unavoidable. Controversy occurs when different or opposing cultures or ideas collide. It is how we deal with and with whom we deal with controversy that is important. With reference to controversial issues, it is my desire to present the facts in a manner that is as uncontroversial as possible. You, the reader, can only measure my success at this.

The circumstances of the moments that I have recalled on these pages are just a few of many that I consider as important, significant or interesting. I can only describe the reality of the moments that I have recalled with the editorial viewpoint of an individual that was deeply involved. There is very little, if any, fiction in what I have written. We inescapably suffer from short perspective if we write only a few years after the events have occurred. I feel that it has been more advantageous to chronicle these events quite a while after the fact. This provides us with a sort of filter on the emotions of the immediate happenings and thus renders a view with a long-term, in-depth perception.

Everyone's life is unique. The daily life of anyone in any given century is unlike that of any other century. I didn't fully realize this when I was very young. We all seem to be directly observing and participating in life from inside our own body and brain. The five physical senses appear to dominate our experience of life. And yet, we have mental feelings and emotions that transcend the physical senses and, in fact, provide guidance for us in our daily life. We may call this sixth sense, but I prefer to call it intuition or being spiritually aware. None of us are exempt from this. The soul is the reality of our being and existence.

I am happy that you are reading this book. Very few pleasures can match the enjoyment readers feel when they are immersed in a story about bygone times and places. This is a type of travel accessible only through the written page. For the very young readers, this is a tale from an era that you never knew, and perhaps you may find it difficult to grasp the full meaning of some of the subject matter. To this end, I have strived to describe the circumstances leading up to the occasions and incidents included in these chapters.

Gilbert Ruley Smith
Lutherville, Maryland
June 2015

A New Life Begins for Little Anna

In the genealogy of Ruth and Ann's family, it is retrospectively evident that the Felger family of the late nineteenth and early twentieth centuries had a significant effect on the twins' lives and my life. This effect would not become apparent to me for decades after I met them.

In the late 1860s, Anna Felger, the twins' grandmother on their mother's side, was a small child living happily with her five siblings in a modest home in Baltimore. Catastrophe struck when her mother fell seriously ill and passed away.

Her grief-stricken father was left with the impossible task of raising his children and earning a living. He could not stay home and keep his job. Two of his oldest children were still in school but old enough to be on their own at home and take care of the family meals and housekeeping for him. However, he couldn't afford day care for his younger children. For a parent in the dire circumstances of that situation in that day and age, it was common to ask the favor of relatives, friends, or neighbors to take one of your children into their home and raise them.

The Ringsdorf family was a nearby neighbor of the Felger family. They agreed to take little Anna into their home and raise her. Mr. Ringsdorf owned a local lumberyard and could easily afford the expense of another child. The Ringsdorfs had three children of their own two boys and a girl. And so, a new life began for little Anna in the Ringsdorf household. There was never any formal paperwork or legal arrangement for this situation. It was all done with a handshake and in total friendship and kindheartedness. Anna's young sisters and brothers were likewise placed in the homes of other friends and neighbors.

Since they lived in the same neighborhood, Anna could often visit her family, but she didn't eat her meals there or sleep there. Logically, a majority of her time was spent in the Ringsdorf household. Fortunately, Anna got along very well with the three Ringsdorf children, and they essentially became her foster brothers and sister.

Anna's experience of close familiarity with the Ringsdorf family would turn out to be very important in the future to the happiness of her granddaughter Ruth and me. Anna would never be aware of this important effect of her growing-up experience. One of the Ringsdorf boys was named Millard. He became fond of his foster sister Anna's daughter Effie, the mother of the twins Ruth and Ann. Thus, he often visited Ruth and Ann's house. This was one of the keys to the future of Ruth and me.

Anna's older brother Charlie Felger was another important person in our lives. Charlie's friendship with his niece Effie would later be significant in our lives.

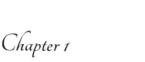
Chapter 1

The Parents of the Twins

Effie's Mother Was Anna Felger

The twin's father, John Moore, was born in Philadelphia in the latter part of the nineteenth century. John's father passed away when he was five years old, leaving his mother as a single parent with the daunting task of raising him and his two sisters. Unfortunately, a few years later, his mother passed away, and he and his two sisters became orphans. Fortunately, John's aunt Rick, his mother's sister who lived in Baltimore, took it on herself to raise him. The fate of his two sisters is unknown.

In world history, it seems that somewhere, at any given point in time, there was turmoil. In the second decade of the twentieth century, when John was a young man, the United States entered World War I. John was drafted into the army. World War I was a war of foot soldiers in the trenches. He soon found himself fighting on the front lines in France. As a result, he was disabled with shell shock and was sent back to the United States for rehabilitation. In a short while, he was released from the hospital and discharged as a disabled veteran. He returned to civilian life with no apparent problems.

John was mechanically inclined and managed to get a good job as a machinist at the Naval Gun Factory in Washington, DC. He commuted daily between Baltimore and Washington by car with several other Gun Factory employees

John had a quiet and laidback personality. He was quite socially active as a young person. In 1922, he met and married the love of his life, Effie Norris. Effie was also born in the latter part of the nineteenth century. Effie's mother was Anna Felger. Effie had an older sister and a younger brother. Effie and John's first home was an apartment in west Baltimore. A couple of years later, they purchased their first home, a typical western Baltimore middle-income town house, or row house, as it was locally described. The houses in the neighborhood were very nice and had all the latest amenities. The street was lined with trees, and there was a small grass plot in the front and back of each house. Also, each house had a large roofed front porch.

For whatever reason, John and Effie did not immediately have any children. In 1931, Effie gave birth to identical twin girls. They named them Ruth and Ann. Ruth was Effie's middle name, and Ann was named after her grandmother Anna. John and Effie realized that they needed help in raising and caring for their twin little girls. Fortunately, they were able to find a very nice lady named Susie to act as a non-live-in nanny and help feed and care for the babies. John was making a good salary and could easily afford to provide for double everything and pay for Susie.

It was in this quality environment that the twins lived as they advanced from babies to toddlers to young children. Neighbors, friends, and relatives visited them often because the event of twins was a rare thing.

Given that we are now in the twenty-first century, the fact that John and Effie were born in the late nineteenth century gives one the false impression that they must be very old. This is not really true. They were about ten years older than the average young couple of that day and age, but this does not make them ancient!

My parents were born in the early twentieth century in that optimistic era before World War I. For those years near or in the middle of a century, it is common for parents, children, and grandchildren to be born in the same century. Logically, this will not happen for those born near or at the end of a century.

Chapter 2

The Early Life of Ruth and Ann

The Twins Liked Nature

The bond between identical twins begins in the womb. For nine months, you are in intimate contact with your twin. Following birth and until you begin to crawl, your twin is nearly always by your side. You share all the necessary baby activities of sleeping, eating, bathing, and entertainment. In this manner, Ruth began her life with her twin, Ann. As toddlers, the twins always had a playmate, namely, each other. Through all their daily activity, they were never alone.

As little girls, Ruth and Ann were very happy because they were identical twins. They shared living their life, side by side. Their likes and dislikes were the same, and they were always together for everything they did and wherever they went. There is a natural, inherent bond between identical twins, and this is reinforced as they share their life together. As identical twins, they liked the same food, toys, clothing, environment, activities, and entertainment.

The twins liked nature in the form of grass, trees, flowers and vistas such as lakes, ponds, hills, and mountains. They also had a deep love for birds and animals. There was always a bright-yellow canary in a cage in their house. They both loved dogs, but their mother didn't, and so, there were no pets in the house. There was individuality expressed here in the fact that Ann loved horses and Ruth didn't. Ruth liked ducks, swans, geese, owls, rabbits, and elephants. Ann tolerated these birds and animals because Ruth liked them. However, Ruth couldn't tolerate any close contact with horses.

The twins' love of nature was expressed in their flower garden hobby of landscaping. As little girls, they spent many hours tending to the very small flower gardens in the front and back of their house. The small grass plots were always well manicured, and the flowerbeds were free of weeds and well watered. Neighbors were always complimenting them on the appearance of their property.

At a very early age, Ruth became aware that her twin sister, Ann, was letting her make most of the decisions in their daily life together. In other words, Ann was dependent on her. This was the first hint that the twins' personalities were different. It was a fact that Ruth was an extrovert with an outgoing personality, and Ann was an introvert who, in general, would rather not talk to people. From this, it seems only natural that Ann would look to her twin for guidance.

As a child, Ruth would attempt to get Ann to take the initiative by asking her to make a decision concerning what doll or what toy to play with. Ann, in typical twin manner, simply replied, "Oh, I'll like anything you choose!" Then, in typical twin manner, Ruth would reply, "Well, I'll like anything you choose!" Here we have a typical twin standoff! It takes a minute or two of iteration for this to resolve, and finally one of them breaks down and makes a decision. Conversations such as this are common with twins and continue on a daily basis for the rest of their lives. As a result of the inherent personality difference, Ann usually backed down and accepted Ruth's decisions.

As young children, the twins began to display a speech problem in the form of stuttering. Ann's problem was worse than Ruth's. This problem continued into their adult years. The cause of this malady is perhaps unknown. Some say that it is genetic, and others cite neurophysiology or language processing in the brain. For whatever reason, Ruth and Ann had it.

Stuttering causes a hesitation in the beginning of a sentence or phrase plus hesitation throughout the speech. During the hesitation, air comes out of the mouth with no words. The first phrase or sentence of a conversation was generally the biggest problem. After that, a sentence or two would come out just fine, but then, the next sentence would cause them problems.

The wisest modern speech therapists don't aim to cure stuttering in adults. Instead, they help patients stutter easily and openly without the breathless struggle. For her moments of hesitation, Ann found that if she substituted the word *anyhow*, words came more easily for her. Consequently, there were many *anyhows* in Ann's speech. Ruth never used the word because she didn't need to, as her speech problem was not nearly as bad as Ann's.

In their adolescent and teenage years, Ruth and Ann continued to have a stuttering problem. As part of this speech problem, they had difficulty pronouncing complicated words, and they would generate their own, unique version of the word. You would often hear some rather amusing words and sentences coming from Ruth and Ann. For instance, the game of badminton was pronounced, "badmington." The meat pastrami was pronounced "pastronomy."

Unfortunately, all this reinforced Ann's inward nature. This caused her to be shy and in a constant state of mild depression. Her twin sister, Ruth, was her shining star and mentor. She relied on Ruth for just about everything. She was happiest when engaged in some activity with Ruth, and this was most of the time.

As a result of her outgoing personality, Ruth often laughed at her own stuttering followed by a comment such as "That, um, didn't come out very good, did it?" Three cheers for Ruth for looking at the bright side of things! As an introvert, poor Ann was always embarrassed or ashamed of her stuttering. It is not surprising that she disliked talking on the telephone or talking to strangers. In contrast Ruth, as an extrovert, was outgoing, curious, inquisitive, and adventurous. Ann had none of these characteristics.

As young children, middle-income family life was good for the twins. There were several other girls near their age in the neighborhood. However, for whatever reason, there were no boys. This imbalance had a significant effect on their lives in that they gained no experience in playing with and interfacing with boys. Bear in mind that the twins always had each other to play with. Thus, the need for playmates was not as high a priority as it was for the average family with children.

The twins' parents never owned a car. Even in the 1930s and '40s, this was unusual. A majority of people and families owned a car and enjoyed the convenience of having a vehicle to use as transportation to and from stores, to visit friends' and relatives' homes, or to travel to attractive destinations. The lack of this nicety made a lasting impression on Ruth and Ann. There were many occasions when the twins sat on their front porch and sadly watched their neighbors and children happily pile into their car and go off on a trip or vacation. Then, when they returned, they listened to them joyfully describe the wonderful places that they visited.

Ruth and Ann accepted their fate and were happy in the confines of their modest home and small grounds. This did not, however, fill the void they felt at being deprived of the convenience and pleasure of having a car.

Birthdays for the twins were always a big occasion. In their day and age, twins were unusual, and the occasion of two children celebrating the same birthday drew a lot of attention and fanfare. They grew up realizing that they were special people, which reinforced their happiness at being twins.

The seasonal holidays were celebrated in their home with gusto. Their mother, Effie, filled the house with appropriate decorations for each holiday. She was also a fervent house cleaner, and everything was always in place, neat, and clean. In addition, she was a good cook, and her kitchen was well used in the preparation of sumptuous meals.

At the age of five, the twins started attending elementary school. Attending school and doing homework was much less of a chore for the twins than it was for the average nontwin student. The twins attended the same classes together, had the same homework assignments, and did their homework together every night. They got the same or similar grades in their tests and made the same mistakes. Teachers were always accusing them of cheating. The school separated them in different classrooms, but they still got the same grades and made the same mistakes! Twins always do this! This was logical and was a result of the fact that they did their homework together.

The twins were leading an idyllic, pleasant, middle-income life. As twins, their life was one of being focused on each other and expressing "twin love" for each other. There were never any arguments or disagreements between them, as is common for the usual siblings growing up.

Somewhere between the ages of five to ten, it became evident that Ann possessed an artistic talent. She found great pleasure in pencil sketching and watercolor painting. This was extended to include painting whatever needed painting with a can of paint and a brush. As a young person, she was a talented house painter. She was content and happy whenever she was painting anything.

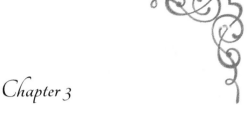

Chapter 3

Crisis

The Life of the Twins Was Steeped in Poverty

When the twins were seven years old, disaster struck. Their father regressed into his shell-shocked state. He was sent to a nearby military veterans hospital for treatment. The prognosis was not good. The doctors stated that it would likely take years to return him to normal. This meant that, for all practical purposes, Effie lost her husband, and Ruth and Ann lost their dad. The small stipend that Effie received from the government was totally inadequate to support a household with a family of three. Fortunately, the house was paid for, and she could stay there. But she needed money for food and utilities.

The United States was still in the process of recovering from the Great Depression of 1929. The economy was not good. Jobs were scarce. Effie had no trade or experience in the working field. She couldn't go to work and earn enough money to pay a babysitter and have anything left for food and utilities. She had to stay home and raise her little daughters. She was in a dire financial circumstance. She solved her problem by renting the second-floor bedrooms of her house.

Unfortunately, this meant that she lost the use of the only bathroom in the house. This was a very serious handicap in their living conditions. Effie and her twins had to live on the first floor of the house.

Their house was arranged with the front door leading into the living room, where the stairway to the second floor was located. To accommodate the person who rented, Effie had to give them a key to the front door of her house. The living room and stairway became public space.

A wide archway separated the living room and dining room. For privacy, Effie had a thin temporary partition with a door installed in the archway between the living room and the dining room on the first floor. The dining room table was removed and stored in the basement. A double bed and a sofa bed were placed in the dining room. This was their bedroom. One of the twins slept on the sofa bed, and the other slept with their mother in the double bed.

Effie and her twins lived only in the dining room and kitchen of the house. There was a toilet in the basement for them to use. The kitchen table was the only table, so they had to use it for everything. This was the way they had to live. It is difficult to imagine what it was like to live this way. Their quality of life was definitely not the best. John's illness plunged his family into virtual poverty.

At first, the young twins thought that this big change was neat and fun. Children always like something different. As the days went by, they began to realize that this change was not so nice after all. They missed having their own bedroom and having the use of the bathroom. They also missed having their nice house to run around in and play.

The basement of the house was dark and dank with stone walls. Light was provided by two pull-chain lightbulbs and a little bit of daylight came through two small windows in the front and rear. The furnace and the coal bin occupied half of the basement. As individuals, Ruth and Ann were afraid to go down there alone to use the toilet. So they always went there together. Ann was always the braver of the two. As a result of this situation, the twins developed a firm dislike of basements. Throughout the rest of their lives, they disliked going down into a basement.

In early twentieth century manner, Effie washed their clothes and bedsheets by hand on a washboard in the utility sink in the basement and wrung them out with a hand wringer. The wet clothes were either hung on a wire in the basement to dry or outside on the backyard clothesline to dry in good weather. Without a bathtub or shower, I don't know how they managed to keep themselves clean. While the twins were still little, their mother bathed them in a large, galvanized tub in the kitchen. After that, they said that they took a "sponge bath."

Effie had to learn to tend to the furnace in the winter to keep the house warm and to see that coal was delivered on a regular basis. They didn't have an electric refrigerator in the kitchen; they had an old-fashioned icebox. Effie also had to see that ice was delivered regularly. These were part of the expenses that she had to meet.

With only two rooms and a basement to live in, there was no privacy. This restriction naturally caused the twins to become cranky and disobedient. Their mother, as a single parent, could not afford to tolerate misbehaving children, so the twins often felt the sting of their mother's hairbrush on their backsides. The twins learned that life had taken a turn for the worse for them. Their outside play area was limited to the front porch or the front and back lawn. Their only pleasure was tending to the outside lawn and flowerbeds. The cold, dark winter months were miserable for the twins because they couldn't play outdoors.

Effie knew how to play the piano, and there was an upright piano in the living room. Effie managed to get a really low rate on lessons for Ruth and Ann from a piano teacher that was a close friend of hers. This was the only luxury that she could afford for them. The twins had to practice on the piano whenever the person who rented the second floor was not home. These lessons continued into their teenage years.

In this period of time, the life of Ruth and Ann was steeped in poverty and in substandard living conditions. Their mother had very little money to spare. There were no amenities or luxuries. Without a car, all travel was done using the city trolleys or buses. Effie had to take her little girls with her whenever she went shopping. The local grocery store was six blocks away. Ruth and Ann vividly remember carrying heavy bags of groceries back home from the store.

As a result of the lack of money, the twins' birthday and all the major holidays were not the same. Effie had to use the decorations left over from previous years to decorate the house for these holidays. Their Christmas tree was very small, and there were only a few presents for the twins. Effie tried to teach her girls to take special care of their belongings so that they would last as long as possible. She knew how to sew and used her sewing machine extensively to mend old and tattered clothing. This period of austerity made a lasting impression on Ruth and Ann. They learned to fully appreciate the things that they had and to not be wasteful. However, this did not lessen their desire for things of quality and beauty.

About once a month, Effie took her twins to visit her mother and father by trolley. The twins looked forward to this with great joy because it was an occasion to get out of their cramped living quarters and visit their grandparents. The twin's father was an orphan, and there were no grandparents on his side. His local area relatives were limited to his uncles and aunts and their offspring. Unfortunately, their father's relatives did not visit the twins very often. Also, Effie's sister and brother didn't visit them very often, which seemed to please Effie! As twins, in their later years, Ruth and Ann couldn't understand why their mother really didn't like her sister and brother. They couldn't comprehend the fact that this was normal in the nontwin world!

Every Sunday, weather permitting, Effie dressed her twins in nice clothes and walked them to church. Sunday school was no stranger to the twins. Ann and Ruth looked forward to Sunday, for both the social aspect and the religious aspect. It is difficult to separate these finer aspects from the fact that Ann and Ruth would go anywhere at any time just to get out of their house!

Whenever she could afford it, Effie took the twins to a movie theater. It would be several years before the twins became old enough to let them go without her. Entertainment was limited to the movies, radio, and records. There was only one small radio in their house and an old fashioned wind-up record player console. They didn't have very many records because they were too expensive.

The twin's father, John, had an aunt and uncle that were very wealthy as they owned a local laundry. The aunt's name was Cora, and she was fond of Effie and her twin daughters. Even so, she did not visit them very often. When she heard of Effie's plight and poverty, she offered to help. She didn't offer help in the form of money or cash. Instead, she provided a kind service to them in the form of free transportation and companionship for them.

Approximately every other weekend, Cora came to their house in her chauffer-driven limousine and took them to an expensive restaurant and paid for the meal. After that, she took them anywhere they wanted to go. Usually, Effie chose to go to the food markets in downtown Baltimore. In those days, the local grocery store was small with a limited stock and was usually a house with the first floor converted into a store. The large downtown food markets provided a much greater variety and quantity of food. In addition, the food would be placed in the trunk of the limousine and thereby delivered to Effie's house.

At Christmastime, Cora took Effie, Ruth, and Ann to the downtown department stores and generously bought new clothes, hats, and shoes for the twins. Effie refused to let her buy clothes for her. Ruth and Ann were delighted with these occasions with Cora, but all too soon, they had to return to their home and a life of poverty, living in two rooms with no bathroom.

To present a view of life in those days, radios had tubes that became very hot when in use. Parents forbade listening to the radio while doing school homework. The twins found that they couldn't cheat by listening to the radio while doing homework because their mother, Effie, would always come and feel the radio to see if it was hot!

Around the age of seven or eight, Ann became infatuated with listening to Nelson Eddy sing on the radio. She persuaded her mother to buy Nelson Eddy records for her and began listening to them on the record player. She would play them over and over again.

Ruth became disenchanted with hearing them and would go to the place farthest away In the house to avoid hearing them. This was a small example of individuality expressed by a twin. Throughout their life, it was always Ruth that expressed individuality and left her twin behind in pursuit of some endeavor.

Fastidious is the best word to describe the twins' mother, Effie. Everything in her house had to be clean and in its proper place. Housecleaning in some form was performed every day. Beds were made every morning. She has been known to delay supper until she finished washing all the pots and pans she used in preparing the meal. She even dusted the rafters in the basement ceiling! Some of these characteristics were inherent in the twins, but they were not nearly as fastidious as their mother.

Chapter 4

Return to Normal

He Returned to a Household of Matriarchy

The twins and their mother lived under these highly undesirable living conditions for three years, at which time their father was finally released from the hospital and returned to home. Three years for children at the age of seven to ten years old seemed like an eternity. It made a lasting, indelible, negative impression on them. Yes, they suffered through these years.

The second-floor boarder was cooperative and moved out on the day that John returned. The family was happily united again. John helped in moving the furniture back to normal and returning all their clothing and belongings to the second floor. Effie and the twins were extremely happy to have the use of the bathroom and their bedrooms again.

Their father returned to a household of matriarchy. His wife and two young daughters had become accustomed to living in an all-female household with all the advantages and freedom of attire thereof. There was now a man in the house! Effie had no trouble in making adjustment to the return of her husband, but Ruth and Ann had difficulty in the adjustment to the male presence of their father. For whatever reason, Ann seemed to have the most trouble with this. This strange, detrimental characteristic of Ann followed her throughout her life.

Both their father and the twins had been robbed of three years of growing up with one another. This relatively short void in their lives had a lasting effect on the twins. Their father was almost a stranger to them. Not having a father figure for three years in their childhood somehow made the twins unfamiliar with the male sex in general. In my opinion, they did not know how to treat a man and had no idea what made him tick.

Fortunately, John was able to get his old job back as a machinist at the Naval Gun Factory. He made a good salary, and the family was able to return to the good middle-income life.

Effie now had two preadolescent daughters to help her with the household chores. As a result, nothing was ever missing or left undone. The twins liked helping with chores around the house, and this characteristic remained with them for the rest of their life. They didn't understand or appreciate the fact that there were two of them, and they got their jobs done twice as fast! This mind-set is typical of twins.

Two years later, after the twins went through puberty, it became evident to John that he needed his own bathroom facility. To this end, a shower stall and sink were installed in the basement of the house. John and his ladies were very happy with this new arrangement.

Since the fourth or fifth grade and on into junior high school, there was a young boy named Edwin who lived near the twins' house and was in the same grade and often in the same class. Ed liked Ruth a lot and was very vocal in exclaiming that she was his girlfriend. However, this was not a two-way street. Ruth didn't dislike him; she just didn't consider him her boyfriend. This did not discourage Ed. She was his girlfriend, and that was that. Ed was a tall, dark, and handsome boy. For whatever strange reason, he did not date Ruth like the usual guy. He never came to her house or invited her to come to his house.

At the age of fourteen, Ruth and Ann had blossomed into very pretty young ladies. All through school, they were the only twins in their school, and as such, they stood out, were very well-known, and were often featured in the school paper. On a small local scale, the twins were celebrities. They became accustomed to their obvious notoriety.

As a result of the time and place, the twins' popularity did not bring about the usual abundance of boys seeking to date them. The fact that they attended an all-girl school contributed to this situation. For whatever reason, just about no one asked either one of them for a date, not even Ed, Ruth's "boyfriend" from school. Ruth and Ann did not have any problem with this lack-of-boyfriends circumstance because they were twins. They had each other and were happy with each other. This significantly contributed to their ongoing relative isolation from the nontwin world and resultant naïveté and lack of experience thereof. The twins always walked together wherever they went, even to the restroom. Unknown to them, this made it awkward for a teenage boy to walk up to them and attempt to talk to just one of them.

Chapter 5

My Early Years

My Mother and Her Siblings Were Musically Inclined

My grandfather on my mother's side of the family was born in Germany. He lost his parents at a very young age and was sent to an orphanage. Fortunately for him, his mother's sister, his aunt who lived in Baltimore, heard about this and made arrangements to send for him. She paid the fare for his ocean trip to America and raised him herself. When he became of age, he met and married my grandmother, who was Pennsylvania Dutch. My mother was one of their six children.

My grandparents on my father's side were born and raised in the farm country of the northern eastern shore of the Chesapeake Bay. My grandfather was a farmer and a carpenter. When he married my grandmother, he built a house for them to live in.

My father followed his father in being a farmer and carpenter. He had one brother and sister. For whatever reason, he was not close to either of his siblings. They never seriously argued or fought with one another; they were just not close.

When my father reached the age of twenty-five, he developed a yearning for the big city and came to Baltimore. He had no trouble in finding a job as a carpenter. It wasn't long before he met my mother. They were married in 1927.

Christmas of 1928 was an emotional time for my parents. I missed Christmas that year. I was born in the hospital on December 26. My parents had been married for a year and a half and were proud and happy to have a healthy baby boy. For reasons unknown to me, my parents did not have any more children. Normally, this would mean that I became a spoiled brat. I am proud to say that this did not happen to me.

We lived in the western part of the city on Mosher Street in the neighborhood called Goose Hill. Obviously, there was an abundance of geese in the area. The houses in the area were low income but had all city utilities, such as electricity, water, and sewage. We were well within the city limits, but in those days in that area, it was normal for everyone to raise poultry and grow vegetables on their property. Everyone had a fairly large backyard that was essentially a truck farm.

Also, all unclaimed vacant property in the immediate neighborhood became the temporary, informal property of the first person to claim it for their own. So vacant lots became small farmlands. Additionally, all kinds of poultry and small farm animals were kept in wooden sheds in the backyard. We had a little bit of the country right there in the city.

In the cities of the 1930s, pigeons were often kept as pets in coops located either on the roofs of houses or on a large wooden shelf supported outside of an upper story window. In my neighborhood, the cooing of pigeons was a constant background sound. I remember hearing it all the time.

For the first four or five years of my life, I lived in the house next door to my mother's parents. My grandparents were the next-door neighbors. Grandfather Cook worked in a carpet factory. Grandmother Cook was the housewife, the backbone of the family. She did everything. My mother's two younger sisters still lived at home. Her older sister and two older brothers were away and married. I was not the only grandchild, but I remember that Grandmother

Cook always treated me as if I were. Every time that I walked into her house, she hugged me and kissed me as if she hadn't seen me for a long time. In addition, she showered me with sweets, desserts, and goodies. I was the recipient of this attention quite often as I lived next door.

Grandmother Cook raised chickens and grew a variety of vegetables in her backyard. In addition, she had a large grape arbor that provided the sweetest grapes that I have ever tasted. I wouldn't doubt that she provided some meals for my parents and me since we lived next door.

My mother and all her siblings were musically inclined and accomplished musicians. They all played the piano and violin and sang. Grandfather Cook played the trumpet. There was an upright piano in the front room, or parlor, of my grandparents' house, and almost every evening after supper, there was an informal concert. One of my mother's brothers and his wife and her older sister and husband often visited in the evening and joined in the concert. They played and sang the popular songs of the twenties and thirties.

Many neighbors would gather on the front lawn to listen. I seemed to be the only child in this gathering, and my mother would put me on the front porch with some toys, and there I stayed, listening as beautiful music filled the air. Perhaps it is genetic, but this furthered my lifelong love of music, singing, and dancing. One of my mother's brothers went on to become director of the Baltimore Symphony. Later, two of my cousins became accomplished musicians.

It was the time of the Great Depression. The Depression was a universal tragedy that affected everyone. No one had any money to speak of. My father, a carpenter and handyman, managed to support his family on just seven dollars a week. Think about that, seven dollars a week! During those awful years, we always had a roof over our head and food on the table. For this, I give my father a great deal of credit. He was not alone. Every husband and father in those years faced the same impossible situation. Some poor souls had to beg for food and shelter.

The infamous bread lines of those times were a harsh reality. The trade-and-barter system was a part of life in those days. Often, my father would bring home a chicken or turkey as part of his pay for his day's work. There was one outstanding benefit from the hard times of this era. It reduced everyone to the same level and brought everyone together to fight the common battle for survival. The brotherhood of man was brought to the surface, and neighbors helped neighbors with just about everything. In that respect, it was a good period of time.

My mother was a telephone operator. For whatever reason, her job was not steady, but she managed to stay employed for most of the time. Her income helped support the family. When my mother worked, I have no idea who supplied the day care for me as an infant and child. I assume that it was my grandparents.

My first home had a furnace and radiator heat, electricity, city water, and sewage, but that is where the amenities ended. The plumbing was all in one place. The bathroom and kitchen were combined in one room in the rear of the first floor. The kitchen sink served as the bathroom sink. A four-legged bathtub sat on one side of the kitchen and the toilet sat in one corner. There was very little privacy! Some neighbors had a temporary standing, fold-up partition or a sheet on a wire to provide a small measure of bathroom privacy, but most didn't have anything.

This lack of bathroom privacy was influential in the establishment of the unique neighborhood culture reflected in the personal hygiene habits and personality of the children that were under school age. There was no modesty among them.

As soon as we were walking and out of diapers, we were sent outside to play. In those days, mothers put their children outdoors to play in the morning and never worried about or thought about them again until lunchtime. Crime was just about unheard of in those days. Boys and girls played together every day on the outside lawns, sidewalks, and the largely empty streets. The neighborhood dogs and cats ran and played alongside the children.

During the warm days of spring, summer, and early fall, hardly any of the children went indoors to use the bathroom. This meant that all of us, the boys and girls, became accustomed to seeing the anatomy of our bodies as we momentarily urinated wherever we were. Yes, this was very unsanitary, but I don't remember having any health problems related to this.

The parents in the neighborhood obviously knew all about this practice, but neither my parents nor any other parent seemed to object or be concerned about it. We apparently lived in a neighborhood that was sufficiently rural to allow this. We were not really hillbillies, but this behavior might certainly be a part of that genera.

On cold winter days, this practice ceased, and everyone went inside to use the bathroom because it was too much trouble and too cold to remove our heavy clothing. Thankfully, our parents kept us indoors on bitter-cold days.

This experience did not cause any psychological problems for me as I grew older. In fact, it was beneficial when I reached puberty. There was very little mystery about the anatomy of the opposite sex. I must add that my memory goes unusually far back in time. I remember things vividly from about one year old.

We had a pet dog, but the day soon came when my parents could no longer afford to feed and keep him. My father put the dog in our car and drove out into the neighboring farm country. He gave our dog to a farmer who said that he didn't mind an extra dog around. This was an emotional experience for me, and I was sad, but I didn't cry about it.

As time went by, my father, being a carpenter by trade, began making home improvements to our house. He installed a bathroom on the second floor. I remember sitting on the toilet upstairs and looking down to the first floor through the unfinished hole in the floor for the sewer pipe.

There was a large back porch adjacent to the kitchen in the back of the house. My father closed this in and made it a nice kitchen for my mother. The wooden planks of the porch floor had a small space between them. A large piece of linoleum covered the porch floor, which was now our kitchen floor. Bearing in mind that the porch floor was totally outdoors, it was not surprising that, when the wind blew hard, it would raise the linoleum up off the floor. To correct this, my father proceeded to pile a mound of dirt around the lower perimeter of the porch. I had a small shovel, and I helped my father with this task. Unfortunately, I often lost my shovel under the porch, and my patient father had to crawl in and retrieve it for me.

There was a little girl my age in the neighborhood named Helen who liked me a lot and was always kissing me. For me, at that age, she was a nuisance, and I was always trying to avoid her.

There was a very large empty lot across the street from our row of houses. Every year, the Ringling Brothers Circus would come to Baltimore and set up their tents on this vacant lot. What a good deal! The circus was across the street! I remember riding on the Ferris wheel and trying to touch the sky when we reached the top!

In the 1930s, the winters were bitter cold. Ice was occasionally two inches thick everywhere, and I often watched people ice-skate on our front street. My father knew how to skate and frequently joined them. He bought me a pair of learner skates and taught me how to skate at a very young age.

The railroad tracks were only a couple of blocks from our house. The trains were very noisy, especially at night. My mother was aware that the train sounds frightened me. Her solution to this problem was to take me to the railroad tracks and wait for a train to come by. It came by with all its huffing and puffing and clanking, hissing and roaring, and the engineer blew his whistle for us. That cured me. I was never afraid of a train again. I became accustomed to hearing train whistles, and even today I get misty-eyed whenever I hear a train whistle.

When I was about five years old, the economy had improved a little, and we moved to a third-floor-apartment house near the downtown area. I never knew why we moved away. Perhaps my father wanted to get away from his in-laws! I started first grade that year in a nearby religious private school. The private school was good, and I had good grades, but I was missing the social and cultural experience of public school.

Two years later, I transferred to one of the nearby public elementary schools. It was here that I learned about bullies. On a relative scale, I was a quiet child. This naturally attracted bullies. Many times I was attacked and often wounded by them in the schoolyard. Sometimes I was hurt badly and bleeding. When that happened, the school called my mother and told her to come and get me. I assume that the school didn't have a nurse to take care of this. My mother lovingly took care of me through these relatively trying times. I learned that the bullies got their pleasure in hearing their victim's scream and cry. So I stopped screaming and crying, and they eventually left me alone. It pays to use your head!

Chapter 6

The Smith Family
Grandparents Home

The Bedrooms Had a Chamber Pot

My interest in things technical and scientific began very early in my life. At seven years of age my interest in astronomy was sparked when I visited my Smith grandparents' farm. In contrast to the city, the country sky was black and seemed totally filled with sparkling stars. As I grew older, I became an amateur astronomer and spent much time looking at the stars and planets at night with my small telescope.

In my first decade, the 1930s, we often visited my father's parents' country home. I reflect on this with nostalgia. From this, I received a direct experience in the country folk life of the late nineteenth and early twentieth century. This greatly broadened my experience. The Smith home had no electricity or running water. There was, however, a telephone. There was also the usual nearby outhouse.

One potbelly stove heated the parlor on the first floor. The heated parlor was a popular place on a cold winter night! There was a twelve-inch square grate in the parlor ceiling that allowed some of the heat from the stove to slightly warm the master bedroom above. After

I was sent upstairs to bed, I always delighted in sitting on the floor next to the grate in my pajamas, feeling the warm air and watching and listening to my parents and grandparents talking below. This was a soothing experience, and I often fell asleep right there on the floor.

Night lighting was provided by kerosene lanterns. Book and newspaper reading was limited to the daylight hours. The nighttime parlor gathering consisted of people talking. The subject of conversation was strictly rural. The major subject was talk of the day's activities on the farm, such as the condition of the various vegetables growing in their fields. The garden was relatively small but large enough to provide an excess of vegetables that, when in season, my grandfather sold by the roadside in front of the house.

The condition of the farm animals was also a big subject of conversation. Much attention was given to the condition of the horses. This was logical because the horses were a critical element for plowing and wagon pulling. Other, seemingly less important topics of conversation consisted of the weather, the neighbors, national news, and everyone's general health. In retrospect, this was a good experience for me.

Each of the second-floor bedrooms had a chamber pot to use as a substitute for a trip to the outhouse in the middle of the night. Grandmother Smith faithfully emptied the chamber pots in the morning and saw that clean ones were there for the night. The beds had feather mattresses that you sank deeply into. On a cold winter night, Grandmother would heat large bricks on the kitchen stove and give each person a hot brick wrapped in a towel to keep them warm when they went up to bed. Wow, did that feel good! The bedroom drinking water jug was often frozen solid in the morning!

The kitchen was heated by a large cast-iron cook stove. The sink was large and was equipped with a hand operated pump handle to pump water from the well. There was a large wooden table with chairs in the kitchen, which also served as the dining room. Storage shelves were everywhere, and a generous supply of wood for the stove filled one corner. As a grandchild, I often had the pleasure of cleaning the pot used to mix the ingredients for the icing that topped the many cakes that grandmother baked.

Grandmother Smith worked hard every day. She prepared, served, and cleaned up three meals a day for all of us. In addition, she fed and attended all the farm animals and attended her flower garden. Also, she washed clothes and hung them out to dry. She kept a flat iron on the hot stove and used it to iron clothes. I helped her carry wood from the wood shed to the kitchen. At the right time of the year, she was busy canning vegetables and fruit and storing them in glass jars for use during the winter months.

For whatever reason, there were no cows on the farm, and I noticed that milk was delivered to the front doorstep on a regular basis just as it was in the city. I was always given the task to gather the eggs from the henhouse. I didn't mind doing this. The elusive fragrance of musty hay and straw greeted my nose as I entered the henhouse. There was always a grumpy hen or two that gave me trouble when I interrupted the privacy of sitting on her eggs! Oh well, that goes with the territory.

The farm had several cherry trees. If I visited when the cherries were ripe, I was given the task to climb the trees and gather the cherries in a bucket. I always liked this duty because I liked tree climbing, and I was free to eat as many cherries as I wanted! The trees seemed to have a special, pleasant aroma that enhanced my experience as I picked the cherries.

My dad and I liked kite flying. This was difficult to do in the city where we lived. So on a visit to the country, whenever the wind was blowing strong, my dad and I flew kites. I remember a big, seven-foot-tall kite that my dad made. It was a monstrous beauty with a long tail. We finally got it airborne and high in the sky with about a hundred feet of twine attached. Then we tied it to a stout fence post. The wind persisted all that day and all that night. When we awoke the next morning, it was still there! Later that day, the wind abated, and our kite came down and crashed in the field.

I liked playing with my toy trucks and cars outside on the lawn in front of my grandparents' house. The nearby road passed by the front of the house. There was very little traffic in those days. One car or truck would pass by in fifteen minutes or so. It was very quiet in the country. The only sounds that I heard were the birds.

As I played on the lawn, I observed that I would hear high-pitched ringing sounds coming from the overhead copper wires on the poles that lined the road about one minute before a car went by. Even though I was very young, I had learned from reading library books that this was due to the fact that sound travels better through solid objects. The sound of the distant car on the road went through the ground to the wooden poles and then to the copper wires. My mother was amazed that I was able to predict the passing of a car a minute or so before it went by!

My grandfather Smith's father, my great-grandfather, visited us one day while we were there. He was ninety years old at that time and seemed to be in good physical and mental condition. I remember having lunch and supper with him that day and talking to him. He was very interested in me because I was not only his great-grandson but the only grandchild in the Smith family. I can honestly say that I spent a whole day visiting and talking with someone who was born in 1845!

One of Grandfather Smith's sheds had a forge, bellows, and anvil that was used to shoe the horses. I was not allowed near there while he was working in there. My father said that his dad often lost his grip while hammering on a red-hot horseshoe on the anvil, and his large hammer went crashing against the shed wall! I distinctly remember hearing the hammering and the crashing followed by a few well-chosen curse words!

My grandfather allowed himself the convenience of an automobile. It was a 1925 Ford two-door sedan. One of his sheds was used as the garage for the car. He reserved his car for infrequent trips to the nearby town general store that was owned by his brother-in-law. I am sure that he received a nice discount because he was family.

Grandfather Smith was a farmer and carpenter. He built the house that he lived in. As he aged, farming and carpentry became too arduous for him, and he realized that he needed another source of income. In the 1940s, he had a small two-pump "Atlantic Gasoline" station installed at the roadside near his house. This seemed to serve his income needs nicely.

He would either sit on his front porch in nice weather or sit in his parlor by the window in bad weather and wait for the infrequent customer to pull up at his pumps and honk their horn. Then he would walk out to the pumps, serve his customer, and always strike up a long conversation with them that sometimes lasted fifteen minutes or more. Most of his customers were people that he knew. Things were very slow, casual, and informal in those days! The fast-paced twenty-first century was a long way in the future.

The Mansion and the Church

The Stairs Kept Us in Good Physical Condition

In 1935, my parents and I were living in an apartment on Eutaw Place. Through the influence of Anna Rieger, my mother's friend, we were attending a church located in downtown Baltimore. There were unusual circumstances surrounding the church that we attended. Historically, in 1924, the church purchased a large, four-story-tall nineteenth-century mansion located on Cathedral Street, across from the Mount Vernon Place Cultural Center, where Baltimore's Washington Monument was located. The mansion was built in 1824.

The church edifice was built on the rear of the mansion's property, where the gardens and stable were originally located. The mansion's massive front doors served as the entrance to the church. A classic large, four-story-tall oval-shaped mahogany stairwell was just inside of the mansion front doors. A large dome and stained-glass window was majestically located at the top of the stairwell. The large stairwell was essentially an atrium.

The church lobby consisted of the large floor area at the base of the stairwell and the large wooden-paneled room at the rear of the mansion. Two large doors were installed in the room to provide access to the church edifice. The church used the rooms on the first and second floor of the mansion for Sunday school classes, a library, and other necessary church meetings. There were many rooms on all floors of the mansion.

My parents had been attending this church for about a year when they heard that they were looking for someone to be a live-in church custodian. The country was still suffering from the Great Depression. Work or jobs were hard to come by. My father immediately applied for the job and was accepted. The church was happy that a church member would occupy this position.

This position was a deal that you couldn't refuse! The church agreed to let us live there rent-free in exchange for a lower salary for my father as custodian. In addition, we did not have to pay for electricity, gas, water, or heating. Also, we did not have to pay for any maintenance of these services. In addition to standard church custodial and cleaning duties, my father provided the church with general repair and maintenance of the church and mansion facility and infrastructure.

My parents and I were given four rooms on the third floor and all the fourth floor of the mansion as our living quarters, or apartment, making a total of fourteen rooms. Most of the rooms were large and quite adequate as living space. Since there was no elevator, we had to use the stairs as access to our living space. The ceilings in the mansion were sixteen feet high. Each floor was about the equivalent of two standard floors. In height, the fourth floor was like the average sixth floor. Climbing and ascending the stairs kept us in good physical condition!

The church caretaker duties that my father provided were not a full-time venture. As a carpenter and general handyman, my father's talents were most always in demand. So my father could take on odd outside jobs that didn't interfere with his custodian duties. The steady background of the church salary made life much easier for my father. We had finally moved up to middle-income living.

As a six-year-old boy, I had no trouble in making the big old mansion and church my home. I learned to know every nook and cranny in the place. I didn't mind helping my father in some of his duties. There were only three church services per week. Church committee meetings were held on weekday evenings. Therefore, most of the time, the church and mansion were empty except for my parents and me.

In addition to the major characteristics of the mansion, there was the emptiness and silence of the place. This was amplified at night. There was very little light. Most people would find the place spooky at night. I overcame this because of my intimate familiarity with the place. I knew what was in the shadows and dark areas. For me, there was no unknown. The unknown is what makes a place spooky. I knew what the place looked like at any hour of the day or night. In addition, I was not afraid of the large dark church edifice at night for the same reason; there was no unknown.

The walls and ceilings of all the rooms on the first three floors were eloquently decorated with nineteenth-century three-dimensional textured, fancy designs as a finish. In addition, they were embellished with large, fancy wall mirrors and cut-glass chandeliers. All the rooms had one or more colored carved marble fireplaces. The mansion was indeed beautiful.

Conversations with senior church members who were there when the mansion was purchased and the church was built revealed the original purpose of the various rooms. For instance, the room immediately to the right of the front door was the dining room. This explained the purpose of the fancy cabinets built into the walls of the room. This was where the dishes and silverware were kept. In addition, there was a small door in the wall for access to a dumbwaiter to the basement below, which was obviously the kitchen.

Across the hall from this was a large front-wall-to-back-wall ballroom or party room. The master bedroom and bathroom was on the second-floor front. Another bedroom and bathroom was on the third-floor front. There was a second smaller stairway for servants that went from the basement to the fourth floor.

Most interestingly, it was stated that President Abraham Lincoln slept there on the night of August 16, 1864. I couldn't believe that Lincoln had actually walked in the same halls, rooms, and stairway where I lived!

As a result of my personality, I was able to adapt to my new environment and enjoy my life. I am sure that some people would not have been able to do this. As a child, I learned to like the old mansion. I was fond of the place. My passion for the old house remained with me for the rest of my life.

The big social disadvantage of living downtown was the car-parking problem. The parking garages and streets were always full. It was difficult to find a parking place. The other transportation options were the taxi and the public streetcar or bus. Relatives and friends did visit us occasionally but definitely not as much as if we lived in a residential neighborhood.

The abnormal circumstances of being raised in the mansion set me apart from the usual person. For me, the advantages of this environment outweighed the disadvantages.

Chapter 8

Inner-City Living

I Had a Nice Growing-Up Experience

The front windows of the mansion overlooked the majestic tall marble monument to George Washington, dated 1829. Our mansion predated the monument! The Mount Vernon neighborhood that surrounded the monument consisted of four small formal grassy park areas with walkways, beautiful flower gardens and shrubs embellished with intricate water fountains, and various statues of famous people. All this was essentially across the street from where I lived. All the streets in the neighborhood were filled with elegant mansions, churches, and prominent world famous institutions such as the Peabody Institute of Music and the Walters Art Gallery.

I often stood at a front window just gazing at the beautiful view and watching the people walking in the gardens and the traffic on the streets. Unfortunately, none of our apartment rooms were in the front of the mansion. In stark contrast, our apartment rear windows faced the typical inner-city view of the roofs and walls of the neighborhood buildings.

The environment in the old downtown mansion was not at all like that of a typical residential area, where there were neighbors to see and talk to. Our third- and fourth-floor rear apartment virtually isolated us from the city around us. On a relative scale, we lived in a silent cocoon. For some, this would be undesirable and intolerable. Fortunately, my parents and I had no problem with this. My father was always listening to the radio in the same manner that we watch TV today. In addition, he was either fixing or tinkering with something mechanical. My mother leaned toward the introvert and readily adapted to the isolation. My hobbies and interests were focused on Amateur Astronomy, things electrical, and reading technical and scientific books borrowed from the main Enoch Pratt City Library located three blocks away.

As a young boy, my playground consisted of the walkways of the beautiful Mount Vernon Place gardens, where I roller-skated and rode my scooter. I was always careful that I didn't interfere with the walking tourists that visited the area. I liked playing in this area better than the surrounding city sidewalks.

As an inner-city child, I had a nice growing-up experience with my parents and friends that included a good balance of boys and girls. In those days, the inner city or downtown area was not really a bad place to live.

My parents never worried about my safety when I played outdoors on the neighborhood city streets. I never had one bit of trouble. There were kids my age out there, but they were few and far between. As a typical city kid, I played in the alleys and streets and walked on top of the backyard wooden fences that were common to the area. We knew the names of all the proprietors in the neighborhood that owned local stores and businesses. In addition, we knew the names and owners of all the pet dogs and cats that roamed the neighborhood with us. Here again, as in my younger experience, I had dogs around me all day as I played.

Even though nearly everyone had a telephone in those days, I never knew the specific address or phone number of any of my neighborhood young friends. When I went out to play, I played with whomever was out there at that time. It was very informal.

The junior high school that I attended was located within walking distance from our new downtown apartment home. On the Monday after the 1941 Pearl Harbor attack, the United States declared war on Japan. As I walked to school that morning, I suddenly found myself confronted by a soldier with a rifle drawn, telling me that I couldn't walk on the sidewalk where I was and that I had to cross the street and walk over there instead. As a kid, I was stunned at this and didn't understand what was happening. I never realized that my walk to school took me past an armory. This was a military outpost and was now guarded by soldiers.

In my preadolescent years, I only played with the boys in the neighborhood. As I grew older and my interest in the opposite sex began to grow, I remember a neighborhood girl named Mary Beth. She was a pretty girl with blond hair. We seemed to like each other's company, but we never had a serious boyfriend-girlfriend relationship. We would often sit and just talk for hours on the front steps of the neighborhood houses. For whatever reason, our friendship never advanced past this. I often wonder what would have happened if we had somehow become closer friends.

About once a week, a "Hurdy-Gurdy" man would come to our back alley and hand-crank his large musical instrument. The sound was loud and sounded like a cross between a harpsicord and a music box. The music or tune was always something pleasant. The instrument was four or five feet tall and was mounted on two wagon-size wheels in a manner similar to a wheel barrow. This made it portable. In addition, a small monkey accompanied the man and performed cute tricks.

The man would play his instrument for ten or fifteen minutes, and people would come out of their back doors and hand him money. They also brought treats for the performing monkey. As long as the money came, he played. When it stopped, he moved on to his next location. I always enjoyed this, and I can still hear the sound when I think about it.

Sometime between the ages of five and ten, I became aware that I was experiencing "sleep paralysis." As I awakened from sleep, I could see and hear everything but I couldn't move or speak for about twenty seconds. Other than this inconvenience, there were no detrimental effects from this experience. As is typical for children, I reasoned that everyone had this experience, and I never mentioned it to anyone, including my parents.

In my early teen years, I became curious about this and consulted the medical books in the public Library. I learned that it was a benign condition. However, some people experienced fright and anxiety with this. I was happy that this was not my experience. In my midlife years, this condition became infrequent and remained so thereafter.

For all my life, I have had motion sickness. As a child, whenever I was in a car, traveling for longer than five or ten minutes, I became seriously ill. My parents were vividly aware of this but never put two and two together to conclude that it was the car ride that was the cause of it. I learned that if I slept through the ride, I was fine. So my motion sickness was a visual thing and not just motion. I assume that my parents had never heard of motion sickness.

As a very perceptive child, I learned through experience that when I either closed my eyes or focused my vision straight ahead, I didn't get car sick. It was the visual side-to-side motion that made me ill. If I sat in the front seat and avoided looking out of the side windows at the scenery flying by, I was fine. This became my posture for riding in a car, bus, or trolley for the rest of my life.

The Important People

The Connection Was Unknown to Me

Of all our friends, relatives, and acquaintances, we never know who is or who will be important in our lives. In retrospect, for Ruth and me, one such person was Millard Ringsdorf. He was a regular visitor to Effie and her family. Millard was a foster brother to Effie's mother, Anna, who was raised with the Ringsdorf family. As such, he was considered as part of the family. For the twins Ruth and Ann, he was their grandmother's "brother" and was Uncle Millard. He was a good businessman and had assumed a responsible position in his family's business. He was also a senior member of the council of a new Protestant Church located in downtown Baltimore. Effie and her family were members of a church near their home.

Millard obviously had a strong influence on Effie as he managed to convince her to try his church. Effie did like his church and began taking Ruth and Ann with her on Sundays. The twins, in their early teens, also liked the church, and they all began regular attendance.

With reference to my family, Millard was a senior founding member of our church. We did not know that this was the same church that Ruth's family was attending. In my teen years, my church and Sunday school duties kept me busy during the time period immediately following the end of the church service and Sunday school. By the time I got to the church lobby, most of the congregation had left, including the twins and their mother. Therefore, I never saw Ruth and didn't know that she existed. This went on for several months. Then, I stopped my Sunday school activities and began attending the church service.

Millard and his sister, Alma, were friends of my family and often socially visited me and my parents at our home. He was definitely no stranger to us. The close connection between Millard and Ruth and Ann's family was unknown to me. I had no idea that he was influential in getting Effie, Ruth, and Ann to attend my church. In Millard's social interface with me and my parents, he never mentioned his friendship with Effie and her twin girls, and I assume that he never mentioned his friendship with my family to Effie's family. Ne'er the twain shall meet!

All the people that attended my parents wedding in 1927 were relatives of the bride and groom except one person, Anna Reiger. She became a close friend of the bride, my mother, about six months before the wedding. Two years after the wedding of my parents, she became a member of the same church that Millard Ringsdorf attended. Anna was successful in getting my parents to also become members of the church. Thus, she was the second most important person in the lives of Ruth and me. As a result of the influence of Anna and Millard, unknown to Ruth and me, we were all now attending the same church.

Chapter 10

My Second Decade

The Mansion Had Its Advantages for Me

Sometime in the preadolescent or adolescent years, life seems to speed up, and everything becomes complicated and serious. The child goes away, and the young adult makes its first appearance. Gone are the carefree days with little or no responsibility, and you slowly realize what they mean by the word *maturity*.

I was aware of the isolation and loneliness associated with living in the old mansion. My loneliness was offset by my interests in things scientific and electrical. Fortunately, the main city library was just three blocks away. I was a bookworm of sorts, was very well read, and a regular attendee of the library. From my borrowed books, I made my own notes, diagrams, and descriptions in loose-leaf notebooks and essentially had my own library of astronomical, scientific, and technical information at home.

My home was in the downtown area of the city. In my preteen years, I was interested in doing the things that my peers did. I sold newspapers at the corner of the block where I lived. I was a city kid!

A large dance hall was located at the end of the block where I lived. It was busy most of the time, and you could hear the music coming from there in the evenings. The dance hall had a dress code.

The men had to wear a tie. I knew that many men were refused entry for this reason. In those days, the five-and-dime stores sold inexpensive ties. I bought several of them and stood on the sidewalk wearing a shirt and tie outside the steps of my home in the early evening, when the dance hall was open. Shortly, a guy without a tie would approach me and say, "Hey, kid! Can I buy your tie?" I would reply, "Sure! Three dollars!" If he balked at the price, I went down a dollar. I was making 100 or 200 percent profit!

When an Electrical Engineer friend of my father visited us, he noticed my interest in things electrical and gave me an introduction to electronics kit. He is the person who launched my career in electronics. In that respect, he is one of the important people in my life. I was soon successfully building complicated radio receivers, transmitters, and other electronic devices. In a year or so, with this experience and knowledge, I established my own radio repair shop at home. As a young teenager, I was in business in my spare time, making lots of money.

This was the time of World War II. There were no new commercial products of any kind manufactured in the United States. You couldn't buy anything new. Every industry was dedicated to making some product to support the war effort. You could buy things in stores, but there was nothing new available. The backlog of whatever was in the warehouses was all that was available.

There were many restrictions in wartime civilian, or home-front life. Food, gasoline, leather shoes, and rubber tires were rationed. A time-limited number of ration stamps for these items were issued to individuals or families. People were encouraged to grow vegetables on their property, and these were called victory gardens. Also, people were encouraged to donate any scrap iron to the war effort. I witnessed the removal of many wrought-iron fences and outdoor window rails.

The United States pessimistically assumed that the Germans had the ability to bomb eastern US coast cities. As a result, each city and community had loudspeakers installed in the streets, and the loud wailing sound of sirens often filled the air, announcing an air raid drill. The problem was, we were never informed whether it was a drill or the real thing! All homes, stores, and buildings were supplied with many sand bags to be placed in attics and top floors for use in extinguishing possible incendiary bombs. For a nighttime air raid drill, a light blackout was imposed, and we were supposed to turn off all lights in our dwelling or install blackout blinds in our windows that would not transmit light.

An official cap and armband was issued to neighborhood air raid wardens. These people were volunteers from each street or neighborhood. Their major duty was to inspect the neighborhood and enforce the blackout. My father was the warden in our neighborhood. During an air raid drill, no one was allowed outside or in the streets except police, firemen, or air raid wardens. If you were driving a vehicle, you were supposed to pull over or park, turn out your lights, and find shelter in a nearby building. The air raid sirens sounded for two or three minutes. When they stopped, all outdoor activity was stopped, and the rules of the emergency were in effect. When the drill or emergency was over the sirens again sounded.

The war had taken most of the young men into military service, thereby removing them from whatever job they had as a civilian and leaving that service empty. There was a high demand for repair of all products, including radios. Repairmen of any kind on the home front were hard to find. Radio repair shops were almost nonexistent. I never had to advertise; my home radio repair business thrived on word-of-mouth recommendation from my customers. There were no new radio tubes. A repairman had to learn to do whatever was necessary to affect a repair. I devised a method to repair the burned-out filaments of the radio tubes.

Living in the mansion had its advantages for me. I had access to the roof, and I installed radio antenna wires between the chimneys. The antennas were five stories high, and the reception was outstanding. During the war, I was an avid shortwave radio listener. As such, I listened to news of the war from around the globe. I found this overseas news to be more accurate, up-to-date, and informative in comparison to the censored local news in the United States. I have listened to the infamous propaganda from "Axis Sally" in Berlin and "Tokyo Rose" in Tokyo.

During and right after the war, my shortwave radio listening also included radio amateur broadcasts. I listened to discussions between radio amateurs. These interesting discussions were not censored and often included what was happening on the war fronts. My shortwave and amateur radio listening often caused me to be up very late at night so as to hear the discussions from various time zones around the world. There was a very active amateur in Bermuda, VP9F. His location was unique, and he was always passing messages from one side of the Atlantic Ocean to the other.

I learned the call letters and the voices of many of the amateur station operators. There was one voice that I kept hearing that was very familiar, but I couldn't place it. One day he gave his name. It was Mel Blanc from Los Angeles! He was the voice of Bugs Bunny and a lot of other cartoon characters of that day and age.

When I was out of school for the summer, I found jobs in the electronic field. One summer, I worked at a nearby radio repair shop. The proprietor of the shop was an elderly man. On my first day, he left me alone in the shop and said that he would be back in the early afternoon. When he returned, he was amazed and pleased that I had repaired every radio in the shop! The next summer, I worked at a shop that installed automobile radios in cars. Car Radios were not standard equipment in those days.

After graduating from junior high school, I wisely decided to attend Baltimore's Polytechnic Institute. This was a highly rated engineering high school whose "A" course graduates were admitted into the second year of college. At that time, I didn't realize that the education that I received at Poly would set me up for life as an Engineer and Scientist. The practical, hands-on education was outstanding at Poly. There were many laboratory and shop-type classes. These classes were far more advanced than the usual vocational school. My teenage high school years spanned the 1940s time of World War II.

At Poly, I quickly learned the ropes and became engrossed in many of the extracurricular, after-school activities. As a result, I seldom got home from school before six or seven at night. Out of self-interest, I attended many after-school clubs and activities. Naturally, I joined the Radio Club and soon became Club President.

As President, I began teaching Radio Theory and Radio Repair after school two nights a week. The class was popular and packed with students. This was the first such class in the school. From this, I learned early on that I had no trouble in public speaking or teaching. In addition, I personally built and tested the first radio amateur transmitter for the club.

I also joined the stagecraft club. The school had a very large auditorium that held 2,500 people with a professional-sized stage that could be used to produce plays or shows. It seemed that the auditorium was always busy with either school assemblies, demonstrations, sports rallies, shows, musicals, or plays. With all this, there was a constant series of rehearsals taking place. The stagecraft club was very busy! My electronic interests were served by the constant need for microphones and speakers for audio amplification. I also enjoyed working the electrical panels for stage and house lighting. From this firsthand experience, I developed a deep appreciation of what it takes to produce a professional stage show.

During the summer before my senior year of high school at Poly, a friend of mine and I built a large audio public address system for the principal to use to speak to or address the entire school without calling for a time-consuming assembly in the auditorium. I spent many hours running wires for the speakers in the hallways. This was the first such public address system in Baltimore City schools.

I hand-built several audio public-address amplifiers with microphones and speakers. During the war, this public-address service was almost nonexistent. When I turned sixteen, my father taught me how to drive on his 1935 Ford. I liked driving, and it seemed to come second nature to me. My pleasure in driving stayed with me for the rest of my life. Driving a car requires a straight-ahead focus, and fortunately, I had no problem with motion sickness.

After I learned to drive a car, I was often busy providing this service to the public. This was another one of my ways to make money. I provided amplification for the local high school football games at the Baltimore City Stadium, shows at the Lyric Theater, wedding reception dances, college and high school graduation dances, and public music concerts at the city parks.

Prior to age sixteen, I naturally needed my parents and a good home to live in, I was always happy with my life. In general, my relationship with my parents was good. However, the older I got, the more it became apparent to me that I was not at all like my parents. In fact, I was not like them in any way. My personality was totally different.

My parents limited their close circle of friends to only those who were acceptable to them in religion, race, culture, and social standing. They looked down on both the poor and the wealthy. I could not and did not accept these standards. There were times when there were serious verbal differences between my parents and me, especially my father. However, as a result of my personality, we never stayed angry at one another. In spite of the differences between my parents and me, they did a very good job in raising me. They did a lot of right things for me, and my youthful experience was good.

Up to the age of sixteen, I needed them. After I reached sixteen, I matured quite rapidly. I developed an independent self-confidence and outlook on life that was well beyond my years. It soon became obvious to me that the tables had turned. My parents needed me! When they were both focused on the duties of raising me, they seemed to get along very well together. Now, I had become independent and really did not look to them for anything except room and board or perhaps benign advice now and then.

I was still living at home with my parents, but without me to raise, they had no one but themselves or each other to think about or deal with. It was then that I became aware of the fact that my parents did not really get along that well together. So I had a job to do. I became an arbitrator. It was me that patiently kept them together through all their quarrels and differences, for the rest of their lives.

Chapter 11

My Social Life

1947 Was a Banner Year for Me

At the tender age of thirteen, I attended my first dance, sponsored by my church. I was standing in the sidelines, just watching the kids on the dance floor. Someone pushed me out onto the dance floor, and I found myself face-to-face with a girl that had no partner. A moment later, we cautiously began to dance. Soon, I got the hang of it, and we were dancing just like everyone else. Dancing in those days was close-up stuff, where you get to put your arm around the girl and hold her close to you. So I considered that this dancing stuff was great and thus began my lifelong love of dancing.

In my early, young teenage life, with few exceptions, I always had a girl to date or go out with on the weekend. Prior to learning to drive, I used public transportation when I dated a girl. This was satisfactory at that time, but I was destination limited and time limited by the public transportation system schedule. All this took place in the early 1940s.

After I learned to drive a car, my social life took a turn for the better. Starting in late 1944 and early 1945, I borrowed my father's car very often and quickly learned to know my city from one end to the other. I felt really grown up because I was taking girls out on dates in my car and staying out late. These were exceptional times because the war had removed all the young men from the home front between the ages of eighteen to thirty-five. As a result, there was no slightly older young crowd out there in the social world. There was almost no competition out there for me. Young "men" like me were essentially "king of the road."

All through 1945, I dated lots of girls. Some of them were nice, but none of them seemed exceptional to me. Some of the friends of my parents had daughters that were my age, and the adults were often making social arrangements for me. As a result of my easygoing personality, I didn't mind this. However, none of these arrangements lasted very long because there was no chemistry between the girls and me.

One of these arrangements was with a girl that was deaf and dumb; she couldn't hear or talk. For whatever reason, she had not learned sign language. So our only communication was with written notes. She had just started to read lips. I didn't dislike her, but there was no chemistry, connection, or commonality between us. We parted friends after a mutual decision to stop seeing each other.

Socially, I was generally with the in crowd. However, I leaned toward the conservative and never got involved in mischievous or dangerous activities that were considered fun. I was occasionally in trouble but never serious trouble. Whenever I was aware that the activities of the young crowd that I was with were indeed unsafe, I always made up an excuse to leave and go home. The reports that I heard the next day verified the wisdom of my decision!

I experienced the usual teenage standoff in relationships with girls my age. The pretty brunettes that I liked and dated didn't like me. Conversely, all the girls that liked me a lot, I didn't like. As a compassionate person, I felt bad about ignoring the girls that liked me, but I had no chemistry with them.

In 1946, when I was seventeen and in my senior year of high school, I met a very nice, very beautiful blond girl named Barbara who was a year older than me. I liked her a lot because, on my relative scale, she seemed so mature and settled in comparison to the other girls that I had been dating. It was obvious that she liked me a lot, in spite of the age difference, and that made me happy.

I was aware that she was not the love of my life, the girl I was searching for, partially because she was a blonde and not the brunette that I preferred. With apologies to blondes, I must say that at seventeen years old and still today, I preferred the company of girls, no matter what color the hair!

We dated for about four months. Then, I found that she had to return to her home in Mansfield, Ohio. I knew that she was visiting and staying with her uncle, but I thought she was here sort of permanently. I was very upset that she was leaving. After she went back to her home, we wrote friendship letters to each other faithfully for about four months. Some of our letters were borderline love letters. Then one day, I got a Dear John letter from her telling me that she just got married! She explained that she had to get away from her dysfunctional home and stepfather. From this, I assumed that it was a marriage of convenience. I hope that it was also a marriage of love. I was upset with her for being untruthful with me for all those months. Oh well, so much for her!

Looking back on it, the following year, 1947, was a banner year for me. In the beginning, it seemed to be just sort of typical of the past year. World War II had recently ended, and the nation as a whole was on a happy, upbeat track. In February, I happily graduated from high school and attended my graduation ceremony. I went to my senior prom with a blond girl named Ginny that I happened to be dating at that time in my life. I had been going with her for several months. Not long after the senior prom, I stopped dating her. She had a good figure and a pretty face, but that was it.

Communication with her was always a problem. She was the type that only told you what she wanted you to know. Consequently, I never knew what to expect from her. I was always being unpleasantly surprised when I went out with her. For instance, she told me that she wanted to go to see a movie. Then, when I get to her house,

I find her all dressed in a formal gown. Without apology, she informs me that instead, we are going to a formal dance! More often than not, she just used me to get out and go places socially where she would essentially dump me until she wanted to go home. So my patience finally reached its limit, and I dumped her!

Chapter 12

One Day in May

It Made Me Happy to Know Her Name

As an only child, I was lonely for companionship. As an adolescent, this desire for companionship naturally focused on the opposite sex. I always had an inner feeling or intuition that the right girl was out there, and all I had to do was find her. For me, this feeling was very strong and positive. To accomplish this, I had no option but to continue to be socially active. Time moves so slowly when you are young. At eighteen years of age, it seemed to me that I had been searching for my girl for an eternity.

Every year, I attended the annual spring youth group gathering sponsored by our church at one of the local state parks. It was a typical outdoor occasion where we played games, had fun, ate lots of food, and had music. All the young people enjoyed it. The basic purpose was to mix the young people together. There were, however, a few couples that attended. At any rate, I never brought a date to the affair. I always went alone. In early May of 1947, I had the date for this occasion marked on my calendar. Usually, I made no preparation, and on the appointed day, I just went. For some reason, this year, I felt differently about it. I found myself thinking about it in advance as if it were a special occasion. Looking back on it, I was unknowingly reading the future. I had no idea what this day would bring.

The day unfolded with the usual lots of fun with my friends. About one hundred people attended that day. For some reason, I felt that something was missing. Finally, it was all over, and people began to leave. For reasons that I could not explain, I found myself wandering aimlessly through the exiting crowd.

Suddenly, there in the crowd, I saw her. I guess that it was pure luck or destiny, but there SHE was. She was a very pretty brunette with a nice smile. From the moment that I first laid eyes on her, I knew that she was THE one. It was love at first sight. I had never felt that way about any other girl. I knew without a doubt that this girl, a total stranger, was the one that I had been searching for. I stood there, gazing at her, transfixed. Essentially, I had been hit by the proverbial ton of bricks.

A moment later, when I came to my senses, I knew that I had to find out who she was. At that time, for reasons that escape me, I didn't go over to her and talk to her. Instead, I quickly started asking all my friends if they knew her. No one knew her name. Fortunately, I had my camera with me. In haste, I raised it to my eye, pointed it at the group where she stood, and snapped it. All cameras in those days used photographic film and were manually operated. I turned my attention to winding the film in preparation for taking another picture. When I looked up, she was gone. She had disappeared into the crowd. My heart sank. I ran in the direction where I last saw her. I couldn't find her anywhere. *Oh god!* I thought to myself. *What if I never see her again?* I was sick with grief when I finally gave up the search and went home.

I could see her face before me when I went to sleep that night. Tears filled my eyes because I loved her, and I wanted to be with her. I was sad because I didn't even know who she was, and I didn't exactly know how I could find her again. The church affair was very informal, and I knew that there was not a list of attendees. Strangely, before I fell asleep, my feeling of anxiety was replaced with a feeling of contentment. I had found her. That was good, and I had her picture. Now I knew why I had been searching. Somehow I knew; something told me that she was out there somewhere.

I didn't fully realize it at that time but, this day, this *one day in May* was the biggest day of my life. I had found her. I had found the love of my life. My life would never be the same again. I didn't care what her name was, where she lived, or what her nationality was. I loved her, and that was that. I was truly happy and in love for the first time in my life.

I told my parents about my experience, but they didn't realize the depth and importance of it all. For them, it was just another girl that I had met. However, they couldn't miss the fact that I was exceedingly happy.

The next Monday, I hastened to the photo store to drop my film off for development. Time passed slowly. I couldn't wait to see if I had her picture. In a few days, I was very happy to find that I did have her picture! There she was, smiling and pretty, standing in the front row of the crowd. I took the negative back to the store and had them make a print, just of her, as large as possible.

A few long days later, I had an eight-by-ten photo of her on my night table next to my bed. Oh god, how I loved her and her picture! She was the first thing that I saw when I got up in the morning and the last thing that I saw before I closed my eyes at night. As the week went slowly by, I continued to pursue my quest for the identity of my girl. I was already thinking of her as my girl! I showed the small copy of her picture to many of my friends, but no one seemed to know who she was.

A couple of weeks later on a Sunday morning, I was pleasantly surprised to see her sitting in the pews of my church. My heart leaped. She was here! I was still too shy to go right up to her and talk to her, so I asked around as to who she was. My friend Millard Ringsdorf was standing nearby. He overheard me asking who she was, and he said that he knew her and her family, and in fact, it was he that had invited them to attend the church! Her name was Ruth Moore.

It made me so happy just to know her name. She went home with a lady that I correctly assumed was her mother. A week later, she came to church again with her mother and also her twin sister. I was surprised to see that she was a twin. I could tell the difference between the two of them right away, even though they were identical twins. I couldn't wait for the church service to end. I made up my mind that I was going to go up to her and talk to her, no matter what.

At the end of the church service, I hurried to the front door and stood there, searching the exiting crowd for her. Finally, I saw her coming toward me. She was alone; her mother and sister were not with her. *This was perfect!* I thought to myself. In the next instant, a lot of negative what ifs flooded my already very nervous brain. "What if she doesn't speak to me?" "What if she doesn't like me?" "What if she is afraid of me?" She was now almost standing in front of me.

I forced all those what ifs into the back of my mind as I spoke to her. "Hi!" I said. "I'm Gil Smith. Are you Ruth Moore?"

She stopped and looked up at me with her beautiful blue eyes. A big smile came across her face as she replied, "Yes, I'm Ruth Moore, how did you know my name?"

"Oh," I replied nervously, "I just asked around and found out." I continued, "I saw you a couple of weeks ago at the church youth gathering. I took some pictures of the crowd, and you are in one of them." Then I asked, "Would you like to have a copy of that?"

She seemed to be beaming radiantly at me as she replied, "Well, sure. Um, yes, I would like a copy very much!" Oh god, she was talking to me, and I was in heaven.

"Well then!" I said. "I'll have a print made for you, and I'll call you when I get it. Oh"—I fumbled—"I don't know your phone number. What is it?"

"Oh," she replied, "it's Forest 5-5235!" I immediately burned that number into my memory banks.

"Great!" I said. "I'll call you!"

Her pretty face with beautiful blue eyes and nice smile were still beaming up at me. She had the nicest, engaging smile that I had ever seen. I had loved her from a distance, but now, with her standing just eighteen inches from me, that love within me was not only verified but considerably strengthened. I was absolutely sure, right then and there, that she was the love of my life. If it were possible, I would have married her on the spot!

Well, I was now experiencing hormonal meltdown. I couldn't feel the floor anymore. I have no idea how long we talked or what we talked about after that. Finally, we exchanged brief good-byes, and she turned and walked away. Her pretty brunette hair bounced as she walked and waved in the breeze as she turned the corner and disappeared. I was so happy that I almost cried as I stood there, gazing at the space where I last saw her. Then, her twin sister and her mother walked by, and I said "Hi!" to them, and they both replied with an equally brief greeting and went on by. I had finally met the twins.

For the rest of that Sunday, I couldn't think about anything but Ruth. After having my first face-to-face conversation with the girl of my dreams, I was sort of in heaven. The next day at work, I saw her face before me all the time, and I went through the day on automatic pilot. I was a mess. I could hardly wait until I came home from work. I was going to call her for the first time for no other reason than just to talk to her.

That evening, as I went to the phone to place my call, all those same negative what ifs, fears, and concerns of yesterday came back to me. "What if she won't talk to me?" "What if she doesn't like me?" "What if she already has a steady boyfriend?" My self-confidence and positive attitude came forward as I pushed all those what ifs out of my mind and dialed her number.

Happily for me, Ruth answered the phone. She seemed pleased that I called and, if anything, overly polite. We had a nice conversation for five or ten minutes, and I found that she lived with her twin sister, mother, and dad. It seemed that her family was typical and normal. I asked her if she would mind if I called her again. She told me that she wouldn't mind at all, and in fact, she would be looking forward to it. Well, that made me feel very happy.

After I hung up the phone, I shouted "Yipeee!" to express my pleasure. I knew that at least she didn't dislike me! I reasoned that she probably didn't have a steady boyfriend because of the way she talked to me, and in addition, she seemed to enjoy talking to me. Needless to say, I called Ruth on the phone several more times that week, just to pleasantly pass the time and get to know her better. I loved to hear her voice and to know that she was on the other end of the line.

Later that week, I told her that I had the picture for her and that I would like to bring it to her house that coming Saturday night. And maybe we could then go to a movie or get something to eat or whatever. To my absolute pleasure, she agreed to the whole thing! She then told me what part of town she lived in and gave me her address. So my first date with Ruth was on Saturday May 24, 1947. That day was one of the happiest of my life.

I had been driving a car for only about three years, which, to me as a young person, seemed to be a very long time. I learned that I really liked a car and really enjoyed driving it. I had no option but to borrow my father's old 1935 Ford. That Saturday, I drove the old Ford to Ruth's house and gave her the picture, which she seemed to be pleased with. Ruth introduced me to her mother, father, and twin sister, Ann. Ann seemed very sweet and pleasant, but I could tell that she didn't have the same personality as Ruth. It was no contest. When I looked at the two of them, I only saw Ruth.

Instead of a movie, I suggested that we go dancing that night. Ruth seemed very pleased at this suggestion and agreed to go. In a short while, Ruth and I hopped into the car. She was all smiles and seemed very happy. I was relieved to see that she was at ease and not at all nervous because she really didn't know me very well. I was still a total stranger to her. If I were a girl, I think that I would have been a little apprehensive.

We seemed to get along very well together, and we had no trouble in having a nice, continuous conversation. I learned that she loved to ride in a car, since her parents had never owned one. I was surprised at this because, even in those days, everyone that I knew had a car. I also observed that riding in a car seemed to relax her; she was very content. I was only aware that this girl, this very pretty blue-eyed brunette who was the love of my life, was with me, and I was in ecstasy.

I took her to the Dixie Ballroom at Gwynn Oak Park, which had a live eighteen-piece dance band. The admission price for the evening was only ninety cents per person. The dance floor was set on a pier that was on the edge of a lake. It was festively decorated with colored lanterns that reflected in the lake. All this, on a warm summer night with the music and the moonlight also reflecting in the lake, made a very romantic setting.

Dancing in those days was close-up stuff, where you get to hug and hold your girl tightly. As we stepped out on the dance floor, I turned and faced her. In ballroom-dance style, I held my left hand up. When I felt her small right hand clasp mine and my right arm went around her waist, there was electricity for me, and a thrill went up my spine. This was my first experience of touching her. Oh god, was I ever in heaven that night! There I was, for the first time, dancing and holding the girl who was the love of my life very tightly.

My love for her was elevated to new heights. Perhaps I had ulterior motives for choosing dancing that night! As the evening progressed, to the pleasure of both of us, we found that we danced very well together. I was very pleased, and I felt that things were going very well for me.

We danced almost continuously that night, which meant that we were close to each other most of the time. She never complained or expressed any displeasure concerning the relatively close intimacy that we were experiencing. Our hearts seemed to be in unison as we talked and laughed and danced the evening away together. Oh, how happy I was. I was with the girl of my dreams.

In those days, every band played "Goodnight Sweetheart" as the last dance of the evening. Typically, for this last dance, the floor is filled with couples holding each other tightly. It was with great pleasure and a little sadness that I danced this last dance with Ruth. The evening ended all too soon, and I reluctantly took her to the car and began to drive her back to her home.

As we drove to her house, she commented on how deserted the streets were, as if she were seeing it for the first time in her life. I thought it was a bit unusual for her to comment on something like that. I had been out and had driven on the streets late at night many times before, and I saw nothing unusual or worth commenting on.

I parked my car in front of her house. We sat in my car and talked a little before we went to her house. She told me that she enjoyed the evening with me very much and that this was the first time that she had been to a dance hall and that it was the first time that she had danced with anyone. In fact, she continued, it was the first time any boy had taken her out in a car! This was her first real "date." I was totally surprised at this.

Then, the explanation came. She told me that she was only fifteen years old and would be sixteen in a few months. *Oh my gosh!* I thought to myself. *She is only fifteen!* To me, she did not look or act that young. I would never have guessed that. On the age scale of young people, she was very young for me, an "older" guy of eighteen years. In those days, the three-year difference was large at our age. Dating girls her age by older guys like me was called robbing the cradle! Well, her age didn't matter to me at all. It occurred to me that if she had never been out with anyone in a car before, then indeed it really was the first time she had seen the deserted streets at night.

I continued talking with her and told her how much I enjoyed the evening with her and that I hoped that we could do it again soon. At that time, she made no comment concerning future dates with me. It was well after midnight. The residential neighborhood where she lived was a very quiet one. I walked her from the car to her porch and front door. There were no other people in sight of the distant streetlight, and there were no sounds. The quiet hush of the late hour caused us to whisper to each other. This was nice because whispering is very romantic. She didn't invite me into her house, and I didn't mind that at all for the first date.

We said good night to each other, and she again told me what a wonderful time she had. I held her hand and gave her a quick hug. This was not really what I wanted to do, but I knew that it was the best thing to do. What I really wanted to do was give her a big kiss and a long hug! I didn't kiss Ruth on our first date because I didn't want to do anything that would upset the pleasant relationship that we had. I stood on her porch as she opened her front door and went in. To my delight, in typical female fashion, she agreed to go dancing with me again as she closed the door. And so ended our first date.

I was the happiest guy alive that night as I drove home through the empty, deserted city streets. In my mind's eye, I could still see her pretty face with beautiful blue eyes, hear her happy voice, feel her close to me, and smell her fragrance. Just spending one evening with her had filled my mind with what seemed a lifetime of wonderful memories! Oh my god, was I happy!

When I got home, I sat on my bed, looking at her picture on the night table. Her picture was now much more meaningful to me. I had wonderful memories of being with her, holding her tight, laughing and dancing with her. My senses were totally filled with the deep love that I felt for her. As I sat there, staring at her picture, I found myself re-living every beautiful moment of the evening that I just spent with her. Right then and there, I reasoned that I was not going to let her young age interfere in any way with the pleasant relationship that I had with her. I loved her, and that was that.

Then, I remembered what I was like at fifteen. I correctly reasoned that she was too young to have any kind of serious relationship with anyone. This, however, did not make me love her any less. I was completely, hopelessly, and seriously in love with this girl. At the time, I didn't care if she loved me; I just wanted her to like me a little. Given some time, as she grew older, I hoped that she would learn to love me as much as I loved her. From this point on, I knew that I had to patiently wait for her to grow up. I was content with it that way because I loved her so very much. I wanted this girl to love me and eventually marry me. Patience is an attribute of true love.

According to her sister, Ann, the next day, Ruth couldn't stop talking about her first date with me. She was so happy. It was an experience of many firsts in her life, and she was hoping that it wouldn't be the last. I was a stranger to Ruth, and she had no way of knowing what my plans were for her. In the back of my mind, I wondered why Ruth's mother let her young daughter go on a date with me, a total stranger that was older.

The answer to this question came many years later in my conversations with Ann. Ruth's mother, Effie, considered that her good friend Millard Ringsdorf would know everyone in the church that we attended, so she telephoned him to ask about me. Well, Millard did indeed know me quite well, and he obviously gave me a good rating! Effie then allowed her young daughter to go out with me.

Millard was also responsible for getting the twins and Effie to come to my church. Obviously, Millard was one of the key people in our lives. Without him, I would have never met Ruth. I am forever indebted to him. I am also indebted to Anna Reiger, who convinced my parents to attend the church that eventually allowed me to meet Ruth. I am also thankful that Ruth had an outgoing personality that enabled her to go alone without Ann and attend the church youth function that day when I first saw her.

Chapter 13

My Life after Ruth

I Soon Learned that I Was Dealing with Twins

After I met Ruth, I stopped dating other girls and began going steady with her. My search for the love of my life was over. The next week, for our second date of dancing, I decided to bring her a bouquet of flowers. That's how I learned that she really loved flowers, especially roses. For every Saturday night thereafter that I had a date with Ruth, I brought her a dozen red roses. There was a Saturday sidewalk flower vendor on one of the streets leading to Ruth's house. This made it convenient for me to buy her the roses, which cost only $1.25 a dozen in those days.

My memory tells me that when I first met Ruth, I loved her deeply, and I proceeded to draw her into my life. Happily I found that she responded by drawing me into her life. It wasn't long in my early dates with her when I took her to eat dinner in a restaurant either before or after we went to a movie. This is when I learned that this girl really loved food and loved to eat. As far as I was concerned, she was very easy to please. In those days, there were many ice cream parlors, or stores, that sold only ice cream products. These were a

Ruth by the Roses

natural magnet to the young people. The adjacent parking lots were always filled with cars. There was always someone there that you knew. Ruth loved being in my car, going to these places, and seeing the young people there.

For a decade and a half, Ruth and her family had lived in a world of relative isolation as a result of not having a car. For Ruth, it seemed so wonderful to ride in my car and to see all the sights on the way to and from wherever we were going. She also enjoyed listening to the music on the car radio while we were driving. These were all the niceties that she had been deprived of for all her life. In the beginning, everywhere we went and everything that we did was a first-time experience for her. No wonder she was happy!

Ruth loved music and was an accomplished pianist. At her house, she would often sit at her piano and play popular music, while I attempted to sing along with whatever she was playing. Unlike her twin sister, Ruth was very adventurous and liked to get out and do new things and go to new places.

It wasn't very long before I kissed her. It seemed to me that I had been waiting for an eternity to kiss her. I remember our first kiss explicitly. I brought her home after a date, and we were in the living room of her house. The soft glow of a small night-light filled the room. It was indeed a very romantic setting. In spite of the fact that she was very young and a little shy, she willingly approached our first kiss. She didn't push me away from her. Her adventurous nature was leading her on, and it is likely that she was expecting it to happen.

When my lips first met hers, I held her very close, there were fireworks, and we melted in each other's arms. I could tell that she felt the same way as I did. I had never held a girl that close before. We were deep in a world of physical intimacy that neither of us had experienced before. This kiss had united not only our bodies but our minds as well. In my entire young life, I had never been as fulfilled or as sexually aroused as I was with her kiss.

She did not kiss like a child! Behind that pretty, shy young teen-age face, there was a fiery, sexy woman! I thought to myself, *No girl could kiss me like that and not love me.* She admitted that she had never kissed anyone like that before either. I knew right then that she loved me, and it was just a matter of me waiting for her to grow up. After that first long kiss, there was no power on earth that could separate me from Ruth. I was personally fully committed to her from that moment on.

It occurred to me that it might be difficult for a fifteen- or sixteen-year-old girl to be what I wanted her to be, the love of my life. I hoped and prayed that Ruth would be able to accept me and understand me for what I was, a guy who was seriously in love with her. I didn't want anyone else; I wasn't searching for anyone else. I had found the love of my life, and I was ecstatic. There was no doubt in my mind, and I had no thought of finding someone better than her. I was going steady with her from the day of our first date. The average fifteen-year-old girl is playing the field and not going steady with anyone.

I wanted to be with Ruth as much as possible. As the weeks went by, on a Saturday, I asked her to let me come and pick her up earlier in the day. I then took her for a ride to some pleasant destination that she hadn't been to and then found a restaurant and had a nice meal. After that, I either took her to a movie or went dancing. Not only was I happy with this but she was exceedingly happy. Of course, she had never been wined and dined before. To my advantage, there were no interstate highways in those days, and it took a lot longer to travel from place to place than it does today. I would always take the long, scenic route to and from wherever we went and thus have more time with Ruth.

It was usually around midnight on a Saturday when Ruth and I returned to her house after a day of social activity. To show her appreciation to me for treating her so nice, she always baked a small cake for me. She would invite me into the kitchen and set me down in a chair at the table. Then she would slice me a piece of cake, pour me a glass of milk, and sit in a chair facing me on the other side of the table. As I enjoyed this treat, I talked to her about the day's activities and other trivia. She sat there, keeping the conversation going while her eyes were looking at the floor. She couldn't look at me. She could kiss me passionately, but she couldn't look at me across the table! It took about two weeks for her to get over her shyness and look at me while I ate my cake.

I knew that Ruth liked me a lot, and I was doing everything that I could to please her and keep her. As boyfriend and girlfriend, we were slowly becoming accustomed to each other. As the guy in this twosome, I was leading our relationship from friendly to romantic. To my delight, I found that Ruth was equally inclined to be romantic.

Not long after I met her, Ruth very shyly asked me if I would mind taking her sister, Ann, along with us whenever we went for just a ride in the country. The average guy would have replied, "Well, maybe just once, but not as a rule!" The average person within me wanted to say no. This was something definitely out of the ordinary. My love for Ruth overcame all this, and of course, I said yes. This began my ferrying of both of them around in my car. For a macho guy, it is a definite plus to have two pretty girls riding around in your car. However, this did nothing for me. I only wanted Ruth.

A couple of weeks later, there came the addition of their mother for these rides. This made sense because their mother had also been deprived of car rides for all her life. She expressed great delight whenever she was in my car. I didn't mind this at all because it made Ruth so happy. This is not what the average guy does who is dating an average girl!

I quickly learned that since I was dealing with twins, I had to do a lot of things twice. For instance, if I took Ruth to see a movie and she really liked it, she would want her twin to see it and would ask to go see it again, this time with Ann. I had to sit through lots of movies twice or go to a tourist attraction twice. Twins are twice!

In due time, I became the chauffer who took Ruth and her family wherever they needed to go. I did this as an excuse to be near Ruth. In this manner, I was able to spend lots of time with Ruth but not on a date basis. I think Ruth realized that I would do almost anything to make her happy. I regularly took them shopping. For the first time in their lives, the twins were able to have the luxury of buying more than they could personally carry home. I also took them to the dentist on the other side of town. Using local transit, this trip would take a lot of time and standing on street corners to change trolleys.

Shortly after I met Ruth, I was in her home when the phone rang, and Ruth answered it. I found that she was overly polite with everyone, not just me. She spoke as if that person on the other end of the line was an old, lifelong friend that she was so happy to hear from and would be looking forward to hearing from them again. In a way, I was disappointed because I thought Ruth reserved that kind of talk just for me. It was her sweet, innocent, outgoing personality. She loved everyone, and everyone who knew her loved her. She didn't realize it, but this loving, charming, come-hither characteristic of hers tended to mislead and confuse all the men in her life except me. I have never known anyone who disliked Ruth.

In our first winter together, I discovered that Ruth had never been sledding down a long snowy hill. There were no sledding hills within walking distance of her home, so she had not experienced this pleasure. Naturally, I took her in my car to a big sledding hill in one of the city parks. It was crowded with people of all ages. Oh my god, did she ever have a good time that day, laughing and screaming as we zipped down the hill on our sleds. A few hours later, we returned to her house. We were both cold and exhausted but very happy. This was another first for Ruth.

By having a car and taking her places, I was introducing Ruth to a lifestyle she had never known. As I participated in her life and her family life, I was surprised to find that I was also being introduced to a lifestyle that I had never known.

I was raised in relative isolation in the big mansion located in the downtown area of the city. There was only my mother, father, and me. Christmas Day for me was a very happy but quiet occasion. After breakfast, we three would go to the living room, where the tree was located, and quietly open our presents.

The next day, the twenty-sixth of December, was my birthday. For all my life, I never had a real birthday party. My parents saved a few presents to give to me on the day after Christmas, there was a small cake with candles, and that was that. For whatever reason, I don't remember attending other children's birthday parties.

I was aware that my parents did not celebrate or even talk about their birthdays. Also, they never mentioned the birthdays of my grandparents, aunts, uncles, or cousins. My birthday seemed to be the only one important to them.

On Easter when I was a child, my parents hid an Easter basket full of chocolate candy for me to find in the apartment. As an only child, this was Easter for me. I did not have the companionship and competition of another child. In like manner, Thanksgiving dinner was a relatively quiet occasion for me.

Three months after I met Ruth, it was August and the twins' birthday. Their birthday party took place at her house. I brought Ruth several gifts and roses. Several teenage girls from the neighborhood were there. I had never been to a girl's birthday party. I was the only guy there! The house was festively decorated in birthday style. There were two large birthday cakes, one for each twin. Their friends had supplied an abundance of gifts, the opening of which brought cheers and screams. This was a first for me.

Then came Halloween. It had always been just another day for me. I had never participated in dressing up in costumes or door-to-door trick-or-treating. In contrast, Ruth and Ann had always celebrated Halloween with much pleasure. For my first Halloween with Ruth, she dressed me up in a scary costume, and we wandered the streets of her neighborhood, trick-or-treating. I didn't tell her that I had never done that before.

Next came Thanksgiving. I decided to have Thanksgiving dinner with Ruth and her family. This was the first time that I didn't celebrate Thanksgiving with my parents. The twins' mother had set a table that seemed to me to be elegant enough for a king! With three ladies in the kitchen, everything went smoothly. I was not accustomed to the pure elegance of that dinner. Another first for me.

Christmas quickly followed this. I spent a hasty, quick Christmas morning with my parents and then ran off to be with Ruth. This was my first Christmas Day and dinner that I didn't spend with my parents. I was happy that my parents seemed to understand my devotion to Ruth and not complain about my absence. My first Christmas with Ruth made me happy beyond words. The Christmas dinner was even more elaborate and elegant than the one at Thanksgiving. Yet another first for me

Being constantly with Ruth and her family for all the usual annual celebrations and festivities taught me that I had indeed been missing a lot by living in the mansion downtown. I loved my new social life with Ruth and her family. In each of our separate ways, Ruth and I were both experiencing a new and wonderful social life together.

As the anniversary of our first date approached, Ruth and I discussed our plans for the grand occasion. As usual, we planned on going back to the Dixie Ballroom for an evening of dancing. We decided to celebrate our anniversary on the last Saturday in May that was in the twenties. The first anniversary of our first date was on Saturday May the twenty-ninth, 1948. We decided to make this date, May twenty-ninth, the official date for celebration of our first date.

It was only normal for a high school girl like Ruth to be excited about the upcoming junior prom dance. She began talking about it a month in advance. There was no doubt in her mind that I would accompany her to the dance. She purchased a nice white full-length gown to wear. I gave her an orchid to wear. I wore my best suit. This was the first time that I saw Ruth in a beautiful long gown and the first flower corsage that I gave her. In my eyes, she made the gown beautiful! It was obvious that Ruth was very happy to be attending the dance. She was all smiles and was giggling and laughing most of the time. I felt sorry for Ann because she didn't have a boyfriend and couldn't go.

Chapter 14

Ruth's Indiscretion

She Had to Know that She Hurt Me Deeply

Ruth and I always discussed the plans for our time together for the immediate and near future. We always looked forward to our weekends together. It was sometime in the second summer that I was dating Ruth when, of all things, she was guilty of telling me white lies. For this particular weekend, we had made plans to attend a church-sponsored informal dance on Saturday. She knew that I had already purchased flowers for her to wear.

On the Friday before, as usual, I called her to confirm our plans. I was astonished at what I heard. She told me that she had decided that she didn't want to go! She claimed that she just wanted to stay home and not go anywhere. When I offered to just come to her house and keep her company, she said, "No!" She said that she just wanted to be alone. She didn't want me to come see her. At this point, I was wondering if this was really Ruth that I was talking to! No matter what I said, the answer was no, she didn't want to see me. I finally gave up and agreed to stay away. Naturally, I was very upset. I had no idea what was happening or what had happened to cause this. I concluded that something was happening that she didn't want me to know about. It was so out of character for her to act that way!

I did not take this sitting down. This girl was the love of my life, and I needed to know what was going on. I had many friends. I called a friend of mine and borrowed his car for the day in return for lending him mine. Early the next morning, I was in my friend's car and parked down the street from Ruth's house. I wore old clothes, sunglasses, and a cap.

Sure enough, at eight in the morning, a car pulled up in front of Ruth's house. Out bounced Ed, her schoolboy friend. He ran to her door and rang the bell. Out came Ruth, laughing and happy as they ran to his car. Then, she jumped out of his car and ran back into her house, shouting that she had forgotten her bathing suit! With bathing suit in hand, she laughed again and got back into his car, and they drove away.

It was easy for me to follow them. They had no clue that anyone was following them. It took a half hour to get to their destination. I was familiar with the local area, and I knew where they were going. They were going to one of the popular nearby beach resorts. I parked near them and watched them get out of the car. He carried his blankets and beach basket with food and set it on the sand. They both went into the beach house to put on their bathing suits. I had never seen Ruth in a bathing suit. Oh god, she was a stunning beauty in her one-piece bathing suit! I knew that Ruth was her usual self that day with him, so overly polite, appreciative, and sweet in conversation and actions. They were both smiling and laughing and having a nice time.

I had seen enough. I couldn't watch anymore. I left there and drove home, crying all the way. As far as I was concerned, I had lost her. I had lost the love of my life. I couldn't believe that she could do this to me and lie to me. I was devastated.

There was more reason for me to be distressed than meets the eye. Each generation of young people have their own immediate-area-oriented specific culture or set of rules of social behavior that is common knowledge to all and is a product of that day and age. One element of the rules was concerned with the girl's bathing suit. In the early twentieth century, girls were still wearing the bathing suit that was a full covering dress that you could get wet. The transition to the one-piece bathing suit that was featured in Hollywood Movies of the 1940s had not yet gained 100 percent approval in the commercial market. The exposure of the arms, chest, back, and legs was considered by some as "indecent exposure," and those that wore such a bathing suit were called brazen hussies.

All the men considered the one-piece bathing suit to be just great! It was difficult for many of the young girls of that day to consider wearing them. As a result of this atmosphere, if a girl dated a guy and went to the beach or a public swimming pool in her one-piece bathing suit, she was announcing that she was in a serious relationship with him, and this was very close to, if not, a commitment for engagement to be married.

Knowing all this, I had purposely not yet taken Ruth to swim at a beach because I didn't want to insinuate marriage and scare her away from me. I assumed that Ed knew all about this and had purposely asked Ruth to do this and establish this commitment from her. I also assumed that Ruth knew what she was doing. For this reason, I was positive that I had lost Ruth. I was overcome with grief.

The next day was Sunday, and Ruth and I always telephoned each other concerning me giving her a ride to attend church. Ruth didn't call me, and I didn't call her. She did not attend church that day. Monday came along, and I went to work, and she went to school. She didn't call me, and I didn't call her. When Tuesday night came, I couldn't stand not talking to her, and I called her. Naturally, I didn't mention that I knew all about what she did on Saturday. I was sure that if she knew that I had spied on her, she would probably never speak to me again. I was sworn to secrecy.

She had to know that she had hurt me deeply. She answered the phone politely and started talking about her day at school. A minute later, she asked me what I wanted to do on the coming Saturday! There was a good movie that she wanted to see, and she wanted to go to our favorite restaurant afterward. I was astonished at what I was hearing! It made no sense to me. I couldn't understand what was happening with her! She was acting as if nothing had happened.

I cautiously asked her if she was sure that she wanted to keep going out with me. Her reply was "Of course! Why wouldn't I?" She seemed a little offended that I had asked! I exclaimed, "Oh, no reason! I'm sorry that I mentioned it!" Having smoothed that over, we continued having what I considered our usual long conversation. I had no clue what was happening. But I was happy. I didn't know why, but I had my girl back! This was the one and only time that such a thing happened between us. Unknown to all, several years later, Ruth's one-day indiscreet incident with Ed was going to backfire!

Many years later, her twin sister, Ann, explained the circumstances of this incident to me. For whatever strange reason, Ed never dated Ruth. In the past, since he lived nearby, he had often talked to her while sitting on the front porch of her house, but that was all. On Monday of the week in question, Ed called and asked Ruth to go with him to his church's annual picnic at the beach. She refused. He then called every day, begging Ruth to go with him. Each time, she again refused.

On Friday, good old softhearted Ruth finally agreed to go with him. Ruth then had the usual pretty girl problem. A date with two guys on the same night! She reasoned that she had known me for only a short time, but she had known Ed for almost all her life. Also, in typical feminine fashion, she just wanted to "get it done and over with!" This was not very complementary to Ed, indicating that she really didn't want to go with him, as evidenced by the fact that she had refused him for four days in a row. Ruth reasoned that he was asking her to do something pleasant, so why not?

Ruth and Ann, in their upbringing as twins, were always together and not active socially. They were never exposed to the world of young people. They had no clue about any of the social rules of behavior of the day. Ruth was totally innocent in going to the beach with Ed that day. For her, it was just a day at the beach, nothing else. She had no idea that Ed considered this day at the beach a commitment of engagement for marriage on her part. Also, as a result of Ruth's bright personality, naïveté, and overly polite nature, Ed interpreted her behavior that day with him as genuine affection for him. He considered that she was his girl and that was that!

I can find no explanation for Ed's detached behavior from this point on. He apparently believed that Ruth was his girl now and that he had nothing more to do than wait for the time and place to come along for him to marry her. Thereafter, about once a month, Ed called Ruth on the phone and talked to her for a bit.

Of course, Ruth greeted him with her usual "Oh, it's so nice to hear from you! I was just thinking about you!" At the end of the conversation, she always said, "I'm so glad you called! Let me hear from you again soon!" He did not know that Ruth talked to everyone that way and that he was not special! To Ruth, Ed was just an old friend that occasionally called to talk to her with no intentions other than that. Boy, was she wrong about that! He was calling to be sure that she was still his girl, his sweetheart! Good old charming, sweet Ruth never disappointed him!

From her sister Ann's overhearing her conversations with him, Ruth let him lead the conversation and only talked about what he wanted to talk about. He apparently never asked her directly about her feelings toward him. He interpreted her pleasant voice and nature as assurance that she loved him. Ruth never told him anything about me. Her conversations with him were about trite and trivial things.

This went on for years! In my opinion, there had to have been something mentally wrong with him. Any normal red-blooded guy would want to be around his girl all the time! Was he so macho and good-looking that he considered himself God's gift to women? Or was it the other way around? Was it Ruth? That is definitely possible. I know for a fact that everyone considered Ruth to have the aura of a goddess because of her loving nature to everyone. Everyone that knew Ruth and me told me how lucky I was to have her as my girlfriend. They also told me that they could tell that there was something special between us.

I was very aware of the amorous characteristic of Ruth. Please understand that she never openly flirted with anyone. It was just her nature to be overly polite and smiling. It was never a serious problem for me, but it was a constant concern. I couldn't help but notice that every guy, every male friend that we were acquainted with told me confidentially that they were distinctly aware that Ruth was very special, beautiful, loving, and amorous. I was very pleased to hear this. The problem was that she was not aware of this. Every time someone conveyed this opinion to her, she cast it off as exaggeration and changed the subject.

This didn't change the fact that it was very real and obvious to everyone, especially me. I was constantly observing this and dealing with it on my own. I knew that Ruth was as faithful to me as I was to her. In refusing to acknowledge this characteristic of hers, she was naively marching through life unaware and unconcerned of the chaos that she often left behind her in the form of the emotional confusion she was imparting on many of the male gender of her friends and acquaintances.

Getting to Know Her

We Both Liked Music and Dancing

Not long after I met Ruth, I mentally married her. More than anything, I wanted this young teenage girl to grow up and eventually be my wife. In those early years with her, I realized that I had to be patient with her and let her catch up to me in experience and maturity. I was careful not to give her the impression that I was eager to marry her. I was sure that this would have turned her off and cause her to leave me. So I had to be satisfied with my plan to keep her happy by doing everything and anything for her and just enjoy myself while courting her.

Whenever I could get off from work early, I would drive to the high school that Ruth and Ann attended, wait for them, and drive them home. We had an understanding that if I was not there waiting for them, they would walk home. Ruth appreciated this favor, and of course, I was very happy to have an excuse to be with Ruth, if only for a short time.

From my standpoint, Ruth was my steady girl. The circumstances of our relationship and the very frequent dates that I had with her verified that she was not two-timing me and seeing someone else on the side.

While shopping alone one day in a downtown department store, a very expensive, beautiful blue velvet dress caught my eye. I knew Ruth's dress size, and I purchased it with the intent of giving it to her for her upcoming birthday. When she opened the box in her living room on her birthday, she gasped in surprise. She was smiling from ear to ear as she held it up against her. "Oh, Gil!" she exclaimed. "It's lovely! Oh! I'm going to try it on!" With that, she ran upstairs with the dress. A few minutes later, she slowly descended the stairs. A beautiful dress on a beautiful girl like Ruth is a sight that a guy cannot forget. She then walked right up to me and gave me a kiss that I also will not forget! After that, whenever we went to some formal occasion, such as a wedding, she wore that dress.

I was so proud and happy with the love-of-my-life girlfriend. Ruth, being the love of my life, was an angel to me. It made me happy to know that she considered me to be her angel.

In the beginning, it seemed that Ruth had a nice family. Her mother, father, and sister appeared to get along well, and I considered that they were an average family. Through the avenue of casual conversation, I was rapidly learning about Ruth's life and family. Getting to know her was fun for me because I loved her.

One day when we were out riding in the car, Ruth became somber and began to tell me the story of her life before I met her. She told me all about her father and his shell shock and how they had to live in his absence. They were in absolute poverty. I had no idea that she'd had such a terrible period in her life just four years ago. This knowledge made me realize why the twins were the way they were.

After that, I began looking around her house to see what she had, or in my case, what she didn't have. I saw that they only had one electric fan that was only four inches in diameter. These were the days before air conditioning, and the electric fan was the only thing you had to keep cool with. I immediately purchased a fourteen-inch-diameter fan and gave it to her. In addition, I found that they only had one of those old-fashioned wind-up record players. Since I knew how to do this, I set myself to the task of building her an electronic record player. She couldn't believe that I had made it myself!

Before I came along, the twins openly shared the details of their emotions and feelings with each other. As a result of the close, loving relationship between Ruth and me, she correctly refrained from telling Ann the details of our romance. When Ann asked for details, Ruth summarized and made it sound bland. As time went on, Ann became suspicious that her sister was not giving her all the gossip. If they were just sisters, this would have been an acceptable and normal practice. However, they were not just sisters; they were twins. For all their life, they openly shared their lives together.

In spite of all the nice things that I was doing for the twins and their parents, I was a problem for Ann. Ann realized that I had driven a wedge between her and her sister. This had never happened before. It was traumatic for Ann. She felt that she was losing her sister and that nothing would ever be the same. This was correct. In her mind, I was the bad guy. Ruth had the biggest problem. Ruth had to balance her new life and love with me against her lifelong love for her twin. I am sure that this was not easy to do.

Ruth was extremely happy that she had a boyfriend like me. At home, she talked all the time about her dates with me. At this point in time, her sister, Ann, did not have a boyfriend and had no experience to reciprocate with Ruth. She said that Ruth talked too much about me! Ann was naturally a little jealous that her sister had found a good boyfriend.

In my presence, whenever she could inject it into the conversation, Ann often said, "Oh, Ruth and I are going to be old maids together!" Ruth never said a word to contradict this statement. However, she never agreed with it either. Ruth knew what was going on. This was Ann's way of letting me know that she hoped nothing serious or permanent would develop between Ruth and me. Ann was a problem for Ruth and me. Ann didn't want me to take her twin away from her.

This attitude of Ann caused a transparent hostility between her and me. Ann was obviously conducting a campaign to discourage her twin from having a serious relationship with me that could lead to marriage and separation from her. This campaign continued for several months. Finally, I noticed that these statements from Ann ceased. Obviously, Ruth had to reconcile her romantic relationship with me with her sister and had succeeded in doing so.

This was not an easy thing for her to do. Her love for me was of a different nature than her love for her sister. But for all her young life, she had only known the love for her sister and mother. Ruth's world changed when I came into her life. I had to get accustomed to the fact that, in the beginning, Ruth truly loved her twin sister more than she did me.

For twins, there is an invisible umbilical cord between them that is made out of a material that is totally indestructible. They do not wish to destroy it, and no one else has the power to. And so the bond between twins remains intact forever.

At that time when I first met her, Ruth was just a few months from turning sixteen, and with her mother's permission and signature, she obtained a work permit that allowed her to hold a part-time job in the evening or on Saturday. With Ruth's outgoing personality, it was only natural that she would want to go to work. She became a salesgirl in the men's department of one of the downtown Baltimore department stores. Ruth liked her job very much and was very successful at it. The manager told her that she sold more goods than any other salesperson.

I am sure that this was a result of her being a very pretty girl. This tells you something about her personality. You cannot be an introvert and hold a job as a salesgirl. In retrospect, I feel that I can take some credit for Ruth as a salesgirl. I had been very successful in bringing her out of her shell.

I took her to work and brought her home as much as I could within the constraints of my work schedule. I didn't like it when she had to take the bus and streetcar to and from work. I worried about her safety, even in those days.

Her twin sister, Ann, being very much an introvert, did not follow in her sister's footsteps in finding a job until years later. Ann eventually found a job that she liked very much as a librarian at the Peabody Institute Library in downtown Baltimore. The Peabody Institute is a world-famous cultural center focused on music and the history thereof. The library was a magnificent old edifice with fancy columns, a large atrium, and stained glass windows. This seemed to fit with Ann's personality.

When I went on a date with Ruth, she would always give me her change or money purse to keep until we returned home. Men always have lots of pockets in their clothing, and it was no problem for me to keep her small change purse. She would occasionally use her own money for something when we were out. Well, she didn't know it, but I would always put some of my own money in her purse so that she went home with a lot more money than she started out with. I did this unfailingly, every time we went out, for years. Obviously, she never kept track of the money in her change purse. She didn't find out that I did this until twenty years later when I happened to mention it in a casual conversation!

As I dated Ruth and spent time with her, it was natural that I learned what Ruth liked and what she disliked. She definitely had a taste for the high-quality, better things and the good life. Perhaps this was a reaction to the relative isolation from society in her youth and a rebound from the period of poverty in her childhood, or perhaps it was just the way she always was. She had a wonderful disposition and a cheerful, up-beat personality.

One significant thing that set her apart from others was that I never heard her curse, swear, or use bad language or profanity of any kind. For that matter, neither did I, at least not very much. This common characteristic of the two of us contributed greatly to our bonding. This went with my personality. I was always very calm about everything, and it took a great deal to make me upset. In fact, I am well-known for facing all kinds of catastrophes and seeing them through to the end with no problem. In contrast, Ruth gets very upset when any situation becomes serious or critical, and she generally has difficulty with it. Well, they say that opposites attract!

She definitely did not try to spend or live beyond her means. As a consumer, she compromised toward the better rather than the cheaper. I really liked her taste in clothing and household decorating goods. She liked bright and colorful but not gaudy or flamboyant things. On the subject of food, she loved to eat and, at a mere 115 pounds, could sit down and eat twice as much as I did and not gain a pound! It was always a great pleasure for me to take her out to dinner at a restaurant because I could see that she enjoyed it a lot.

Of course, Ruth was in heaven when she was riding in my car. I was pleased that she was not the usual dizzy, babbling teenager. Ruth was uncomplicated and very easy to please. From my standpoint, her only complication was being a twin.

We both liked music and dancing. We went dancing together as much as possible. We loved to go to the movies, especially the musicals. We enjoyed this immensely. We loved being close to each other and always had a wonderful time when we were together. From the start of our friendship, Ruth never acted or behaved like she was unhappy with me in any way. This, of course, made me very happy. She would never have allowed our relationship to become close if she didn't love me. It was obvious to everyone that we loved each other, even though we were still teenagers.

Ruth and Ann had no cousins from their father's side of the family because the whereabouts of his sisters was unknown. There were many cousins from their mother's sister and brother. However, only one cousin, named Adel, occasionally visited them or contacted them. The rest were aloof.

In my family, my father's brother and sister had no children. As a result, I was the only grandchild on the Smith side of my family. My father disliked his brother and sister. As a result, there was no family unity expressed on the Smith side.

In contrast, my mother was one of six children, all of whom had children. From this, the Cook family, I had many cousins. There were two formal Cook family reunions every year in addition to the many informal birthday, anniversary, and holiday family gatherings. This included all my uncles and aunts and their children, my cousins.

Not long after I met Ruth, I started taking her to visit my many cousins, just to show her off. I was very proud of my new love-of-my-life girlfriend. All my cousins loved her, and we started going on double dates with them. Ruth took to my cousins like a sponge does to water. She had never fraternized with or had a social life with any of her cousins. She loved my family, and in response, my family loved her.

Chapter 16

Our Relationship

Sexual Feelings Were Impossible to Avoid

Ruth was learning about men from me, and I surprisingly found myself learning about women from Ruth. Naively, I thought I knew a lot about girls. After I met her and began to get close to her, I found that I was wrong. I had a lot to learn about girls! Ruth and I were mutually and keenly aware of one thing that we had in common. Our parents had given us zero information or guidance on the subject of sex. Sexual education was almost nonexistent in those days.

I was not your typical egotistical or macho male; therefore, there was no subject about which Ruth and I could not talk. Consequently, we learned everything that we needed to know about sex by sharing personal information and experience. Remember, there is one thing that a twin knows how to do better than anything else—share!

Long before, I had searched the bookstore shelves and had purchased all the books that I could find on the subject of sex. I was well read on the subject. In contrast, Ruth has never been to a bookstore. The library at her high school had no books on the subject of sex. Being around Ruth taught me that I was missing one critical thing—experience!

I had no idea how complicated the average girl was just because she was female. I did not realize how extensively the female body changed during menstruation. And I didn't realize how extensively the female mind deviated from normal during menstruation. In my opinion, this whole thing was just awful to endure. I was very happy that I was a male! However, from this intimate knowledge, I developed a new and very high respect for the female gender.

Very early in our relationship, I was doing everything that I could to help Ruth through her menstrual periods. I was sensitive to her needs and feelings and tried to be especially nice to her or do something especially nice for her. This was not hard for me to do; she was the love of my life, and I loved her very much. In retrospect, I was probably doing more for her than the average married man did for his wife!

Ruth and I were very much in love. She was my girl, and I was her guy. From the beginning, love began to unfold for each of us like a beautiful blossoming flower. We were both lovers and best friends. We knew that everything between us was strictly confidential. She trusted me totally and completely, and likewise, I trusted her.

To be lovers of the present day means that you are likely to be living together or sleeping together. Well, it was not that way back in the forties and fifties. Back then, kissing and hugging was about as far as you were supposed to go until you got married. Our relationship was definitely not lukewarm or conservative.

On the other hand, it was not extremely radical either. In my opinion, it was a mix of conservative and radical. It was what we both wanted it to be. We found that sexual feelings were a like a cup, filled to the brim and waiting to be drank. As very close individuals of the opposite sex, Ruth and I also learned that sexual feelings were impossible to avoid and wonderful to enjoy. And enjoy them we did.

Early on, Ruth and I found satisfactory release from the lust of our very strong sexual attraction through many avenues of benign intimacy. We were teenage lovers. The subject of teenage lovers always brings a raised eyebrow and skepticism to parents and mature adults. This skepticism is justified because, most of the time, teenage love is puppy love, is just the brand-new experience of pure lust and sexual attraction that is short-lived and temporary.

This, however, was not true for Ruth and me. Over and above the sexual attraction, we were blessed by being truly in love with each other. Through warm love, affection, trust, and confidentiality, we lived in a wonderful world of our own where there was nothing about each other physically or mentally that we did not know and understand completely. Did we have a good relationship? You bet we did!

We could go for days without having a passionate moment alone together. This did not bother us at all because we were content in the knowledge that when the time and place was right, we would surely have our intimate, wonderful time together. Essentially, we developed an intelligent, controlled intimacy with one another.

I don't think that either Ruth or I appreciated how good our relationship was, or how unique it was, until years later. As time passed, we both could see that the average relationship was lousy compared to ours. As a result, we always tried to nurture and maintain our relationship. It was not hard; we had true love on our side.

We also understood what pornography was, and we avoided it. The pornography of today is bad because it is a directed and planned display of sexual acts between couples that illustrates one-sided domestic abuse at its worst. There is nothing natural, educational, wonderful, or desirable about it.

Ruth learned to divide her love between her sister and me. Coming from a twin, this was a great sacrifice and a significant accomplishment. This demonstrated how much she really loved me. I was distinctly aware that Ruth's love for me was far greater than any love that could have come from a nontwin girl. This was the significant thing that set her apart from other girls.

Ruth and I had become totally different individuals as a result of our close relationship. I was sure that Ann was aware that her twin had changed. After sharing everything with her sister for years, Ruth had to shut her out from these details.

This had to be difficult for a twin. Yet Ruth did not appear to have any difficulty with this matter. In this area, she had stopped acting like a twin and was acting like a nontwin or normal person. When a twin has a relationship with a nontwin, the twin must make difficult, serious sacrifices. The twin must do things that are against the grain of twinship.

I was very happy that we had an intimate and close relationship. In those days, it was common to cement such relationships with a friendship ring for the girl. Ruth eagerly accepted the suggestion that we get such a ring for her. I took her to one of the downtown jewelry stores to purchase the ring. After much consideration, she chose a beautiful large opal ring. It was quite costly, but I didn't care; it was for the girl that was the love of my life. She wore the ring almost every day for the rest of her life.

Ruth was never stingy with her kisses for me. If she wasn't kissing me on the lips, she was throwing or blowing kisses to me. We kissed a lot. Ann said that we kissed too much!

It was obvious to both Ruth and me that dancing was going to be a large part of our life. In support of this, we both decided to take lessons at the Arthur Murray Dance Studios. We enjoyed this immensely. We learned to dance to everything that was popular at that time. We found that we both enjoyed dancing to Latin rhythms, and this became our preference.

It was so much fun, and we had such pleasure at the dance studio that we decided to continue by taking more lessons at the local Dale Dance Studio. Upon completion of this, we were very polished ballroom dancers.

Thereafter, whenever we went to a dance, we were always the first couple on the dance floor. We never sat down until the orchestra stopped playing. Did we enjoy dancing? We sure did!

Ruth made the comment that she would like to be a dance instructor. In addition, she said that she would like to be a model. As a very pretty and outgoing girl, she would have been very successful at either of these ventures. I was happy that Ruth didn't follow through on her desires. As such, she would have opened up a broad social life for herself, and I would have had much competition in keeping her as my steady girlfriend.

History shows that it didn't take long for the automobile, or the car, to become the vehicle of transportation and privacy for the young crowd. This was certainly true for Ruth and me. She loved being in my car, and of course, I loved having her in my car. Early on, for all the time that I was dating Ruth, I was using my father's car, which first, was the 1935 Ford. Then, my father got a 1941 Ford, which was much better and roomier.

At twenty years of age, I grew disenchanted with not having a car of my own. In late 1949, I purchased my first new car. It was a green two-door fastback Plymouth. Ruth liked my car a lot. She had never experienced a new car before and liked the smell of the interior. She immediately began making herself at home in my new car by filling the glove compartment with all her stuff. Of course, I didn't mind that at all!

On this subject, happiness for young people has not changed over the years. Happiness for me was being in my car with my girl. Happiness for Ruth was very definitely being in my car with me. This was literally the center of our world of happiness.

With music as a large part of our life, it was natural for us to have favorite songs. We decided that the song "Again" was our song. The words seem to fit us. It began with "Again, this couldn't happen again. This is that once in a lifetime . . ." We also liked "Near You" with the words "There's just one place for me, near you . . ."

With Ruth, my education on the opposite sex was almost a daily thing for me. After a night of dancing, we returned to her house, and I expected the usual, which was sitting on her living room sofa and smooching. This time, she asked me if it would be all right if she first went upstairs and got ready for bed. I couldn't imagine that this would be a bad thing, so I said, "Sure, go ahead."

About twenty minutes later, she descended the stairs in a pretty flowered housecoat. Then I saw her hair. Her hair was filled with shiny metal curlers! Up until this moment, I thought she had naturally curly hair. I didn't say a word as she sat next to me on the sofa. I had the radio tuned to the usual soft, romantic evening music. As she snuggled up close to me, her head naturally rested on my shoulder.

This time, the cold, harsh metal of a curler and clamp rested on my ear.

Again, I didn't say a word. I quickly learned that this girl, the love of my life, had a very uncomfortable nighttime presence. However, I was happy with whatever went with her. I didn't fully realize it at that time, but this was going to be my nightly experience for the rest of my life!

Prior to this, my only experience with the nighttime appearance of females had been my mother. My mother didn't have naturally curly hair, but she didn't use curlers. Instead, she used the electric curling iron before going to bed or just after she arose in the morning.

Chapter 17

Learning about Twins

They Consider Themselves as a Unit

At that time, I knew of no books that you could read to learn about twins. Through the process of direct observation, I learned that identical twins are very different from the average or normal person. It took me quite a while to get all the twin stuff together. It came gradually, slowly. The learning curve was not very steep. Along the way, I found myself asking questions like, "Why does she think that way?" "Why does she act that way?" "Why did she say that?" "What does she mean?"

If you consider that these questions are a result of the words or actions of a twin, then you know where I am coming from. Before I met Ruth, I thought that a twin was simply just another person—like me, for instance—that had someone who looked just like them. Sure, identical twins look alike and have almost identical bodies. That is the easy part! The tough part is their minds. They think alike, talk alike, and act alike. These three features are an impossible achievement for the average, nontwin person.

Ruth & Ann

The mind of a twin is borderline supernatural. The world that a twin lives in is totally different from that of the average, or normal, person. Yes, the mind of a twin is very abnormal. But from the standpoint of twins, it is our normal minds that are abnormal! They look at us and wonder why we think, feel, and act the way we do. In fact, they recoil in disgust at the way we think and act.

The mental attraction and connection between twins is uncanny to us. Twins are so accustomed to it that it seems natural to them. With a little understanding of the rules of the game, a normal person can get along fine with a twin.

A twin has much more difficulty in tolerating the rules of the nontwin world that surrounds them. To them, everyone out there is odd except another set of twins! This has to be difficult to live with. To us outsiders, it is only the twins that seem odd, and they are only two people. The rest of the population is still all right!

The psychology of twins is a separate chapter in that field. They consider themselves as a unit, not separate individuals. Twins are psychic with each other. And this is natural for them. The life of a twin is one of never being truly apart from each other. This would drive the average person crazy. We normal people have to be left alone sometimes in order to survive. In contrast, when twins are separated, they find it a terrible, if not impossible thing to endure. Through the school of direct experience, I was learning about the many idiosyncrasies of twins and, of course, about my wonderful girlfriend.

All through her life, Ann was very happy with all the decisions that she and Ruth made, until I came along and into Ruth's life. She became afraid that Ruth's relationship with me would lead to marriage and separation from her beloved twin. To deal with this, Ann had to make decisions on her own without Ruth. This was very difficult for her. Ruth, in supporting her relationship with me, was expressing individualism.

Ruth and Ann were different than the average identical twins in that their personalities were divergent. Most twins are so much alike that they get great pleasure in playing the game of switching places with each other in a social gathering. It is easy for them to fool the average person. My twins could never do this. It was impossible for

Ruth to act like Ann or Ann to act like Ruth. To my knowledge, they never tried this

Ruth and Ann had many of the characteristics of average twins. In this context, and as a background, this was what I was constantly dealing with. They never fully accepted or understood the fact that the average nontwin person had difficulty in long-term dealing with the behavioral characteristics of identical twins.

Ruth never realized how many times I had to come to terms with twin stuff, learn to accept it, and just go on loving her. She was, however, aware that our close relationship was something rare and special. This was a product of us, our love for each other. Most average people find twin abnormality too much to deal with and terminate their relationship with them. Later in my life, with the knowledge of my life with the twins, many of my male friends have told me, "Gil, I don't know how you did it! I could never, ever, do what you did!"

Chapter 18

My Career

I Was the Only Person that Qualified

With reference to my career, it seemed that my life was going forward by leaps and bounds. Immediately following graduation from Baltimore Polytechnic High School, I got a job as a Laboratory Assistant at the school. I seemed to like being at and working at an educational institution. The school also offered advanced technical courses at the level of today's Community College. I concurrently enrolled, and in two years, I received a Diploma in Electrical Engineering.

Many of the Poly graduates went on to College at the local prestigious Johns Hopkins University. These College students knew that Poly was a very good school, also prestigious in nature. One day, two Hopkins graduate students came to Poly, recruiting and looking for a senior or graduate that was proficient in both Optics and Electronics to do research work for the Professor that was the head of the Physics Department. As an Amateur Astronomer that was skilled in electronics, I was the only person that qualified. Yes, I took the job. Thus began my career at Johns Hopkins University. At Hopkins, I immediately started attending Night

School. I was rapidly accumulating experience and knowledge while working with the graduate students earning their PhDs.

Ruth was proud of me for getting my advanced Diploma in Electrical Engineering at Poly, for getting the job at the University, and for going to College at Hopkins night school. I was happy that my girlfriend was pleased with me!

Chapter 19

Life after High School

I Was Happy to Know that She Wanted to Marry Me

I t was with great pleasure that I accompanied Ruth to her high school senior prom. Ruth was eighteen years old. In my eyes, she was even lovelier than when I first met her three years before. I was so proud of her. At twenty-one years of age, I felt that I was among the older guys at the prom! Ruth was happy that Ann had a date for the prom with a boy from our church. He took her separately, which suited us fine. We wanted to be alone.

In 1950, Ruth and Ann graduated from high school. Their parents and my parents and I attended the ceremony. Through all the years of their high school, they were the only set of twins in the school. It was obvious that twins were still a rare occurrence. They were very surprised when a local newspaper reporter and photographer came to their house to interview them as "Local Twins Graduating from High School." In the newspaper, it was a rather large article with two photographs of Ruth and Ann together. The article discussed their hobbies and interests and outlook for the future. This experience strengthened their self-opinion and bolstered their notoriety.

Shortly after graduation, Ruth quit her part-time job as a department store salesgirl and went to work for the Travelers Insurance Company as a claims agent. She liked her new job very much, and the salary was higher.

Ruth and I had been together for three and a half years. Our love affair could only be described as "beautiful." Our relationship was solid. I was dedicated to doing everything that I could to please her, and she did the same for me.

Now that Ruth was out of high school, I figured that it was time for me to assert myself and announce my intention to marry her. With the knowledge of Ruth's beauty and extreme attractiveness to the opposite sex, I didn't want any other unknown guy to come out of the woodwork and propose marriage to her before I did.

I went to the jewelry store and purchased a nice solitaire diamond ring for her. I told no one about this. That Saturday night, after bringing her home late from a dance, I knew that everyone in the house was asleep. I proposed to her on my knees in her living room and presented the ring. With wide eyes and open mouth, she took the ring and placed it on the proper finger. It fit perfectly. Tears filled her eyes as she hugged me and kissed me.

I asked her, "Do you like the ring?"

"Oh yes!" she replied. "It's beautiful."

I then said, "Well then, when can we get married?" There was a pause, and we sat on the sofa.

She continued, "I love you, Gil, from the bottom of my heart, and I do want to marry you. But you don't understand the situation with Ann. It would break her heart if I got married right now or soon and moved away from her. I love her too, you know." I understood this, coming from a twin.

As a twin, Ruth strongly empathized with Ann's feelings. She would never purposely do anything to hurt Ann's feelings. Unfortunately, Ann's inward personality made her overdependent on Ruth. "All along," Ruth continued, "Ann has had difficulty in dealing with the idea that ours is a serious relationship and that we will one day get married and move away from her. She relies upon me for so many things. I'm working hard on it, and I hope to get her to the point when she can do without me."

I said, "Well, I already knew that!"

Ruth, being the secure person that she was, then said, "I would also like to spend some time in the working field on my own. So please, can we just not get married or engaged right now?"

I was intelligent enough to know that this was her bottom line. We then talked for a long time about our love and our life. The situation was so serious with Ann that Ruth didn't want me to tell anyone about my proposal or the ring. Not even my parents. She didn't want the physical evidence of the ring, and she reluctantly gave it back to me. In a way, I was content that we would continue to be close lovers with the definite intention of getting married. We both agreed that we were officially but silently engaged to be married. There were many romantic and amorous secrets between us, and this was just a very big one!

I was glad that I had proposed to her and happy to know that she wanted to marry me. My proposal was good for our relationship. I noticed that after that, whenever I greeted Ruth, there was a different, special sparkle in her beautiful blue eyes when she looked at me.

As you know, I liked driving a car very much, and Ruth loved riding in one. This added a great deal to our compatibility. Whenever I offered to take Ruth on a picnic, I meant to Central Park in New York City! We would leave very early in the morning, and I would drive 250 miles to Central Park, where parking was then no problem at all. We would spread our blanket and have a nice picnic lunch by a lake and watch the ducks. No one ever disturbed us.

We all know that Central Park is definitely not that way today! After our picnic, I would drive to Radio City, park the car in the garage, and we would go to see the show. After that, if any time was left, we would do a little shopping at Macy's or Gimbals. Without sleep or rest, I then drove her home without any problem. On the way home, we would stop at Howard Johnson's for supper on the then new New Jersey Turnpike. Howard Johnson's was one of the good places to eat in those days. We always got back at two or three in the morning. Ruth would have told me if her mother was concerned about the late hour. Her mother was very discerning and seemed to trust me, and she never expressed anxiety or worried about us at all.

There were many things that I took for granted that Ruth had been deprived of in her youth, before she met me. An individual such as myself, who had been driving a car for years, was quite familiar with my hometown. In the spring, I knew what streets and what neighborhoods were filled with either blossoming dogwood trees or the dazzling blossoms of azaleas and tulips. I had visited the zoo many times and had enjoyed the green acres of all the public parks. I had been to all the historical landmarks and to all the well-known movie theaters all over town. I knew where all the young people hangouts were and had been to most of them. On the fourth of July, I knew where the best fireworks displays were located. In the fall, I knew what country roads had the prettiest fall tree foliage.

At Christmastime, I knew what streets and neighborhoods had the best outdoor lights and where the Christmas garden train displays were located. In addition, there were many places that Ruth had never seen that were within a hundred-mile radius of Baltimore. We went on day trips to Philadelphia, Gettysburg, and Hershey Pennsylvania. Also, she had never visited nearby Washington, DC. We saw the Japanese Cherry Blossoms in the spring. We went to the US Capitol, the Smithsonian Institute, the White House, the museums, the Washington Monument, and the Jefferson and Lincoln Memorials. Not all in one day, of course! In addition, I took her to see Annapolis, the capital of Maryland.

Poor Ruth had not seen any of these things until I started taking her everywhere with me in my car. It was as if she had been a country girl that had never been to the city. I knew that she was very happy just going places with me, but I really didn't appreciate the magnitude of joy that she was experiencing until later. When you have a car, it is an easy, almost casual occasion to go visit your friends or your relatives. For Ruth, this was not true before she met me.

In late 1950, Ruth's father began to regress into his shell shock state, and unfortunately, he kept getting worse as time went by. He would forget to do things, not remember where he was, and become very upset over nothing. Finally, he was not going to work and became physically more than his two daughters and wife could handle. He became irrational about everything. He had to go back to the hospital. Naturally, I volunteered to take him back to the hospital in my car. Ruth's mother had to go with me to sign the hospital admitting papers. That was a sad day for everyone. It was very stressful for the ladies, and it took them a long while to recover from it. Their dad was gone again. He would not return to home again except for brief visits.

At this point in time, Ann found a boyfriend that was my age and attended our church. His name was Jim Preston. His family came from a lower-middle-class neighborhood in the southern part of the city. He had two younger sisters and an older brother. We seldom went on double dates with them. Most of the time, he wanted to take Ann out separately. In that respect, he was normal! Otherwise, he was much less mature and intelligent than me and always in competition with me for silly things such as how fast he could get from one place to the other in his car or that he knew something that I didn't know about. Jim didn't have a profession or trade, and as a result, he didn't earn much money. At any rate, it was good for Ann to get out by herself without Ruth. Ruth was elated that Ann at least had somebody!

In August of 1950, Ruth turned nineteen. Her other "boyfriend," Ed, who lived near her house, had a hobby of photography. He had a professional photo center and dark room in the basement of his parents' house. He asked Ruth to come to his house for a portrait photo. She agreed to do this. He took two very good black-and-white photos of her. These photos are among my favorite photos of Ruth. Prior to this, all other professional photos were of Ruth and Ann together as twins.

Ann was now working at the Peabody Institute Library as a librarian, a job that she liked very much. It was quiet and peaceful and went with her inward personality. Ruth was working at the Travelers Insurance Company as a claims agent, a job that went with her outgoing personality. Ruth liked her office environment with lots of people chattering, telephones ringing, typewriters clacking, and filing cabinet drawers slamming shut. It was noisy there! It was a big day for her when she got a brand-new Remington typewriter. To celebrate the occasion, there was an office party with a cake, candles, and balloons! Ruth was very happy with her office environment as it went well with her personality.

Ruth considered Ann's job at the Peabody as dull and stuffy. In response to her culture as a twin, Ruth began lobbying Ann to quit her job and join her at the Travelers, where it was more "fun." After two and a half years at the Peabody, in response to her culture as a twin, Ann quit her job and joined Ruth. They both enjoyed the daily notoriety and attention of being identical twins in the office. For the rest of their lives, Ann managed to successfully follow Ruth in her career. It was a struggle for Ann to be outgoing as this was something that she was not. Ann's struggle was apparently transparent to Ruth. Ann's success depended on the fact that Ruth was there to help her and support her.

Ruth & Ann-Office

Chapter 20

Separation

I Was Not Sure I Would Ever See Ruth Again

The Korean War was in full swing, and young men like me were being drafted into the military service in the manner similar to World War II. My work at the Hopkins University was highly scientific and technical and advancing the state-of-the-art in the field of Experimental Physics. On December 1 of 1950, I received my first draft notice. I was very upset about this. Hopkins Personnel Department forwarded a letter to the draft board, asking for a deferment for me on the basis that my work was funded by military government money from both the Naval Research Laboratory and Air Force Cambridge. As a result, I was granted a sixty-day deferment.

At the end of January 1951, my deferment lapsed, and the draft board refused to extend it in spite of appeals from Hopkins. So my fate was cast. On February 22, 1951, I was going to be drafted. I was very unhappy about this. I went about getting my life together and things together to prepare for my departure from civilian life.

Separation was a terrible thing for Ruth and me. We both cried a lot. The involuntary long-term separation of two people like Ruth and me, who love each other deeply, creates a special kind of agony. In addition to the separation, there was the fact that I was going to war and could be killed. On the day before my induction, I went to see Ruth, and we hugged and kissed and cried a lot. The next morning, I tearfully said good-bye to my parents, and then my dad drove me to the induction center, where I hugged him and left him standing at the door waving to me.

I soon found myself on a bus filled with fellow inductees, on my way to the nearest army base at Fort Mead, Maryland. There, we were sent to an evaluation center, where they interviewed each person. I filled out many forms, asking about personal history, education, and skills. We were told that we would be there for a week or two before being sent to basic training in Georgia.

When my qualifications were reviewed, they wanted to send me to Officers Training School. This appealed to my ego, but I was told that I had the option to refuse, so I did. Everyone knew that they needed officers to send to the battlefield. I didn't want that!

I had a strong background in electronics, so immediately after basic training in Georgia, they told me that they were going to send me to a radio operator's school at the same camp. This was a five-month training school. This was five months that I didn't have to spend at the front line in Korea. Next, the inductees were sent to the base hospital for immunization shots. These shots gave me a terrible headache and nausea that lasted for a day.

On the next day, Sunday, I was pleasantly surprised to find that my parents and Ruth came to see me. I was so happy to see Ruth. I hugged her and kissed her. My mother brought me some warm chicken soup. That was great because I hadn't eaten for a day. We went to the Base Chapel to attend the Sunday Church Service. The Chaplain announced that there wouldn't be a service today because there was no one to play the piano. Ruth immediately stood up and announced that she would be happy to play. And so she did. This tells you a lot about her personality. Of course, I would rather be holding Ruth's hand as she sat next to me, but I was proud of my sweetheart.

A few days later, I was on a troop train headed for Georgia. This was my first experience at sleeping on a train. We picked up more cars and inductees at each city on the way. It was a long train when we finally arrived.

At Camp Gordon, we were issued GI clothing and gear. Apparently, the army was not yet up to speed and ready for this war. There were no new shoes and no mess gear. I was issued used shoes that did not fit and only a spoon to eat with. A week of walking in painful shoes followed. Finally, I got shoes that fit and all my gear. And thus began my basic training.

This was not a good time for Ruth and me. I was not sure I would ever see her again. After basic training, I wrote a love letter to her almost every day and called her on the phone as many times as I could. I loved hearing her voice. A few months had passed, but it seemed to me that I had been separated from Ruth for an eternity. Before my induction, I was Ruth's boyfriend and lover. Now, I was her soldier. Movies and real life stories from World War II of soldiers and their girlfriends left behind at home were still firmly remembered by everyone, including Ruth. For Ruth and me, the agony of these stories had become a reality of life. It was a shock for both of us.

When I called Ruth on the telephone, we often talked for a half-hour or more. Often, she wrote me two letters in one night. We were desperately trying to keep close to each other by whatever means of communication possible. Ruth's love letters to me were wonderfully poignant. She would tell me what she was doing that day and how she would often stop and think of me. I don't know what I would have done without her letters. In my letters to her, I would tell her how much I missed her and missed home. For me, it was difficult to describe what my life was like during basic training. It was awful. Ruth could read between the lines that I was going through a relative hell. After I started my military radio operators school training, she could tell that my life was better.

About halfway through my school training period, they gave us a three-day holiday, centered on the Fourth of July. We had to stay at camp; there was no long-term leave allowed. When I first learned of this welcome break in my training, I mentioned it in telephone conversations with my parents and Ruth. A couple of days later, I learned that my parents had decided to drive from Baltimore to Georgia to see me during the break, and Ruth was coming along! To say that I was overjoyed was putting it mildly. I assumed that Ruth must have told Ann that she was just coming to see me, and that was all. In her letters to me, Ruth was talking about marriage! I counted the days until their arrival.

Finally, they arrived. At that time, Ruth was nineteen, and I was twenty-two. It was all I could do to hold back my tears of joy when I first saw Ruth again. I only had two days and one night with her. I hugged her and kissed her. Then, I hugged my parents. My parents had reservations to stay at an upscale hotel in the nearby town. After checking in at the hotel, my father drove us all around the town to see the sights.

All this was agonizing for me because all I wanted was to be left alone with my sweetheart, Ruth. Early in the evening, after supper, we returned to the hotel room where my parents and Ruth were staying. There was not much to do. Ruth and I sat on the sofa with our arms around each other. Here we were, two young people, deeply in love with each other, desperately wanting to be alone together. This day was the most emotionally charged day of our lives. I could tell by looking into Ruth's eyes that she wanted to be alone with me. For some reason, my parents went out for a while and left us alone in the hotel room. Perhaps they knew we wanted to be alone. What a blessing that was for us. We were so happy to be alone together.

The circumstances of the moment dictated to both of us that this might be the last time we would ever see each other. We held each other tightly and kissed and hugged. In the hotel room, there was a large, empty walk-in closet. We both knew what we wanted. We dashed into that closet and closed the door. We were both being driven by our raging hormones. The activity in that closet became a sequence where unrestrained intimacy prevailed for both of us. We stayed in there for a long time.

We heard my parents open the door and enter the hotel room. We quietly stayed in there until we were ready to come out. When we heard them leave the room again, we both came out. They heard us and exclaimed, "Where were you? We didn't see you!" I glanced over my shoulder and noticed that the room had large glass doors that led to an outdoor balcony.

I replied, "Oh, we were out there on the balcony! It's nice out there!"

My mother said, "Oh! We were wondering where you were!"

I then said, "Ruth and I are going for a walk. We'll be back soon!"

The soft night lighting on the hotel grounds led the way through wandering paths that were filled with beautiful, fragrant flower gardens. It seemed that Ruth and I were experiencing paradise. We were alone. We saw no other people. While we walked, we stopped and hugged and kissed. Then, we sat down in a bench and talked. Ruth said, "Let's get married right away! Tomorrow if we can!" I eagerly agreed to that!

Then we began rationalizing the effect of this action. I knew that my parents would be happy about it. Ruth said, "My mother would be happy for me. She likes you a lot, Gil!

"But," she continued, "Ann would be devastated and heartbroken. I love you very much, honey, and I didn't want you to go off to war without telling you in person that I want to be your wife! That's why I came here!" I tenderly kissed her again.

"Well," I said, "I've been thinking too. If I get killed, I wouldn't want you to be a war widow!" There was a long pause.

Ruth finally said, "Well then, maybe we shouldn't do it! What do you think?"

I reluctantly agreed.

Then, we again walked slowly through the gardens. "Sweetheart," she said, "I can't tell you how much I have enjoyed this day! Especially tonight!"

"Same here!" I replied and kissed her tenderly. We were both smiling broadly as we entered the hotel room and greeted my parents. They both remarked that we seemed so happy, and they were pleased.

I agreed that it would be best if I didn't stay at the hotel with them that night. I returned to the army base and then met them for breakfast bright and early the next morning. The next morning passed all too quickly, and soon it was noon and time for Ruth to go back home. It was heartbreaking for me to watch them drive away. Tears filled my eyes as I watched Ruth wave to me from the car until it disappeared in the distance. Then, I cried very hard as I was engulfed with the awful thought that this might be the last time I would ever see her. The statistics were bad concerning how many men were being killed on the battlefield. Oh god, I loved her so much.

When I returned to school the next day, they announced that the school was getting overcrowded, and they were going to split it into two groups. They asked for volunteers to attend a night session of the school. I immediately volunteered for the night school. I correctly rationalized that this would be a better deal than day school.

We were moved to an isolated barracks area where we could sleep during the day and not be disturbed. We had a separate mess hall where we had breakfast at seven in the evening, lunch at midnight, and supper at five in the morning. We were isolated from all the military protocol that occurred during the day. This was a definite advantage. We had more time to ourselves to write letters to home, call home on the telephone, read, listen to the radio, and enjoy the recreation room. On a relative scale, it was nice!

Needless to say, I kept in touch with Ruth as much as possible. Since her visit to me, her love letters were even more intimate and personal. She happily informed me that she got her period on time! Naively, Ann always wanted Ruth to read aloud her letters from me. Ann wanted assurance that Ruth and I were not getting serious or planning marriage. So I always wrote two separate letters to Ruth. One letter to read to Ann and her mother and the other for Ruth only. I don't know where she hid them, but Ruth apparently was successful in keeping my personal letters away from her sister!

For the next three months, I attended the night session. As the end approached, I could tell from reading between the lines in Ruth's letters that she was getting upset about the prospect of my having to go to Korea soon. Along with thousands of young men like me, I was going to war. This was very stressful. Like the rest of my buddies, I was trying to push all this into the back of my mind.

At the end of my training, I graduated and received my Military Radio Operators License. After that, there was a one-week period of waiting at camp for an assignment, most likely overseas. During this period of the war, the army was in need of replacement soldiers on the front line in Korea. Ninety percent of the men were assigned to the battlefront. Sure enough, I received orders to go to Korea. I was given ten days at home before embarking to Korea.

I devoted most of my ten days at home to being with Ruth. It was very stressful for us. As a couple, we were living through what thousands of couples had lived through during World War II. We remembered seeing this scenario many times in the movies of the 1940s, never dreaming that we would one day be living through the same hell!

My last day at home finally came. I tried to give my parents as much attention as I could. They were doing the same for me. My dad was too young for World War I and too old for World War II. He had never been in the military. It was especially hard for him to see his only son go off to war. My mother lovingly cooked a nice big breakfast for me. I placed a planned last telephone call to Ruth, and we tearfully said good-bye to each other. My parents, of course, realized how much Ruth meant to me.

Later, I was in uniform, I had my army duffel bag packed, and my orders and airline tickets in hand. The time drew near for me to leave. I stood gazing out of the front window, wondering if this would be the last time. My future was bleak. My dad was standing by to drive me to the airport. Then, the doorbell rang! We weren't expecting anything or anyone! What was this all about? I was shocked to find that it was a telegram for me! I hastily opened it and read it. I couldn't believe my eyes! It was from the Adjutant General's Office, the Chief Administrative Officer of the US Army!

It was addressed to me, with my name, rank, and serial number. It said, "Disregard current orders for overseas duty! Instead, report for duty in research at the Squier Signal Laboratory at Fort Monmouth, New Jersey, in ten days!" Was I dreaming? Was this true? I read it again and again. Sure enough, it was for me. My name and serial number and my current order number was correct. It came from the Pentagon in Washington, DC! It had to be true and official!

As the reality of the telegram sank in, I began shouting for joy! My god! I was going to stay in the States! If the telegram had arrived five minutes later, I would have been on my way to the airport! My mom and dad couldn't believe it either! I still have this telegram in my possession.

Someone, somewhere in the military had reviewed my résumé, my qualifications and experience, and decided that the army could best make use of me in army research! To this day, I have no idea who that was, but I thank them from the bottom of my heart. Essentially, my brain saved me from going to Korea!

I glanced at my wristwatch. Ruth wasn't at home; she was now at work. I called her at her office number. Someone else answered and said that she came in crying and hadn't been able to do any work. I told them who I was and to get her to the phone. I never called her on her office phone, so she knew that it must be important. I carefully explained about the telegram and what it meant. She was astonished. She couldn't believe it. She was so happy. She knew that it was absolutely real when I promised to pick her up after work and go out and celebrate. And so we did!

When I arrived at the Laboratory at Fort Monmouth, I was assigned to work on early transistor fabrication with a world-famous Physicist at the Solid State Physics Branch. I was able to significantly contribute to their effort from the first day of my arrival. Whoever reviewed my records and qualifications knew exactly what they were doing by sending me to that location.

While I was gone, Ruth went on with her life. She went to and from work on the bus and walked to the grocery store. Her life returned to the status it was in before I met her. For young people like us, this two-year period seemed eternally long. She missed me because she loved me, but I know that she also missed my car. When I came home to see her, Ruth just wanted to get out of the house and be alone with me. We spent very little time at her house. Instead, we got in my car and just went places. On Saturdays, I took her shopping. In those days, not a single store was open on Sunday.

We went dancing and dining all over town. For all the major holidays, I was able get a pass to be home for a week. I was very grateful that I was able to do this. At any and all times, I was very, very thankful that I was in the United States and not in Korea, fighting the war!

Best of all, I was able to go home and visit Ruth for the weekend about once or twice a month. In the weeks that we were apart, we missed each other terribly. My assignment at the research laboratory was for a nine-month period. Long before the end of this period, I investigated and learned the military protocol for this type of assignment and, on my own, managed to get myself another assignment at the Ballistic Research Laboratory at nearby Aberdeen Proving Ground, in Maryland.

Upon departure from Fort Monmouth, I received an unsolicited letter of recommendation from the colonel in charge. This turned out to be the best letter of recommendation that I have ever received.

At Aberdeen Proving Ground, I was assigned to the Atomic Cannon project. The project was in the stage of field and environmental testing. I was able to make significant contributions to the project in troubleshooting and problem-solving. This would see me through 1952 and into early 1953, the end of my two-year term in the army. Before leaving Aberdeen, they offered me promotion and assurances of advancement if I stayed in the military service. Alternatively, they offered me a job in civil service with assurances of advancement. I turned them all down.

After what seemed an eternity of time, in February of 1953, I was finally released from the military service. I was so happy. I drove right to Ruth's house and ran to her arms. The next day, I returned to Hopkins University and got my old job back. It really felt good to be back to normal civilian life. I vowed to never again complain about anything in civilian life!

Chapter 21

The New House

The House Only Had Two Bedrooms

This time of separation taught Ruth and me that our love was indeed an enduring one. Our relationship was founded on much more than pure physical attraction between members of the opposite sex. We loved just being with each other. We loved sharing every aspect of our lives. For us, love seemed to overcome everything that we encountered in life. I was ever so happy to return to civilian life and once again be with Ruth on a full-time basis. We were in heaven again.

It seemed that we were now at another crossroad in our lives. So I asked Ruth again about us getting married. This was the third time that we discussed marriage. Ruth replied, "Oh, Gil, I want to marry you more than anything, but there are some issues that you don't know about!"

"What are they?" I asked.

Her reply was, "It's still Ann! I don't think she is ever going to be able to live without me! So whenever we get married, both she and my mother will have to live with us, or we will have to live with her

120

Ruth & Donkey Cart

and my mother! Would that be all right with you?" That was a loaded question! My deep love for Ruth prevailed.

A smile of relief filled Ruth's worried face as I simply replied, "Sure!"

Ruth then said, "Oh, Gil! I was hoping you would say that! Oh, I love you so much!" and she kissed me tenderly. I knew then that for the rest of my life, I was going to be helping Ruth in dealing with Ann. "Now," she continued, "the next issue is the house where I live. The house is more than thirty years old. Since you've been away, we have found that we need a new roof. In addition, we need a new furnace and new windows. Ann's salary and my salary are supporting the house and our mother. All those needed home improvements will cost a lot of money that we don't have, so we have decided to move, to find a new house. We would much rather put the money in a new or newer house.

"In addition," she continued, "if we got married now, we would not have a bedroom! There are only two bedrooms. Neither Ann nor I would consider sleeping in the basement! That's out of the question!"

"Well," I commented, "this certainly puts a hold on our getting married!"

Ruth replied, "I know it does, honey, and I am just as upset about that as you are! I hate it!" Ruth then said, "Oh, please don't ever mention to Ann or my mother that we plan on getting married soon. Ann is still having a very hard time accepting the fact that we are in a serious relationship, much less marriage!"

Again, my deep love for Ruth prevailed, and I said, "Okay!"

With little-girl shyness, Ruth then said, "You know, Gil, we could never find a new house or move without you and your car. Will you help us find our new house?"

I replied, "Of course I will, sweetie!"

The ladies scoured the newspaper ads for houses for sale. Based on location, price, and style of house, on a weekly basis, they piled into my car on a Saturday, and off we went to inspect the chosen locations. This put a dent into the social life of Ruth and me, but we always managed to get some time to ourselves. This went on for months

The ladies finally decided on a two-story brick house on Belvedere Avenue that was on the end of a row with a nice size lot. So we went there to tell them that we wanted to buy the house. When we arrived, the For Sale sign was down. The ladies were very disappointed, considering that it wasn't for sale anymore and perhaps was sold. I was more assertive. I went to their door and rang the bell. Sure enough, it was still for sale!

I noticed that the house had only two full bedrooms. The third room on the second floor was very small and would be filled by a double bed. It would make a nice nursery for a baby. I privately asked Ruth about the lack of a third bedroom for us. "Oh," she replied, "I've thought that out! We will add a third bedroom on the side of the house, there's plenty of room for it!" That seemed reasonable to me. Then began the arduous task of buying the new house, selling the old house, and moving. As everyone knows, this is a lot of work!

The sale of the old house was complicated by the fact that the twins' dad was hospitalized. Selling the house involved both government and private lawyers and many trips to the courthouse. Their dad or the government was to receive half of the price of their current house. This meant that Ruth and Ann would have to take a bigger mortgage to buy the new house.

Since we were all going to live together, Ann finally accepted the fact that Ruth and I would soon get married. This was a significant accomplishment! At that time, I had very little money in the bank. While I was in the service, I bought a new car. I was still paying for it. My noncom military pay was not that great. The ladies used the sale money from the old house as down payment for the new. They assumed a relatively large mortgage for the new house. They had to support this on Ruth's and Ann's salary. They could just barely make it. The deed for the new house was in Ruth's, Ann's, and their mother's name, but that was all right with me.

I offered to contribute some money to help. They happily accepted this. In addition, we all had to contribute to a savings account to accumulate enough money to add a bedroom wing to the side of the house for Ruth and me. In those days, everyone saved their money until they had enough to buy what they needed. Then, they paid cash for it. I made this an arrangement just between the ladies and me. I knew that everyone else would not approve of this arrangement. Especially since I wasn't even living there.

Our new house was only three years old, but it needed cleaning from top to bottom. This required a lot of labor and work on our part. We went to the empty house and began cleaning. I pitched in, and for the first time, I worked side-by-side, elbow-to-elbow with Ruth and Ann. This circumstance was of great benefit to me. The twins had never worked with a man before. Ann liked my work! In fact, she requested that I help her with some of the cleaning work instead of Ruth! She said that her sister didn't do as good a job as I did! For the first time, I had bonded with Ann!

It made Ruth very happy to see Ann and me working together. I was happy too. This effort took two weeks. I could see that Ann had developed a new respect for me. I was overjoyed at this. I didn't dislike Ann. I actually liked her. After all, she was Ruth's twin. She was a very pretty girl. Whenever anyone complimented her on her beauty, she always said, "Oh no! I'm not the pretty one! Ruth is!" This tells the psychologist a lot about her!

Ann obviously had an inferiority complex that was the size of Texas! This was reinforced by the fact that she was an introvert. Ann worshipped Ruth and would lie down and die for her. Ann had trouble with anyone or anything that she considered was reducing the love that Ruth had for her. Ergo, me! Also, something in her personality and mental makeup caused her to generally distrust and dislike men! This was what both Ruth and I were battling!

It was fortuitous that I had succeeded in some measure in bonding with Ann. Throughout the rest of my life, whenever I was having trouble or was down and out, she took up for me and helped me through whatever crisis I was having. There was some measure of love buried in her! At other times, she just tolerated me. I realized that, in order to live with Ruth and Ann, I had to learn to tolerate Ann!

All the months of house hunting and moving severely limited the social life of Ruth and me. It didn't matter to either of us because we were with each other all the time, sharing the load together. All that mattered was that we were together. Finally, the move was complete, and Ruth, Ann, and their mother were in their new house.

Ann's boyfriend, Jim, didn't seem to want to help with either the house hunting or moving effort. That tells you something about him. I used my talents to replace defective electrical wiring, hook up the gas stove, replace broken door hinges and window locks, and adjust door latches. I was able to deal with all the problems in a house.

We needed the bedroom addition to the house. The major drains on our money were the large house mortgage, the general cost of living, and the savings for the addition. The cost of the addition was equal to the mortgage. In order to get married in a year's time or less, all our money would have go to the mortgage and savings for the new addition to the house. In that situation, we would have to live like paupers. Ruth and I had some serious decisions to make. After much consideration, we decided to live better and postpone our marriage. For us, this was not an easy decision to make.

If Ruth were not a twin, this situation would have been totally different. We would have been married by now. This is the baggage that came with Ruth. This is what made my life so different and so difficult. Ruth was very perceptive, but she never fully realized that it was as difficult for me to embrace this decision as it would have been for her to ignore her twin.

At this point, it was now early 1954, and there was nothing that Ruth and I could do but wait until the money for the addition was saved. Ruth and I were unhappy that we couldn't get married and live together. I had to live with my parents, who, by now, had become accustomed to my regular absence.

By now, I had learned to respect Ruth's intuition or feelings. She felt that it was right for us to wait. It was very hard for Ruth and me to put our marriage on hold. However, we had each other, and I was with Ruth almost as much as if we were married. On the relative scale, we were happy, and we enjoyed our life.

On the absolute scale of two people deeply in love, getting married, without the involvement of identical twins and their mother, Ruth and I would have been married long before this. Unfortunately, we were not just two people. We were four people. I would have been happy sleeping on a sofa bed.

As soon as they moved in, Ruth and Ann began making flower gardens in the yard. I was an important part of their effort as it was my car that took them to the nursery and hauled the plants back home. In a short while, our grounds were ablaze with colorful flowers and bushes. Their passion and hobby was gardening and landscaping. Our grounds never looked shabby.

I was with Ruth and Ann a lot more now. As usual, I was the provider of transportation for all their shopping. I was essentially the man of the house, who didn't live there! What a distinction!

At all times, my reward for my effort was Ruth. We didn't mind staying up late at night at her house after Ann and their mother had gone upstairs to bed. We looked forward to our time together. We would turn the TV on and turn the sound down low and snuggle on the couch together. Later, our desire for intimacy would conclude in the kitchen!

As time went by, our new house was alive and festive with all the happy occasions such as holidays and birthdays. I ate supper at Ruth's house many times during the week. I always spent all day Saturday and Sunday with Ruth. On most Sundays, after church, I took Ruth and Ann and their mother for an hour-long trip to see their dad at the veterans hospital. He was always very glad to see us.

As time passed, things changed. We were dismayed to find that the Dixie Ballroom, our favorite dance hall, was going to close. Other dance halls in the area were either closing or changing their format, making them less desirable for us. It seemed that there was no place for us to enjoy dancing in the Baltimore area.

I then turned my attention to the nearest large city, Washington, DC. I found that the most highly recommended place for dancing was at the Shoreham Hotel on Connecticut Avenue. Brochures showed that there was weekly Saturday night dancing on the attractive Shoreham outdoor terrace with the Bob Cross Orchestra.

With eager anticipation, Ruth and I decided to give it a try, and on a Saturday night, off we went to the Shoreham Hotel. When we arrived, we couldn't believe how nice it was. The terrace was a beautiful outdoor dance floor setting amid lovely floral gardens with a large water fountain. The dance floor was huge with colorful tables, chairs, and umbrellas on the perimeter. It was truly magnificent. A large poster indicated that Peggy Lee would be singing with the orchestra. She was a famous singing star of that day and age. With that knowledge, I considered that this would be an expensive evening for me.

Alfred, the maître d', informed us that the cover charge was only $1.50 per person for the evening, including dancing and a floorshow! I expected a much bigger charge than that. We arrived early, and there were only a few people there. We found ourselves an up-front table and ordered drinks. Soon, there were hundreds of people there, and the band began to play. The music was terrific, and we danced continuously with the night stars shining above. The whole setting was beautiful and romantic. Ruth and I agreed that this was the place for us.

We came back to the Shoreham Terrace for dancing very often after that. To our delight and pleasure, we found that many singing stars, musicians, and movie stars came to the Shoreham just to dance. We found that we were rubbing elbows with many famous people. Nelson Eddy came there several times to sing, and of course, Ann came along with us. We also heard Tony Martin sing. On another occasion, our table was next to Al Hirt, the famous trumpet player.

Every time that Nelson Eddy came to the Shoreham, Ann was sure to be there. More than once, life and family circumstances dictated that Ruth and I could not attend Nelson Eddy's concert and take Ann with us. Ruth, being the loving twin that she was, arranged for me to take Ann.

I will never forget the day that Ruth and I were on the dance floor with movie star Susan Hayward and her partner. As she danced and talked, her voice sounded just like it did in the movies. It was crowded, and everyone naturally bumped into one another while dancing. We bumped into her several times. After that dance set, Ruth and I sat at our table. With my dry sense of humor showing,

I said to Ruth, "I can honestly say that I have bumped rumps with Susan Hayward!"

With a slight frown on her face, Ruth replied, "Gil! Really! You're bad!" This was neither the first nor the last time that Ruth called me bad!

Chapter 22

Engagement and Wedding Plans

Everything Went Wrong with Those Plans

As the months went by, I openly expressed my impatience concerning getting married. Ruth's loving manner counteracted this and always made my life seem worthwhile. After what seemed to Ruth and I to be a very long two and a half years, we found a contractor to build our addition for a reasonable price. I was proud that my architectural drawing of the addition was the one accepted by the city! In 1956, Ruth and I officially announced our engagement. We were so happy.

I took Ruth to the jewelry store to pick out our rings. I liked the plain gold wedding band for myself. Ruth chose a large diamond with two smaller ones beside. She set our wedding date for June 22, 1957. Unfortunately, in that same year, 1956, I had to go on a month-long field trip to White Sands, New Mexico, as part of my job at Hopkins University. While I was gone, Ruth and I wrote love letters to each other. These letters were precious to me, and I still have a few of them.

Gil & Ruth 1957

Planning a wedding is a big deal. It is a once-in-a-lifetime occasion. Ruth and I made sure that we got the big things right. We could have easily gotten married in our church. That would have been our first choice. In consideration of Ruth's father in the hospital, we decided to get married at home in our living room. Her father never went to church and seemed to dislike churches, for whatever reason. He was not an atheist, he was married in a church, and he always said grace before a meal. According to Ruth's mother, Effie, he never objected to his family attending church services, but he never went with them. In the ten years that I had known Ruth, he never attended a church service.

When we visited him at the hospital the next weekend, we told him that we were getting married. He seemed very pleased that his daughter was marrying me. When we told him that the wedding would take place at our home, he seemed even more pleased. This told us that we had made the right decision.

Ruth, Ann, and their mother didn't have any problem with the fact that I would be living in the same house with them. However, in those days, just about everyone in the world outside of twins considered this to be "shocking" and a big "no-no." I kept hearing from everyone, "You're going to live in the same house with her unmarried sister? Oh my! I don't see how Ruth can allow that!"

Whenever I mention anything about the ways of the world outside of twins like this to Ruth, she always gave me the same answer, "Oh, Gil! You're just exaggerating it!" and cast it off as unimportant. However, this issue was certainly a reality for me. All my friends and relatives were expressing the same serious concern to me. I couldn't convince them that there would be no "hanky panky" in the household. Everyone was convinced that I would be having sex with both girls! All my guy friends were envious of me and wanted to hear regular reports of my "escapades." My own mother didn't approve and asked me, "How are you going to tell which one is sleeping with you!"

I answered, "If that happened, I guess that I wouldn't be able to tell!" She seemed to be satisfied that I used the word *if*.

I was always telling Ruth about the ways and thoughts of the average person and comparing it to the twin way. Ruth appreciated my gems of wisdom because it helped her understand some of the puzzling manners of nontwins. I would often tell Ruth and Ann that they were doing or thinking twin stuff.

Ruth had three wedding showers from her friends and relatives. One of them was a surprise. She enjoyed these showers very much. She was just overflowing with joy and happiness. Of course, Ann went to the showers with Ruth. Ruth wanted me to attend her showers, so I did. I was glad that I attended as I was the only one taking quality 35 mm film photos.

It was nice that Ann was enjoying the happiness of participating in all of Ruth's prenuptial parties and planning. At this point in time, she had broken off with her boyfriend, Jim, and had no other boyfriend.

The new bedroom and bath addition to the house was finally completed. The twin's mother was in her seventies and was having difficulty with the stairs. It was only right that she get the new bedroom on the first floor instead of Ruth and me. We took the upstairs bedroom that her mother had.

Ruth and I went shopping for our bedroom furniture. Her taste was formal, and mine was modern. We compromised and purchased furniture that pleased us both.

We knew that I had to pay for the wedding because Ruth's father was permanently hospitalized, and there was no money. I went with Ruth to pick out and purchase her wedding gown and the maid-of-honor gown for Ann. I also paid for all the flowers, the wedding cake, and the decorations. I had saved enough money for a two-week honeymoon trip to Miami, Florida, with a side trip to Havana, Cuba, which was then a very romantic city.

Everything went wrong with those plans. One week before the wedding, termites invaded our house by the million. The ladies were frantic. They had spent all their money on the addition to the house and the wedding and had nothing to spare for emergencies like this. So it was up to me to use my honeymoon money to have the house exterminated. There went our honeymoon to Florida! As it turned out, that was when Castro started to take over Cuba and close the country to Americans, so we wouldn't have been able to go to Havana.

Chapter 23

The Wedding

There Was the Problem of Ruth's Mother's Sister

The sky was clear, and the sun shone warm for our wedding day. I was happy about that. Early in the morning, at Ruth's request, I drove thirty miles to the veterans hospital where her father essentially lived. I picked him up and drove him to Ruth's house to attend the wedding. Then, I went to my house and got dressed in my tuxedo. My parents were very glad that I was marrying Ruth.

I arrived very early at Ruth's house for the two o'clock wedding. In accordance with tradition, Ruth stayed upstairs to get dressed so I wouldn't see her. Ann and her mother and a few other ladies were also upstairs, helping her. Helping a bride get into her wedding gown is, of course, an exciting and momentous occasion for the ladies. I could tell by the giggling and laughing that they were having a good time.

I was glad that I arrived early, because there were some problems. The wedding cake had just been delivered and was sitting on the dining room table in its box. When the box was opened and the cake removed, the screams of many female voices filled the air. It seemed that the freshly delivered wedding cake was covered with fruit flies! Apparently, the flies came from the delivery truck. What a terrible situation! We made a desperate emergency call to the bakery, and they first apologized and then agreed to bake another cake and deliver it just in time for the reception.

As if this was not enough, there was the problem of Ruth's mother's sister. She was a nice enough lady but a little overbearing. She proceeded to meddle into everything. I will refer to her as "she." She had rearranged all the tables set up in the dining room for the reception and even rearranged the table decorations! Ruth, Ann, and her mother had spent all the previous day and evening nicely decorating the house for the wedding and arranging things the way they wanted them.

I yelled upstairs to the ladies and informed them of this travesty. Ann and her mother immediately came down and scolded the mother's sister then put everything back the way they wanted. Unfortunately, she still continued to meddle.

I knew that the minister who was to marry us had arrived and was somewhere in the house. She saw a closed door and mumbled that it should be open as she boldly pushed it open. I couldn't believe my eyes when I saw what was in the room! There stood the minister, clad only in his underwear, with a look of shock on his face! He had gone into the room to change into his vestments for the wedding!

What a terribly embarrassing situation that was! She was equally shocked and just stood there, staring at him, her hand still holding the doorknob. I gathered my composure and apologized to him as I quickly pushed "she" aside and closed the door. That did it! Ruth's mother came downstairs and gave her sister a few words of advice that were, shall we say, strong! I had never seen her that angry and using curse words! Apparently, she was accustomed to hearing her sister talk that way to her and didn't seem at all upset about it! Things calmed down after that.

Frankly, I missed the excitement, and the next hour of waiting seemed like an eternity. Finally, it was time for the wedding to begin. By that time, the house was packed with people. All our immediate family and some close friends and neighbors were gathered. A good friend of mine was best man, another friend played the piano, my cousin Maynard, who had a nice tenor voice, was the soloist, and

Ann, of course, was the maid of honor and only bridesmaid. The piano played the wedding march. It brought tears to my eyes to see Ruth, my beautiful bride, walk slowly down the stairs to the living room for the ceremony.

My cousin Maynard then sang "O Promise Me." The Reverend then proceeded with the traditional wedding ceremony. Neither Ruth nor I were nervous. We were just plain happy. After I kissed my lovely bride, Maynard sang "Because." To me, it was the most wonderful, memorable wedding ceremony in the world. The depth of my happiness could not be put into words, and I knew that Ruth felt the same way. There was the usual postwedding throwing of the bridal wreath, which Ann caught, and removal and throwing of the garter.

Following the wedding, we had a nice reception right there at home with the opening of presents. I had not enlisted the services of a formal photographer, but I made sure that an abundance of pictures were taken using my high-quality 35 mm camera. This worked out very well. Prior to the reception, the bakery kept its promise and delivered a replacement wedding cake. We were grateful for that.

Hours later, Ruth and I were finally free to put last-minute luggage in the car. We were very heavily showered with rice as we ran to the car. Then, we waved good-bye to everyone and drove off with tin cans in tow. A short time later, I stopped at a gas station to wash all the painted words off the car and snip off the tin can strings. It was a bit overdone, and I couldn't see to drive!

In retrospect, we had too much luggage with us, but we were inexperienced. Ruth and I had collected all the money that we had in the world, which amounted to just a few hundred dollars, to use for our honeymoon.

We decided to just casually, without any hotel reservations, make our way north to Niagara Falls, the old honeymoon standby. We were going to see how long our money would last and base our length of stay on that. On our wedding night, we reserved a room at the Shoreham Hotel in Washington, DC. We knew this was not in the direction of Niagara Falls, but we liked the dining and dancing at the hotel. This was definitely where we wanted to be on our wedding night.

Wedding Day

Chapter 24

The Honeymoon

Nature Was Good to Ruth

Ruth and I had been dreaming of this for years, and now, here we were on our honeymoon. In those days, air conditioning in automobiles was not common. As we happily drove down the highway to the Nation's Capital in the very warm summer air, the car windows were down. Suddenly, Ruth let out a scream. I anxiously asked her what was wrong. She told me that a wasp had blown in the window and was now in the front of her dress between her bosoms.

I pulled the car to the road's shoulder, got out, ran around to the passenger side, opened the door, leaned in, pulled the front of her dress down and searched for the wasp. Sure enough, there it was, lodged in her bra. I reached in, calmly picked it up by its wings, and threw it out of the car. The look of horror was still on Ruth's face as I told her it was gone.

We waited a long time for Ruth to calm down before resuming our drive. Apparently, as the wasp blew into the car, it hit Ruth's bare upper chest with such force that it was stunned and just sort of fell into her bra. We were fortunate. I hesitate to imagine what would have happened if that wasp had stung her there in her tender parts. I would have spent our wedding night in the hospital with her!

As I was removing the wasp, I couldn't help but notice that Ruth's chest was covered with red spots. I asked her about this, and she said that it was just hives. Apparently she had this condition every time she was in an emotional situation. I agreed that a wedding was indeed an emotional experience.

When we arrived at the hotel entrance, Ruth and I got out of our car and walked into the lobby, leaving a heavy trail of rice behind us. Everyone knew that we were honeymooners because rice was constantly falling to the floor behind us. After settling into our room and changing clothes, we went to dance at the beautiful outdoor terrace that we both loved. We had been there many times before. We held each other very close as we danced, and as our very pleasant, romantic evening progressed, thoughts of the imminent honeymoon night filled my mind.

We both were finally going to get to do what we had dreamed of for so long, to be together all the time. Now, I didn't have to go home at night! Dancing in those days was close-up body contact! Well, there I was, dancing very close to Ruth for hours on end, feeling her warm, sexy body just two layers of clothing away! As a result, I was almost constantly experiencing an erection. This was perfectly normal under the circumstance. I didn't realize that this was going to be detrimental for me. To say that I was getting anxious for the evening to end was putting it mildly!

Finally, it was time to return to our honeymoon suite and go to bed. By this time, all my sexual organs, including the prostate, were in pain! I informed Ruth of my problem and remembered hearing that it was a result of prolonged erection. She was very sympathetic with my problem. I explained to Ruth that it was a typical male problem. I knew that I just had to wait for my condition to improve. It took about four hours for my pain to subside. It would have been much better for me if we had sex first and then danced later. This never entered my mind, and I went with the logical flow of events, which caused me to experience the pain.

Nature was good to Ruth. She informed me that she had just gotten over her period. I then proceeded to consummate our marriage! That night was one of the happiest nights of our lives. I still remember every detail of it. The next day, we got up late because we were both very tired from the physical and emotional activity of the previous day and, of course, night! As we headed north in our car, we went through Baltimore without even thinking of stopping at home!

On the way north, I took a short, unscheduled detour in north-eastern Maryland to have a brief visit with my grandmother Smith. She did not expect us, but she was very glad to see us. I took lots of pictures. I was very glad that Ruth got to meet her in person. That was the last time we saw her before she passed away.

We got back on the main highway and continued north. We were not in any hurry, so we stopped in New York City. On our second night, in a downtown Manhattan hotel, we attempted to continue our honeymoon, but we found it almost impossible. The atmosphere was so lousy in that hotel room that it even dampened the spirits of lovers like us. The room was very small, dark, and unromantic. The walls gave you claustrophobia. It was a good place for a one-night stand. We were happy to just cling to each other and finally fall asleep. All night long, we kept hearing people talking, laughing, and screaming in the hallway outside of our door. Ah well, so much for our second night.

The next morning, we got up early because we were very anxious to just get out of that hotel! We left the congestion of New York City behind as we drove north on the New York Thruway toward upstate New York. The drive was pleasant and scenic, and we made good time. On our third night, we stopped at a motel in Geneva, New York. With a last name like Smith, they were suspicious of us, and I had to show them our wedding certificate in order to get a room. Another sign of the times!

As we prepared for bed that night, I realized that something was missing. I took Ruth by the hand, and we both knelt by the bed and said our nightly prayers together. I found that Ruth had never done this with Ann. This became our nightly practice.

Well, that motel room was so nice and so quiet that we were able to resume our honeymoon and make up for the previous night! That was another night I shall never forget.

The next day, we arrived in Niagara Falls, New York, and had no trouble finding a motel room. Then we went to see the falls. It was more impressive and more beautiful than we had imagined. I, of course, took lots of photos and movies.

We were finally feeling like married people. We were so happy and so in love. It wouldn't have mattered where we were; we were just happy to be together. As I mentioned earlier, we did not have reservations anywhere for our trip. We just optimistically assumed that we would not have any trouble, and we didn't. I guess that this too was a sign of the times. Throughout our trip, we had no trouble finding a nice place for meals.

That night, we called home to let everyone know that we had arrived safely at our destination. After we called my parents, we called Ruth's mother and sister. Ann answered the phone, and Ruth immediately started telling her how happy she was and what a wonderful time she was having. Unfortunately, that was the last thing her twin sister wanted to hear. She was hoping that Ruth was ready to come home. Ruth's twin was miserable without her. She was crying and said that she had to take all the wedding decorations down on the night of our wedding because it reminded her that her sister was gone.

Ruth and I understood that this was a perfectly natural twin reaction. Then her sister again asked when we were coming home. Ruth replied that before we left, it was understood that we didn't know how long we would be gone. Basically, her twin was very unhappy. Ruth won her argument by telling her sister that, as her twin, she should be happy that her sister was having a good time. After that, Ruth had a nice conversation with her mother, who was very pleased that her daughter was happy.

Ruth was really having a wonderful time on our honeymoon. I could tell that she wasn't at all worried that her sister was unhappy at home. Ruth was learning that love and sex were just as wonderful, if not better than twinship. I knew that Ruth was not giving up twinship; she was just adding true love and sex to her life.

The next day, we crossed the border and visited Niagara Falls, Canada. It was even more beautiful than the American side. Then, we drove to Toronto, Canada, to visit the James Gardens, which had a very nice walkway through floral gardens with scenic bridges and lakes. Ruth was very impressed with the gardens.

We woke up the next morning knowing that we had to start our journey back home. We did not want to drive back home over the same crowded East Coast corridor, so we drove west out of Niagara Falls and went by Erie, Pennsylvania, and into Ohio. In eastern Ohio, we turned south. In the evening, we stopped at a nice motel in Youngstown and continued our honeymoon there.

In the morning, we continued on to Pittsburgh, where we picked up the Pennsylvania Turnpike to Harrisburg, Pennsylvania. From there, it was a short drive back to Baltimore. In a way, we were sad that our honeymoon was over, but we knew that at home, our nice new bedroom was waiting for us. After a weeklong honeymoon, we were back, obviously a very happily married couple.

Ann was overjoyed to have her sister home again. Everyone could see that Ruth and I were very happy. It was our first night at home, and it was nice to be in our own, newly furnished bedroom. It was well after dark, and Ann was so happy, sitting on our bed, chatting with us about everything.

On one hand, Ruth and I were having a nice time talking to her. On the other hand, we were anxious to try out our new bed and enjoy our first night at home. We didn't know how to tell her that we wanted to be alone. Then, her mother called to her from the foot of the stairs. "Ann!" she said. "You come down here now, and you sleep with me! They need to be alone!" Ruth and I looked at each other in astonishment as Ann said good night and obediently descended the stairs. We both laughed quietly at this for a couple of minutes. Then, we knelt and said our prayers and jumped into bed. It was nice to continue our honeymoon in our own bed, in a room we didn't have to pay for! That was the beginning of our married life at home.

Chapter 25

Life and Love at Home

We Were in Heaven When with Each Other

When I arose the next morning, I realized that I was in a very new and different environment that I was not accustomed to. I had a lot of adjustments to make. I was already accustomed to seeing the house decorated and filled with the pretty, colorful, and lacey feminine touch.

However, I had never been involved with the female getting dressed and bathroom activities in the house in the morning before breakfast. The bathroom countertop was filled with ladies accessories. Items of feminine attire were everywhere. There was nothing masculine anywhere. The bathroom was a very busy place! I had to wait a long while to get in there! Ruth and Ann definitely dominated the bathroom in the morning and, as I found later, in the evening before going to bed. It became clear to me that the toilet in the corner of the basement was going to be mine!

While I was sitting in my bedroom chair, waiting to use the bathroom, Ruth came in and promptly made the bed. In the past, I was aware that the beds were always made, but I had no idea that they were made while the beds were still warm!

Ann had bigger adjustments to make than I did. The twins and their mother had been living in a matriarchal environment for the seven years since their father went away to the hospital. Now, there was a man in the house! He was sleeping with her sister in the bedroom next to hers. Her twin sister was not going to sleep with her anymore. I fully appreciated her problem and point of view.

Ruth loved me and trusted me. Otherwise, she would never have consented to having me live in the same house with her twin, her equally beautiful sister. For the average macho guy, this situation would surely end in disaster! I have a great deal of self-control, but I must confess that at first, living with two equally beautiful girls was difficult for me. Ann's prudish nature was the water that extinguished any fire within me. Nonetheless, for inbred masculine reasons, this didn't prevent me from occasionally drifting off into a sexual fantasyland. In this respect, I was a normal guy!

I noticed that every time Ann went to the bathroom to use the toilet, I could hear water running in the sink all the time. Finally, I asked Ruth about this. She said that Ann didn't want me to hear her peeing in the toilet! Oh boy, that was an indication of the total discomfort she felt with my presence in the house! In addition, Ruth came to me later and said, "I can't believe it! Ann doesn't want to put her soiled underwear in the same clothes hamper with yours! Oh my! I don't know what I'm going to do with her! After all, she has known you for ten years! You are not a stranger!"

All this was confirmation of her warped mental view of men! I couldn't help but notice that in the house, Ann never let me bump into her or touch her. She leaned away from me when passing me. Good grief! In my opinion, Ann possessed a negative attitude toward the male gender. I do not understand how this came about or where it originated.

A couple of days later, I was sitting in the kitchen in the morning before we had breakfast. Ruth was busy with her mother. Ann took the opportunity to speak with me alone. She stood in front of me with her fists on her hips, a sign of confrontation. With a firm, almost angry voice, she said, "Now look here, Gil, we are not going to cook different, special meals just for you! You'll have to eat what we have always had!"

I was startled by this but quickly recovered and replied, "Sure, that's okay with me!" With that, Ann briskly left the kitchen. In the few days that I had been here, I had never asked for anything special to eat. I had no idea what prompted that outburst from Ann.

A little while later, I told Ruth about it. She frowned and said, "Oh, that's just awful! Of course you can have anything you want!" She knew that I was not a fussy eater. She went off to speak to Ann. I don't know what Ruth said to her but, after that, Ann became very cordial with me. Apparently, Ruth told Ann to come to her with any complaints about me. After that, Ruth communicated with me concerning any issues Ann had with me. In a way, I felt a little sorry for Ann. Once again, she got her hand slapped by Ruth. I am sure that Ruth shielded me from many of Ann's complaints.

In the same manner, I had many minor confrontations with Ann that I never mentioned to Ruth. I considered that this was something that I would just have to get used to. I learned to settle some of these minor disagreements on my own. They were all based on Ann's lack of familiarity with the male sex or lack of familiarity with the ways of a nontwin individual. Unlike her, long ago I learned how to deal with my problems with twins. Both Ruth and Ann never fully appreciated my problems with them.

It was obvious to everyone, thankfully, that Ruth and I had no trouble with each other's presence twenty-four hours a day. We were in heaven when with each other. No period of adjustment was necessary for us after we were married. To love and be loved is the greatest joy on earth.

A few days after we returned from our honeymoon, a letter arrived in the mail addressed to Ruth. I watched her open it. A frown came over her face as she read the contents. I could see that she was distressed and upset with it. She said, "I don't understand any of this! It's inappropriate!" She handed me the letter.

Oh my gosh! I thought to myself. *It's a letter from her old boyfriend, Ed!*

He wrote as follows:

Dear Ruth,

I called your house last week to talk to you, and your mother answered the phone. I asked if I could speak to you, and she informed me that you weren't there, that you were away. Then, I asked where you were. She informed me that you had just gotten married and were away on your honeymoon. Well, I couldn't believe my ears. I have not been able to sleep since I heard that. How could you do this to me? I thought you loved me and were waiting for me. I just finished college and was getting my life together. I was going to ask you to marry me. I am so disappointed and upset. This is just devastating for me.

—Ed

I completely understood the letter, remembering that he took her to the beach once and then called her on the phone regularly to satisfy himself that she was still waiting for him. Ruth's usual manner of being overly polite and full of compliments had convinced him for years that she loved him and was waiting for him.

I had seen some of the post cards that Ed kept sending to her. They were all from a college town out of state and covered a period of six or seven years. Instead of signing them "Love," he signed them "Fondly." I thought that was a little odd. He had to have come home sometime while he was away at college. If so, why wouldn't you have gone to visit the girl you loved? I don't understand! There was definitely something wrong here.

I told Ruth that I understood the letter. I tried to explain to her that it was the day at the beach that convinced him that she loved him and wanted to marry him. Then, it was just her sweet, polite conversation with him over the years that convinced him that she still cared. Then I said to her, "Look, Ruth, a guy doesn't ask just any old girl to marry him! This came from his heart, and his heart is now broken! He deserves an answer to this letter!"

"Humph!" Ruth said. "I don't see why I have to answer him. His letter is way off base and inappropriate. I should think that if he were a friend, he would be happy for me, not upset with me! I don't want to answer it!"

"Oh no," I said, "he wasn't a friend! He was a lover!"

"Well," Ruth replied, "I never considered him anything but a casual friend! I don't know where he got the silly idea that I loved him, and I never got the impression that he loved me! I'm not going to answer him!"

I knew that it was really Ruth's fault. She should have known not to go to the beach with him in her bathing suit that day. Also, she should have known that a guy doesn't call you on the phone regularly unless he likes you a lot or loves you. Sweet, innocent Ruth had no idea that she was leading him on for years. As far as she was concerned, she had done nothing wrong. She obviously never mentioned anything to him about either me or our engagement or marriage.

This letter from Ed was a perfect real-life example of how Ruth's personality affected the male gender. However, in my opinion, Ed was not your typical guy. He went to college to become a minister. Not many people choose that line of study. A normal, average guy would have dated and courted the girl that he intended to marry. I don't understand his abnormal behavior.

Without being pushy, I kept reminding Ruth that she really should answer him. About a week later, Ruth finally gave in and asked me to compose the letter, and she would write it and sign it. I wrote the following: "Dear Ed, I'm very sorry that you are upset. I'm sorry if I ever did anything or said anything that made you think that I loved you, because I don't. I'm sorry that I unintentionally gave you that impression." Ruth wrote it, signed it, and mailed it. We never heard from him again.

With marriage, the love between Ruth and me grew even deeper. We became closer than ever. Every day, we looked forward to our life and love at home. We celebrated all holidays by making a special effort at lovemaking that night, and sometimes the night before too! Ruth and I learned a lot about married life together and quietly considered ourselves experts at it. We were aware that many relationships were founded on just enduring each other until the brief time when the pleasures of sex could be enjoyed. That kind of relationship can't last very long.

As identical twins, Ruth and Ann were accustomed to sharing everything. This included clothing, shoes, and jewelry. Nothing belonged to just one of them; everything was shared. They always shared a bank account together. This was perfectly natural for them, but not for me. I had great difficulty with this. In our house, Ruth and I singularly owned our bedroom furniture and all the wedding gifts given to us. Everything else in the house was owned by the corporation called Ruth, Ann, and their mother, Effie.

Not long after I moved in, Ruth informed me that we were going to pay half the cost of the new coffee table for the living room. I suggested that either we or Ann buy it. I was unaccustomed to this sharing stuff. Ruth was upset with me for suggesting this. It interfered with the way the twins were used to doing things. I had great difficulty in dealing with this. I made a list of things in the house that belonged to Ruth and I. Ruth couldn't understand why I did this and was upset with me for doing it.

This was a prime example of the difference between twin thinking and nontwin thinking. This was most always the cause of any friction between Ruth and me. Fortunately, we loved each other enough to see us through these times of crisis.

Our married life was different and complex. With other people always around, we could not do what we wanted to do, whenever we wanted. To the average couple, such an arrangement would be totally unsatisfactory. However, the magnitude of sexual gratification and satisfaction that Ruth and I experienced together was far greater than that of the average couple. The major reason for this was the depth of Ruth's love.

Ruth had two distinct loves in her life, her sister and me. Think about that. Two channels of love flowing from one person. The magnitude of Ruth's love was beyond measurement. She was made of love. I could distinctly feel this. It was as if she were two people, one who loved her sister and the other who loved me. Whenever Ruth was expressing love for me, and especially during sex, I was aware of a love that was very, very deep. I believe she was able to funnel some of the love to me that she felt for her sister. I was very fortunate to be the recipient of such great love.

Was our life at home different than average? It certainly was! Was our life together filled with an unbelievable love? It certainly was! Every night, we looked forward to our time together in bed. And it was wonderful beyond description. For us, sex was a beautiful, loving togetherness, an expression of the fullness of our love for each other that gave us both an almost magical sense of pleasure, fulfillment, and release.

Making love in the privacy of our own bedroom was very nice. However, on the subject of sex, you must realize that both Ruth and I have a little twinkle of devilment in our eyes. It wasn't long before we decided to expand our territory of lovemaking beyond the bedroom. This was a challenge in a house full of people! This distinctly added fun, excitement, and increased pleasure to our activity. So did it matter that we couldn't do whatever we wanted, whenever we wanted? Not at all!

We had only been married a couple of months when Ruth and I decided to have a large, wide, floor-to-ceiling mirror installed on the wall of our bedroom, next to our bed. As uninhibited lovers, this was a logical step to take. We really liked our mirror! The rest of the family thought our mirror made the room look twice as large and brightened it up. Well, Ruth and I considered these as secondary features!

Back then, most beds had wooden slats to support the box spring and mattress. If the slats fit tightly, they didn't move, and there was no problem. Unfortunately, our bed had loosely fitting slats. So in time, with just normal use of the bed, the loose slats would slowly get shifted at an angle and fall out, causing the box spring and mattress to fall to the floor. It doesn't take much imagination to predict that lovemaking will cause this to happen very often! And it did for us! When our bed went crashing to the floor in the middle of the night, it woke Ann up and caused her to wonder if we were hurt. So I had to fix the slats so they wouldn't move. I did this with some reluctance because Ruth and I thought it was kind of fun to crash the bed!

Ruth and Ann kept the house and the grounds of our home looking good all the time. They liked good quality mahogany, cherry, and walnut furniture, and this was obvious all over the house. Their love of flowers was also reflected all over the house in the form of flowered drapes, table coverings, bed covering, furniture upholstery, and many vases of artificial flowers. In short, the flower motif was everywhere. In addition, the outdoor flowerbeds were always ablaze with the bright-colored flowers of the season.

We were only there for a couple of years when the twins started home improvements. Outside of the back door, there was a small wooden landing and a wooden stairway to the backyard. The ladies wanted a back porch, so we replaced the landing with a ten-foot square concrete porch and stairs. This was in the days before wooden decks. This was a nice addition. After that, we spent out leisure time sitting on lawn chairs on the back porch.

The ladies always admired a house that had bow windows. This desire for a bow window surfaced, and we had the single window in the front of our house replaced with a larger, very expensive bow window. Naturally, this enhanced the appearance of our house and provided much more light in our living room. Ours was the only house in the neighborhood that had a bow window. Following that, we replaced the rotting wooden supports of the front porch roof with brick columns. We now had the best-looking house in the neighborhood!

My parents were not nearly as socially active as Ruth and Ann. My parents were always invited to attend all the birthdays and other celebrations at our house. They didn't attend those celebrations that involved lots of people that they didn't know. We didn't mind this at all.

Chapter 26

Ruth's Personality

She Was a Very Special Person

Ruth had established a good relationship with the neighbors before I moved in. This good relationship changed to even better after we got married and I moved in. Apparently, a married couple attracts more social attention than a single person. According to Ruth, the neighbors, especially the men, became much more friendly after my arrival. This seemed logical to me. As a married guy, I would feel more at ease talking to a married neighbor lady than a single neighbor lady. As time went by, I noticed that the married men in the neighborhood were freely expressing their complimentary comments to me concerning the overly polite and friendly nature of Ruth.

One day, my good neighbor Calvin and I were sitting on his front porch, having a nice talk. He began talking about Ruth. He thought that she was a very special person and was so nice and polite to everyone. He said that he could tell that she was a very loving and amorous person and that she had the characteristics of a goddess. I agreed with him.

I had a similar conversation with another neighbor, George, who lived next door to us. He was very perceptive. He asked if Ruth's amorous nature was any problem for me. I told him that it definitely

151

was a problem for me because she refuses to recognize that she is that way, and she didn't realize how she attracts and affects men by just talking to them. I also told him that men who are perceptive recognize that it is just her nature. However, most men are confused and don't understand that she is not attracted to them. He said that it was good that I understood the problem.

Our neighbor Alice, who was of my parent's age, often spent evenings after supper with us. She liked us all, and she freely expressed it. One evening, she and I were sitting alone on lawn chairs, admiring the sunset. She said that she admired the harmony among the members of our household. She leaned toward me to speak confidentially. She softly said, "I don't know what kind of arrangement you have with Ruth and Ann, and I don't want to know, but you seem to be keeping both of them very happy!" I was astonished.

My god! I thought to myself. *She thinks that I am having sex with Ann!* I did not contradict her. I knew that as an average person of her age, just like my mother, she was totally convinced that I was "servicing" both girls! So I just smiled and said, "Thanks!"

Chapter 27

Life Goes On

There Is Something Special between You Two

At this point in time, my job at the university required me to go on two weeklong field trips on a regular basis of every six weeks to the White Sands Missile Range in New Mexico for the next year and a half. It was our first year of marriage, and I wasn't happy being separated from Ruth that much. On the professional side, I was learning a lot, and it was very interesting. I could tell that Ruth was very unhappy with this. She was always upset when I had to leave. I was just as unhappy as Ruth, but I was gaining a lot of valuable experience in my job. If I had to leave Ruth all alone in the house when I went away, I would have refused to go. Since she was with her mother and sister, I reasoned that it was okay. I was very happy that Ruth didn't divorce me in our first year of marriage!

For our first anniversary, we went back to the Shoreham Hotel in Washington for an evening of dancing and entertainment on the terrace. This was a repeat of our wedding night a year before and another very nice evening that Ruth and I will not forget.

As a married couple, we could now plan more than one-day trips or vacations. This opened up a new world for Ruth and Ann. Ruth, being a good twin, wanted her sister and mother to also see Niagara

Falls. So in the following summer, we planned a ten-day vacation by car that included a tour of some of New England followed by Niagara Falls. For whatever reason, the twins' mother wanted to see the city of Boston. Ann and her mother had never traveled outside of Maryland.

Having traveled it often, the way north to New York City was nothing new to Ruth and me. On the way, we crossed the Hudson River at the Tappan-Zee Bridge and traveled through upper Connecticut and Rhode Island and into Massachusetts. As we reached the Boston area, out of self-interest, I drove past Harvard University and Harvard Square in Cambridge and the Massachusetts Institute of Technology on the Charles River.

Then, we visited the Boston Common Park, the start of the Freedom Trail and the Emerald Necklace, a system of connected parks that winds through quaint old neighborhoods. We then visited some of the Boston churches, such as the Old North Church, as this is what the twins' mother wanted to see.

We spent the night in a motel outside of Boston. On the following day, we headed west, crossed the Hudson River, and drove across New York State to Niagara Falls. At Niagara Falls, I essentially repeated the honeymoon trip Ruth and I took from the year before. Everyone enjoyed that trip.

Every now and then, Ruth and I would go for our usual Saturday night dance at the Shoreham Hotel in Washington. We would first check in to a nearby, less expensive motel and then go to the Shoreham for dancing. After the dance, we drove to our motel and spent the night. This gave us the opportunity for great lovemaking. Motel checkout time was usually one in the afternoon, so in the summer months, we would sleep late then go to the swimming pool for a dip before returning to our room for more lovemaking. You know, we never even thought about breakfast!

Everyone noticed that we seemed to be a very happy and loving couple. Ruth and I were often told that, "It is obvious that there is something special between you two!" As the years went by, Ruth and I enjoyed our married life very much. Sure, there were little ups and downs, but nothing of any consequence ever came between us. We went dancing regularly and never refused any invitation to attend a dance. If Ruth and I are an example, then those who dance well together will live and love well together.

Since Ruth and Ann were raised in a family that never had a car, they didn't know how to drive. They wanted to learn. So I personally and successfully taught both Ann and Ruth to drive a car. In the eyes of the general public, this was a significant and nearly impossible accomplishment. Almost any husband you ask will firmly refuse to even attempt to teach his wife to drive. Such a venture usually leads to shouting and screaming sessions between couples. Not so for Ruth and me. We never had any problems while I was teaching her or Ann to drive. This accomplishment was another testament to the very deep love between Ruth and me.

On the home front, our kitchen had a gas stove. Ruth and Ann's mother always had a gas stove and was happy with it. At this point in time, the twins' mother had lost most of her hearing and was quite deaf. In addition, she would not wear a hearing aid. To converse with her, it was necessary to shout at her. With reference to the kitchen gas stove, their mother couldn't hear the hiss of the gas in the oven, and she was responsible for several *ker-booms!* As a result, she refused to have anything to do with the oven.

As the years went by, their mother did less and less cooking and finally left all the cooking to her daughters. This was fine except for the fact that Ruth and Ann were essentially afraid of fire and flames. They disliked cooking on that stove! They positively would not light the flame in the oven. Sometimes, supper would not get started until I came home from work and lit the oven! This was too much! So I started a successful campaign to buy a new electric stove. With an electric stove in place, meals were always on time!

For our second summer vacation, Ruth, Ann, their mother, and I went on a two-week trip to Miami, Florida. It took two days to get there by car using US Route 1. Ruth and Ann helped me with the driving. We stopped at all the beaches and towns on the Florida East Coast. We toured St. Augustine, as it was one of the first settlements in America. At Daytona Beach, I drove my car on the famous hard sand right at the water's edge. The Palm Beach Gardens were very nice. Finally, we were in Miami, where we stayed in a motel and enjoyed the beach for several days. We then drove to Winter Haven, Florida, to see Cypress Gardens. The floral gardens were outstandingly beautiful. Then we went to see the famous and spectacular water ski show at Cypress Gardens. We had seen portions of the show many times in movie travelogues, but it was much better seeing it live.

On our return trip north, we drove inland to Ocala in central Florida to see Silver Springs. This was a beautiful garden and wild life preserve, where there were river boat rides through a jungle filled with all kinds of wild life and beautiful birds. After a night's stay in Ocala, we began our trip home through Georgia and the Carolinas. We enjoyed that trip very much.

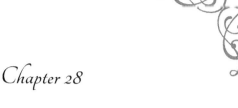

Chapter 28

Another Wedding

A Strange Marriage

Three or four years after Ruth and I got married, Ann started dating her old friend Jim again. Jim's major problem was that he had never broken away from his family. A lot of guys are that way. Other than that, he seemed like a nice person.

To make a long story short, Ruth was always telling Ann how good married life was with me. Ann always looked to Ruth for either advice on a specific subject or opinions on life in general. As a result of constantly hearing good things about marriage, Ann considered that this marriage thing might not be bad for her. So Ann decided to marry Jim! Of course, Jim was anxious to get married, because Ann was a beautiful girl with apparently no bad habits. In retrospect, what Ann needed was a guy like me, not Jim. Unfortunately, this was just a "me too" marriage. Not good!

A wedding day was set, and Ann had several nice wedding showers. Ann insisted on doing the same thing that Ruth did. She wanted to get married in the same wedding gown that Ruth used. So the wedding gown and the bridesmaid gown were going to be used twice! We just switched girls! She engaged the same church pastor to marry them, and she wanted to be married at home in Jim's parents' living room. All this was more evidence of the "me too" nature of the wedding

On the day before their wedding, I was where I usually was in the early morning, in the basement, shaving. No one, not even Ruth, had ever come down in the basement while I was there using the toilet or shaving. That morning, I heard footsteps coming down the stairs. It was Ruth. I could tell that she was upset.

She exclaimed, "I don't know what I am going to do with Ann! She wants you to talk to Jim and tell him that she doesn't want him to fuck her or have sex with her! Oh my! I can't believe it!"

I replied, "Good god! Why the hell is she getting married then?"

Ruth said, "She's not! Unless you ask him and he agrees!"

I said, "This is very serious, isn't it? She should have said something earlier. Oh, boy! She is the one that should be talking to him, not me. This is positive evidence that she is very prudish. If Ann doesn't want to have sex with Jim, then she isn't in love with him, and they shouldn't get married!"

Ruth said, "Yes! I see what you mean. However, there isn't going to be a wedding unless you convince Jim to accept her terms."

I replied, "Okay, I'll call him and meet with him right away! I can't promise you anything about the outcome of this."

Ruth gave a sigh of relief and said, "Thank you, sweetheart."

Jim and I talked very briefly. I tried explaining the unusual anti-male psychology of Ann to him, but I was not sure he got it or understood it since he was a little less perceptive than the average person. He finally accepted the "no sex" stuff with the understanding that it would not be permanent and that they would eventually get into it. Personally, I would not have done that. If I were in his place, I would have called off the marriage.

I conveyed this to Ruth, and she conveyed it to Ann. Ann was still hesitant about the "eventually getting into sex" but finally agreed to go through with the wedding as planned. Whew! Ruth and I breathed a sigh of relief. It would have been terribly embarrassing to tell everyone that the wedding was called off.

The next day, this completely wrong and fake marriage took place. Ann went through with the wedding with a smiling face and apparent happiness. Personally, I couldn't see what she was happy about since there was this "no sex" thing. In my opinion, when she repeated the marriage vows, she was essentially lying! Ruth and I were constantly worried that she would leave him at the altar! Apparently, Jim had not discussed our private conversation with anyone in his family. If he had, I am sure that they would have told him to call off the wedding.

It was obvious to everyone outside of his family that Jim was one of those individuals that had not broken his mother's apron strings. The problem was more than his mother; he was overly attached to his entire family. This situation generally makes marriage difficult, if not impossible. Earlier, I had voiced my opinion that, for this reason alone, Ann should not marry him. Unfortunately, this advice fell on deaf ears, and Ann was now Mrs. Jim Preston.

When Jim and Ann went off on their honeymoon, Ruth and I took advantage of the relative privacy of having the whole upstairs to ourselves and ramped up our sex life. We were essentially on our second honeymoon!

When Ann and Jim returned, we noticed that there was not this love flowing between them like Ruth and I had. We were sad about that, but what can you do? Everyone is different. Ann needed and would rather have had a guy like me for a husband. A guy like me would have broken her prudish shell and transformed her into a normal female, eager to enter into matrimony and intimacy with the opposite sex. Ann was a beautiful girl with an equally beautiful body. It seemed such a shame to waste it!

Jim was nothing like me at all. He was more married to his job and his family than he was to Ann. I don't think Ann could have lived alone with him. Ann's focus in life was Ruth and her mother. She more or less tolerated her husband. With the addition of Jim, we now had five people living in our house. The big advantage was that we now had four working people incomes to support our house.

In 1961, I quit my job at Johns Hopkins and took a higher-paying job at Westinghouse as an Engineer. At Westinghouse, there was a lot less travel and a great deal of job satisfaction for me. It was a good move. Ruth loved having me home more, and of course, so did

I. We soon became a part of the ongoing social life of the employees at Westinghouse. There were many dances, parties, and picnics. In addition, when I had to go away on business, it was always with my boss and his wife and Ruth and I. When we got to our destination, my boss and I attended to the business, while Ruth and his wife went shopping and became tourists.

In early 1962, we received the sad news that Ruth and Ann's dad passed away at the hospital. It took a while for the twins and their mother to recover from this. Ruth seemed to recover more quickly.

In the few years since Jim married Ann and moved into our house, I had been casually observing and analyzing his abnormal personality and behavior. I do not harbor any ill feelings toward Jim in spite of the fact that he was difficult to live with. He seemed to occupy the position in the household as a complainer and irritant.

He was the way he was through no fault of his own. I was the only one in the family that tried to help him. Unfortunately, I was not successful in this effort. I recognized that he often did not realize the full meaning of his words or actions.

His personality was that of an individual that was immature, insecure, and generally lacking in self-confidence. He never liked to be in new or unfamiliar surroundings. From this, it could be seen that he didn't like to travel to new destinations. He made himself comfortable in the immediate surroundings of his home, neighborhood, and workplace by becoming overly familiar with the people thereof. In this, he was always boasting "that everybody knew him there." This gave him a feeling of self-importance. He would never take anyone in his car to a place that he had not been before. He was afraid that he would get lost, which he usually did. To this end, he often went driving on his own to explore new places.

His insecurity was quite extensive. He would not go on an extended vacation with Ruth, Ann, their mother, and me simply because he wouldn't be familiar with anything. However, he gladly spent his vacation every year with his family for a week or two at the same ocean resort nearby. Unfortunately, there was a great cultural and personality difference between Ann's and Jim's family. As a result, Ann refused to go with him.

In like manner, Jim's family couldn't understand why Ann refused to socially associate with them. This is evidence of the fact that we seldom see ourselves as others see us. This was my problem in dealing with the twins and their problem in dealing with us singletons.

Our friends and acquaintances are generally people whose company we enjoy. Jim didn't enjoy strange places and new people. Ann didn't in any way enjoy the company of Jim's family. Marriages that unite the involved families are a blessing. Unfortunately, this is not always true.

Chapter 29

Cross-Country Trip

The King-Size Bed

In our day and age, Hollywood movies and New York stage shows were the pinnacle of entertainment. New York City was only a few hours' drive away, and Ruth and I had seen several New York stage shows. She and I especially liked Radio City, and we went there quite often. Ruth often expressed the desire to visit Los Angeles and see Hollywood. To fulfill this desire, I proposed that we drive to Los Angeles for our vacation that year. That way, we could see some of the country on the way. The ladies enthusiastically approved this suggestion.

I had driven my car across the country and back on business in 1956. This gave me confidence in my ability to plan and execute a big, long vacation trip to Los Angeles and back. I knew of the extreme heat in the desert southwest. Air conditioning was still not common in cars. So I had air conditioning installed in my car in preparation for this trip. In June of 1962, Ruth, Ann, their mother and I embarked on this trip. As usual, Ann's husband, Jim, did not want to go with us.

On the day of our departure, I took a five-hour nap in the afternoon so as to be able to drive all that night and the next day. I awoke at five in the afternoon. The ladies were very excited about this trip and had the car already loaded with suitcases, pillows for sleeping in the car, and other provisions. Something told me to check everything, so I did. That was a good move on my part. I found that they had forgotten my suitcase! The ladies were embarrassed and apologized. Finally, we were on our way.

I knew that we would make much better time by driving at night. My goal was to get west of the Mississippi River as quickly as possible. After an hour or so of driving, I was headed west on the Pennsylvania Turnpike. For supper, we had prepared a picnic-style meal to eat in the car as we drove.

As we entered the Ohio Turnpike, I made a restroom stop. It was 10:00 p.m. and dark. I was hoping that we would not have to stop again until morning. By 11:00 p.m., the ladies had made themselves comfortable and were asleep. There was no more conversation. There was just the road and me. I turned the radio on very low to keep me company.

There was very little traffic as the white-painted highway lane markers went flashing by in the headlights of the car, hour after hour. Radio stations faded, and new ones took their place. Happily I had no trouble keeping awake.

At seven the next morning, we all needed a break, and I made a rest-and-breakfast stop. Soon, we were on our way again. At noon, we made a quick rest stop and picked up some sandwiches to eat in the car for lunch. I relentlessly drove westward. At 5:00 p.m., I had been driving for twenty-four hours. The car odometer indicated that I had driven 1,000 miles! We were finally approaching a bridge across the Mississippi River.

I wanted to drive on to Des Moines, Iowa, but the ladies declared mutiny on me and wanted to just get out of that car! So I crossed the bridge at Davenport, Iowa, and found a Holiday Inn motel. After a nice supper, I crashed in bed and slept for twelve hours.

We decided to stay at the Holiday Inn motels en route. The Holiday Inn brochure indicated where their inns were located. Each day, I estimated the distance that I would drive and, while at the motel, had them call ahead and make the reservation for that evening This worked very well for me.

The next day, we got a late start, and the weather was terrible. It was raining hard, and there was a strong wind. Iowa is open farm country. The high wind picked up dirt or soil and made the roads very muddy. As a result, we couldn't see very well and had to drive slowly. In twelve hours driving, we only covered about 450 miles across Iowa and to Lincoln, Nebraska.

I started letting Ruth and Ann take turns in giving me a break in driving. That helped me a lot. I gave them instructions on what route numbers to follow. However, I found that they were not very good at following a map or route signs. Often, I found that they were on the wrong route, and I would have to get us back on the right one.

The next day the weather was clear, and we made it to Colorado Springs, Colorado, where we could see the famous Pikes Peak in the near distance. We also visited and enjoyed the grandeur of the red rock formations at the Garden of the Gods. Later, we visited the impressive Air Force Academy.

On our way west, we visited the Petrified Forest, which was not a forest at all. It was a stretch of barren land with scattered petrified tree logs lying on the ground. It was interesting to see. We made it to Flagstaff, Arizona, at the end of the day and stayed overnight there. It was June, and due to the high altitude, I found frost on my windshield in the morning.

As we continued west, we drove across northern Arizona. I knew that the Grand Canyon was nearby, but I decided not to go there because we didn't have time. In northwestern Arizona, scenery was not very good. The land was barren with large black rocks and mountains. It was very hot, and we were glad we had the car air conditioner. We drove across the Boulder Dam. Halfway across, there was a parking area that served as a scenic overlook area. We stopped there and took pictures. It made us feel small to be standing on this huge concrete dam.

A short drive later, we made it to our next destination, Las Vegas, Nevada. We stayed at the local Holiday Inn. The casinos were magnificent. We saw one show and visited several casinos, where

Ruth and Ann lost money. In contrast, when I gained ten dollars, I quit! We couldn't help but notice that the food was exceptionally good and reasonably priced at the casino restaurants. This made sense. The casino owners didn't want their patrons to be unhappy in any way. We only spent one day at Las Vegas, as this was not our final destination.

The next day, on the road from Las Vegas to Los Angeles, I was doing seventy-five miles per hour, and cars went by me like I was standing still! I don't want to know how fast they were going! At that time, there was no speed limit in Nevada.

We were very happy to finally make it to our destination, Los Angeles. We found the Hollywood Travel Lodge Motel, right where Ruth wanted to be. We walked down Sunset Boulevard, Hollywood Boulevard, and Vine Street. Ruth was overjoyed to be there. We stopped to eat at a restaurant on Hollywood Boulevard. When we entered, we found that it was pitch-dark inside. We could barely read the menu much less see the food! That was an experience! I assume that this was a fad in Los Angeles at that time.

We saw Grauman's Chinese Theater with the footprints of movie stars in the sidewalk. We couldn't get Ann off the footprints of Nelson Eddy! The next day we visited Disneyland. It had recently been completed and opened. The Disney theme was everywhere. A floral Mickey Mouse face was at the entrance to the park. The ladies enjoyed the rides, while I preferred to just sit and watch because of my motion sickness. Ruth enjoyed the spinning teacups ride. I couldn't even watch it! Later, we visited the Movie Land Wax Museum.

On the following day, we visited Knott's Berry Farm and Ghost Town. We enjoyed that more than Disneyland! It was so interesting and so much fun! Ruth wanted to go back the next day, but with our limited time, we couldn't afford to.

Marine Land was excellent. Following that, we toured the well-known MGM Movie Lot and CBS's Television City. That was enough for that day! We were tired that night! On the next day, we drove slowly through the streets of Beverly Hills. Oh my, did Ruth and Ann enjoy that. We saw the magnificent homes of most of the movie stars. Then, we drove through the beautiful San Fernando Valley area

On our final day, we visited the famous Palladium Theater on Sunset Boulevard. We were surprised to find that there were no tables or seats. It held 3,500 people, but it consisted of a large stage and large dance floor. It was a huge dance hall. Then, we visited the impressive Hollywood Bowl and drove to beautiful Laguna Beach, where we stayed for the rest of the day.

The next morning, with reluctance, we started our drive back east. We were on our feet a lot on the last couple of days, and I was happy to be able to just sit and drive! On our way to California, we drove halfway via the northern route. On our way home, I planned to take the southern route all the way.

On the first night, we stopped again at Flagstaff, Arizona. As we drove east the next day across Arizona and New Mexico, I noticed that a very dark cloud to the north seemed to be following us. We stopped for the night at the Holiday Inn in Roswell, New Mexico, and, for supper, went to their restaurant that was a separate building. As we were eating, it became very dark, and the storm hit. A deluge of rain and wind continued for almost an hour. The storm was so fierce with its lightning and thunder that it frightened the ladies. I had been through such storms in the area before, and I was not worried. I told the ladies to observe the local people, the waitresses, and the cashier. They were not at all concerned and were laughing and talking as if nothing was happening. This calmed the ladies.

Shortly, the storm subsided, and the rain stopped. I paid the bill, and we walked to the door to leave. Our waitress darted ahead of us and calmly unlocked the door. They had locked it to keep the wind from blowing it open! When we looked outside, water was a foot deep, everywhere. The waitress informed us that it would be at least an hour before the water went down. Then, she giggled and told us to remove our shoes and stockings and walk barefoot the short distance to the motel. Somehow, my ladies thought that it would be a lark, and they began laughing as they removed their shoes and hose! I took off my shoes and socks, rolled up my trouser legs, and walked through the water with them.

The next day, we drove across northern Texas. Western Texas had mountains and dry, barren deserts. Eastern Texas was flat, green, and damp, much like Louisiana. That evening we stopped for the night in Little Rock, Arkansas.

The last stop of our journey was at the Holiday Inn at Oak Ridge, Tennessee. The last leg of our trip to Baltimore was uneventful. I was very glad to be home again and not driving all day long anymore! Upon walking through the front door, Ruth exclaimed, "Now that was a really nice vacation!"

In the motel in Los Angeles, Ruth and I slept in a king-size bed for the first time. We liked having acres of bed on which to make love, so as soon as we returned home, we went shopping and bought a king-size bed. In fact, we bought a whole new set of French provincial bedroom furniture to match. We were very excited and pleased with this. We stored our old bedroom furniture in the spare bedroom, basement, and attic. We still liked our old bedroom furniture and didn't want to give it away. When our new bedroom was finally ready to use, we could hardly wait to try it out.

The rest of our family at home was generally naive about things like that, and it was obvious to Ruth and me that they didn't understand fully why we were so thrilled about it. Ruth and I celebrated that first night in our new big bed. As far as we were concerned, we christened it! Oh god, did we have a good time! The next morning, we were casually, calmly, and naively asked how well we slept in our new bed. Ruth and I glanced at each other with a gleaming look of devilment in our eyes, knowing we hadn't slept much at all! I gained my composure first and, with one eyebrow raised, answered, "Oh, just fine!" This was another one of those many times when our family failed to understand why Ruth and I gave each other a quick, firm hug.

Ruth and Ann were working for the Travelers Insurance Company as claims agents. The *Travelers Beacon* was their semi-monthly employees magazine. One year, the magazine featured an article about the sets of twins that were working for the company. The article for Ruth and Ann was titled "Real Togetherness." It featured a photograph of the two of them sitting with one of Ruth's crocheted afghans across their laps. In the article, Ruth succinctly described what it is like to be a twin as "A most exciting experience where you feel that our individual lives are not our own, but part of the other's." This clearly expresses the inherent lack of individuality in the twin experience.

Ruth and I were blessed by having true love flowing between us. However, neither one of us were angels. We were normal in that we did have some disagreements in our life that sometimes left us upset with each other. This was always over something silly and not really serious. Most of this was Ruth's lack of understanding how the average nontwin like me thinks and acts or my lack of understanding of twin stuff. Such occasions were very few and far between and did not last very long. We both knew what it was like to experience the joy and rapture of making up.

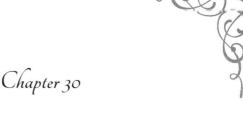

Chapter 30

Children

Ann Wanted a Girl!

During the first few years of our marriage, we were neither trying nor not trying to have children. We were just enjoying life together. Finally, after five years, Ruth and I mutually decided that we would like to have children. We thought that this would be no problem. We assumed that she would get pregnant if we just had unrestricted sex whenever we could. For us, this was almost no change at all in our physical lifestyle. The only change was that we began to mentally think "baby." Several happy months went by, and nothing happened. So this made us start to think about it more.

We knew that there was a best time in her monthly cycle to conceive. Because we loved each other so deeply, for us, this period of time became wonderful beyond imagination. We made desperate love to each other for months. We were marvelously happy and quite sexually satisfied all the time, but we still had no baby! The months turned into a year. Nothing happened.

Finally, we concluded that there must be something wrong with one or both of us or that we were doing something wrong. It was obvious that, as a couple, we had a difficult time conceiving. One of our options was to go to a doctor and find out if either one of us was sterile. We decided to postpone that for a while longer. I hit the books and learned that conception could only take place during the very limited twelve to eighteen-hour period following female ovulation.

Ovulation was positively identified as coincident with the drop in the female morning temperature reading. I purchased the proper thermometer, and during the proper time period, we began to keep a written record of Ruth's temperature before she got out of bed in the morning. The first month showed only a very vague, small temperature drop for one morning. We concluded that this must be ovulation. So we gave it everything we had that day and for days afterward. Nothing happened.

The next few months showed the same kind of small temperature drop, and we were still not successful. On the morning of December 24, 1962, her temperature took a different, sharp, clear drop, a plunge like we had not seen before. She was definitely ovulating! That morning, we were so excited that we could hardly contain ourselves. The problem was the timing. It was terrible! It was Christmas Eve, by gosh, and we all know that means a lot of celebration, festivity, social interchange, family visiting, and church going. It was an exceptionally busy day, and Ruth and I wanted to do the impossible, stay home in bed!

We acted strangely that day, but no one picked up on it. We did seem to have a very naive family. We thought up every excuse in the book to get everyone to go out, leaving us alone in the house. Surprisingly, we were successful at this and were able to devote ourselves to the pleasant task at hand. Think about it, here we were, two people who were deep lovers, desperately wanting a baby, suddenly getting the green light! Ruth and I will never forget how we celebrated that Christmas Eve, Christmas Day, and the day after that, and the day after that!

Later, to our absolute delight, we found that Ruth was pregnant! The morning temperature method worked very well for us. It also made us happy to know that neither one of us was sterile. After six years, we were finally going to have a baby! Ruth claimed that our new king-size bed brought us good luck.

We assumed that Ruth was pregnant when she missed her period by several weeks. To verify this, we went to see her gynecologist. Sure enough, it was true! Shortly thereafter, we decided to announce it to our family in the evening when everyone was in the living room watching television. When we told them were going to have a baby, they all just turned to us and said, "Oh! That's nice!"

Ann said "How did that happen?" as if it were a mistake! Then, everyone just turned and went back to watching the television. No hugs! No kisses! No congratulations! We had the impression that Ann thought it was terrible!

Obviously, they had no idea that we wanted a baby or were trying to have one. I guess they were not paying close attention to us. This was another example of the naive nature of our family. Ruth and I looked at each other in astonishment. We were stunned at our family's complacent reaction. Ruth was very hurt at this. We went upstairs to our bedroom. Ruth said, "Oh! I can't believe that!" and began to cry. I hugged her tightly. Ruth quickly recovered and said, "I don't care about them! We are having this baby, and I am very happy about it! From here on, it's just you and I! If that's the way they feel, we don't need them!"

There was no excitement in the family. No cheerful calling of friends and relatives to announce the big occasion. Ruth told everyone at her office, and I told my parents, all my relatives, and everyone where I worked at Hopkins. We received the standard reaction of cheer from them! Ruth and I were indeed on our own at our home, having this baby. No one at home expressed any interest in keeping up with Ruth's condition.

Ruth's term of pregnancy only served to draw us closer together. I went with Ruth for her regular visits to the gynecologist. I noticed that I was the only man in the waiting room. The doctor always called me into his office to discuss the results of the examination. I asked questions, and I learned a lot from that! He explained the reason why we had such a hard time conceiving. He said that Ruth's uterus was bent instead of oval shaped. This meant that it was difficult for the sperm to navigate the bend and also explained why she had such a hard time with her menstrual flow. Sometimes, Ruth's period was so bad that it caused her to even dislike me!

We were thankful that Ruth had no complications during her pregnancy. Occasionally, morning sickness would get to her, but the bedside dry cracker seemed to solve the problem. We lived in a relatively crowded house, but we were essentially alone in tending to her pregnancy. During Ruth's pregnancy, no one else in the family sympathized with the wonderful everyday nuances of bearing a child.

Ruth's mother, having been through childbearing thirty some years ago, would occasionally tell a story or make a comment that struck home with Ruth's experience. It was a big occasion for us when we could finally hear the little heartbeat. Ruth used a stethoscope, and I laid my ear on her belly. One thing was for sure. Our baby was very active! It moved a lot. Often, as she was walking, Ruth would stop cold in her tracks and hold on to anything that was nearby. A wide-eyed look of surprise would fill her face, followed by a big smile, and she would say, "Oh my, that was quite a kick!"

During her seventh and eighth months of pregnancy, Ruth had two falls while walking, causing us to be concerned about the baby. The gynecologist assured us that there were no adverse effects from these falls.

Physical and mental love flowed freely between us during all those nine months. I truly felt as if I were having the baby too. It was, of course, three o'clock in the morning on a cold, rainy September night that Ruth declared it was time to go to the hospital! Our obstetrician earlier stated that Ruth's hip and pelvic bones were positioned such that she would have a very difficult and painful time with a normal delivery. For that reason, Ruth would have the baby through cesarean section.

In those days, there was no up-front technique to determine the sex of the unborn child. Ruth and I didn't know what we were going to have. Earlier, we had picked out a name that we liked for both a boy and a girl. The cesarean section went well, and our beautiful baby boy was born. We named him Thomas and called him Tommy. We both loved him so much. When he was born, a third channel of love began to flow from Ruth to him. Ruth was wonderful. Her love had no limits.

Ann, with her inherent anti-masculine attitude, had totally convinced herself that her sister was going to have a girl. She wanted a girl! At the hospital, when Ann heard that her sister had a boy, she exclaimed, "No! That's wrong! There must be a mistake! It has to be a girl!" When the nurse brought our newborn baby to the window for all to see, Ann shouted, "It's a girl, isn't it?" The nurse shook her head no and lowered his diaper so that everyone could see his masculinity! That did it. Ann was very disappointed. She then said, "That's terrible! I wanted it to be a girl. I guess I should have known that Gil would have a boy." In typical Ann fashion, I was to blame!

This gives you an insight into how different the personalities of these twins really were. All this goes back to the twins' childhood, where they were raised by their mother, without a father. The effects of this masculine void were still with Ann. She still didn't really know what to do with a member of the masculine gender. This uncertain feeling about the masculine gender was projected toward our baby son.

The occasion of bringing a newborn baby home means that nothing will ever be the same as it was before. This is not a bad thing; it is a good thing. Nothing brings more love to a home than a baby or children. Cesarean sections in those days were much more serious operations than today. It was twelve days before Ruth and our baby could come home from the hospital.

It was a grand, happy, and glorious occasion when we brought Ruth and Tommy home. At home, Ruth was still flat on her back, recovering from the operation. She could not care for the baby at all. We had not expected this. Ruth was very upset and cried because she couldn't care for her baby. Earlier, while she was pregnant, Ruth and I had attended a baby care course with the expectation that we both would be taking care of the baby.

The world of baby care had changed so much since Ruth's mother had her twins that her mother was overwhelmed with everything. Ruth and Ann had not been involved in babysitting when they were young, so Ann had no experience at this sort of thing. As a result, the burden of responsibility for newborn care fell singularly on my shoulders. Boy, was I glad I had taken that baby care course!

In life, there are always problems. On the very day that Ruth and Tommy came home from the hospital, the sewer line from our house became clogged. What a terrible time for that to happen! When our good neighbors who lived across the street heard about this, they very kindly offered to let us use their bathroom any time we needed it. That was very nice, and we took them up on that offer. We began walking back and forth, across the street. Ruth was essentially bedridden and couldn't walk very far at all. She had to use the bathroom in our house. With just her using it, there didn't seem to be a problem.

Our plumbing contractor began working the next day. He had to dig up our front lawn to replace the broken and clogged pipe. What a mess that was! A few days later, it was all fixed, and our household returned to normal.

Ruth and I again realized that we were surrounded by people, but we were alone in bringing our newborn son home and caring for him. I took vacation days from work to stay home and take care of our newborn baby. After several days of watching me take care of the baby, Ann and her mother began to help with the baby care effort. When Ann started to care for our baby boy, that was the beginning of a lifelong love affair between her and him. He won her heart over with ease. She learned to love him almost as much as Ruth did. Later, she confessed, "I had no idea that a baby boy could be so sweet, cute, and cuddly!"

Gosh! I thought to myself. *What did you think he would be? A tough, macho monster?* Apparently, for Ann, "sweet, cute and cuddly" could only be for girls! Our baby son had effected a permanent change in Ann's personality. Her attitude toward men and me in general improved greatly. The power of babies and children! Ruth and I considered this a milestone in Ann's life. We all need more happy occasions like this one.

Because of our deep love, Ruth and I had no problem in assuming parenthood and raising our son. The third small, unoccupied room on the second floor of our house served as the baby's room. I have always been the type of person who could quickly get up in the middle of the night to attend to something and then have no trouble in going right back to sleep. Not so with Ruth. Whenever her sleep was interrupted, she always had a hard time in getting back to sleep. So I was the one who always got up whenever the baby cried or needed attention.

Ruth wanted to take care of her baby, so she always got up too. Therefore, while I was up and taking care of the baby, a sleepy Ruth would come stumbling into the room to help. A lot of couples have a mild or sometimes serious marital problem with the arrival of a new baby. The mother focuses on her child and neglects to give her husband the affection he needs. This never happened with Ruth and me. Great love just seemed to naturally flow between Ruth and me and our new baby. We were so happy and so grateful to have an obviously happy, healthy, and normal baby boy.

At that time, with reference to church and religion, we were wandering Protestants, not firmly attached to any place of worship. We were married by a Presbyterian pastor. When our baby son was six months old, we had him baptized at the Methodist Church near our home.

We were now a family of three, and we had the health, well-being, and happiness of our newborn son to consider. A lot of our time and effort was now focused on this new responsibility. This tended to isolate us even more from the other members of our household. Ruth and I were very busy with our new lifestyle as parents. It was up to the other members of the household to make adjustments so that they might better fit into our lives. Otherwise, Ruth and I would have just gone on with our lives without their participation or assistance.

For Christmas 1963, the baby that we were trying so desperately to conceive on Christmas Day 1962 was here! What a wonderful Christmas it was. Ruth and I got so much pleasure buying lots of Christmas presents for his little three-month-old eyes to see! No baby or child ever had a better Christmas than our son, Tom, did that year. For us, all holidays took on a new meaning and perspective. We now had our child to share everything with us. Our child was the center of attraction for us. We were so proud of him. We never put him in his crib upstairs and alone when we had an adult party. He was in his baby seat, right there with us, all the time.

Ruth & Tom

Chapter 31

After Tommy

Our Daughter Was Totally Different

After Tommy was born, we waited a year for Ruth to completely recover from her cesarean section before thinking about having another baby. Then, we were casual about it, not caring if she became pregnant or not. Our love was as strong and as deep as ever. We went on like this, enjoying life in general and sex specifically for months. In that time, our baby grew to be a child. Ruth and I knew that we would be happy if we became parents, but we had no idea it was going to be so wonderful.

After two years, we decided to get serious about it, and in 1966, we got out the old thermometer and again started recording her morning temperature. Apparently, this was the only way to get her pregnant. Just as it was in 1962, each month, her temperature only took a slight, subtle drop with her ovulation. We made love like crazy every month at the proper time, but nothing happened. Many months of happy lovemaking went by.

Then, in May 1967, her temperature took an obvious big drop instead of the usual subtle drop. This was it again! We were just as excited as we were the first time. So that day and for days afterward, we devoted ourselves to the pleasant task at hand. This time, happily, there was no holiday to interfere with our efforts. We were able to go about it with much more vigor than the first time. Ruth and I will definitely never forget the experience of trying to conceive our second baby. And sure enough, Ruth again became pregnant!

When Ruth's gynecologist declared that she was pregnant, we announced it to our family. Unlike the first time, we were greeted with a normal, happy reaction. As before, we loved each other deeply while she was pregnant. Her second pregnancy was normal and uncomplicated, much the same as her first one, except that she was much larger, and our second baby was not nearly as active as our first one.

In February 1968, through another cesarean section, our beautiful daughter, Judy, was born. A fourth channel of love began to flow from Ruth to her. I think that if Ruth had ten children, she would have been able to give each one the same fullness of love. I cannot tell you how happy I was with my family. I had a good home, a wonderful wife, and two beautiful children. No man could ask for more. I was truly blessed, and I thanked God for everything.

Ann, of course, was very happy that her sister had a girl. Ruth and I were also happy because we now had one of each gender. We loved and cared for our new daughter in the same way we did our son. Holidays, birthdays, parties, and other occasions were even more joyful for us because we now had two sets of sparkling eyes and two faces of happy children to behold. We made certain that our children were having the best time possible within our financial means and environment.

With our two children, our family totaled four, which made us the majority in the household. The rest of the family only totaled three. By now, the other members of our household had adjusted to living with us, with our young family. Ruth and I welcomed any amount of assistance that our household members would give us. We had built-in babysitters whenever Ruth and I wanted to take a Saturday night off and go dancing or participate in some adult function. Since we became parents, we had not been able to go dancing as much as before. This did not bother us at all. We were very happy just attending to our two young children.

We soon found that our daughter had a totally different personality than our son. This was evident in her actions and manner at the tender age of one. A year later, we realized that we had a tomboy on our hands. Our little daughter was rough and tumble! She was pretty and cute but also tough as nails! Ruth had difficulty dealing with this. She expected her to be sweet and feminine, like her mother! As a child, our daughter seemed to always have a black eye or bruise on her face. This was self-inflicted as a result of her boisterous nature of running into furniture, a doorframe, or a wall! Of course, we loved our daughter, no matter what!

When our son was a few years old, he became a sleepwalker. We had to place a gate at the top of the stairs so that he couldn't fall down the stairs. We never knew where we would find him in the morning. One morning we couldn't find him! We knew that he had to be somewhere. His bedroom door opened into the hallway. The door was open and against the hall wall. Somehow, he managed to curl up in the small space behind this fully opened door! Fortunately, this stopped when he was seven years old.

It was fortunate that I was making enough money to support the family without Ruth's income. We were keenly aware that many of our friends who were young parents were faced with the situation where both had to work to support their family. They had to use babysitters and childcare centers.

To raise our children, Ruth quit work and stayed at home. This meant that she not only took care of our children, she did all the cooking and house cleaning. This period of time was difficult for Ann, who was now working alone, without Ruth at the office. She was without the usual help, companionship, and assistance of her twin. This was very stressful for Ann. During the workweek, Ruth received many phone calls from Ann at work.

The stress was too much for Ann. She was gritting her teeth so much that her jaw hurt, and the dentist gave her a soft plate to insert in her mouth while she slept at night. For whatever reason, Ruth did not seem to be overly concerned about Ann's physical problems. Personally, I would have recommended that Ann quit her job, take a vacation, and find another job that suited her inward, introvert personality

Ruth stayed home with the children for eight years, until our young daughter started school. After that, she went back to work. By that time, Ann's condition had worsened. The medical profession seemed no longer able to help her. I was tasked with the job of properly adjusting a heat lamp on Ann's side ribs while she reclined in bed to alleviate the pain that she was experiencing. She claimed that no one adjusted it right but me.

With reference to my career, I quit working at Westinghouse and took a job with the federal government, NOAA and NASA, in the Washington, DC, area as a civil servant in the new field of instrumentation for satellites and spacecraft. This was again a higher-paying job, and the job security and benefits were the best. The only disadvantage was the long commute of a little more than hour.

On two occasions, Ruth and I looked around for a place to live that might be closer to my work. Each time, we ended up only liking the homes in an area that was fifty minutes or more from work. So we reasoned, why bother to move? For one thing, it would have meant uprooting the children from the stability and familiarity of their friends in their neighborhood, church, and schools. Also, the cost of living in the Washington, DC, area was much higher. I commuted and stayed with the federal government.

Ruth & Judy

Chapter 32

Necessary Home Improvements

We Had Twice as Much Space

O ur home was always different than the average because there were twins living in it. Two married couples, a mother-in-law, and two children were sharing the same roof. For the average person, this scenario would be totally unacceptable and indeed intolerable. The two married couples situation is the big impossibility. My brother-in-law was the only person who had any serious difficulty with this living environment.

The end-of-row town house that we lived in for the first years of our marriage has quite a history to it. The house was satisfactory until our two young children became old enough to need separate bedrooms. Our two-year-old daughter, Judy, was sleeping in her crib in the same small room with our seven-year-old son, Tom. That room was very crowded! We considered ourselves fortunate that Tom did not complain about this arrangement. Our options were to add a second floor to our first-floor addition, make a bedroom out of the basement clubroom, or move to a bigger house. Our house had seven people in it.

When Ann and her husband, Jim, got married, they recognized that they needed more income to meet their expenses. They invested

Ann's income in home rental property, namely, the town house next door to us. The house mortgage was paid off, and the rental money was full income for them. The lease on the house ended in two months. Ann and Jim agreed that they would not renew the lease and thereby render the house empty. Finally, there was an empty house next to us.

The town house next door was ours. We could expand into it. This was the solution to our problem. Ruth and I agreed to pay Ann and Jim half of their usual monthly rental fee. There was a common wall between our house and the one next door. We chose to have two doorways in the common wall: one in the kitchen and one in the living room.

As a result of my higher income, Ruth and I were saving money in the bank. We had more than enough money saved to pay for the home improvements. So we paid for it all, and Ann promised to pay her half to us whenever she could. We hired a contractor to break through the walls and make one big house out of our two adjacent town houses. This doubled our living area. It was with great relief and satisfaction that we expanded our cramped living quarters into the second house. It was really nice to have some space. We had five bedrooms, three bathrooms, and the children had their own basement playroom. Our double town house was a blessing.

With a family of seven, including our two children, it was evident that we needed a larger back porch. So at the same time, we had our small back porch replaced with one that extended the entire width of the back of the corner house with a hard roof, rain spout, and awnings. We could now sit out there even if it was raining! There was a large concrete covered area underneath our big, new back porch. During the summer months, in this covered area, we placed a small, ten-foot diameter aboveground swimming pool for the children. Ruth and Ann couldn't resist the temptation to get in it too! Our new double house was an idyllic setting.

It was 1970, and this was a very good time in our lives. As part of our home improvements in both houses, we expanded the second-floor rear bedrooms into the adjacent small bedrooms to make one large bedroom. My in-laws, Ann, and her husband took the new larger bedroom in the rear of the end house. Our two young children each had modest-sized front bedrooms, one in each house. Our daughter, who was only two and a half, took our previous bedroom in the front of the corner house. Our son, who was seven, took the front bedroom in the second house.

Ruth and I had the nice, new larger bedroom in the rear of the second town house. We liked this arrangement very much because we were isolated from the rest of the adults in the household, and we had our own bathroom. In contrast to the previous arrangement, there was no reason for Ann or Jim to be in the hallway outside of our bedroom door. Tom's bedroom was near us, but he had a quiet personality and was at an age when he rarely bothered his parents for anything in the evening or at night.

Ruth and I loved our relative privacy. We immediately changed the style of our lovemaking to fit this new, better environment. When it came to lovemaking, Ruth and I were definitely opportunists! This subject was always foremost in our minds, but we rarely let it show to other people.

Judy was still a toddler and had difficulty sleeping so far away from Ruth and me. She was in the house next door, and we found that, if she was frightened by something, it would take her little legs about fifteen seconds to run from her bedroom in the other house to our bedroom. However, she never wanted to go back to her room when she ran and jumped into our bed.

To help this problem, I installed an intercom between her bedroom and ours. She could call me at any hour of the night if she was frightened, and I would talk to her. This helped her a lot. When there was a thunderstorm, naturally, both children ran and jumped in bed with Ruth and me. It is interesting to note that when our children were very young, they never had any problem identifying Ruth as their mother, even though an identical twin was living in the same house.

With two young children in the house, holidays, birthdays, and things like that took on a new dimension. Our house became a social center for children. We reciprocated with friends who had children around the same age, attending their birthdays and just parties in general. Ruth and I became socially very busy. All this in no way interfered with our personal relationship. Sure, we had less time for each other, but our love continued to be as wonderful and deep as ever. Our love survived the challenges of being young parents.

We tried to have a third child, but we never saw a clear drop in Ruth's temperature again. We were not as consistent and faithful about it, and it is entirely possible that, for various reasons, we missed the chance. In retrospect, we both assumed that at the time when she was ready, we were in a circumstance that disallowed us to either know about it or respond to it. We accepted it as divine providence that we were not going to have any more children. As the parents of two young children, it goes without saying that we were leading a busy, very full life. Ruth and I were very happy, but when bedtime came, we were often very tired. Even though we didn't have as much time for each other as we did in the past, our love life did not suffer.

As life seems to go, the unforeseen occurred. Ruth and Ann's mother developed Alzheimer's disease. She kept getting worse, and finally, she reached the stage where she did not remember who we were. She could not be trusted or left alone. Ruth and Ann had to take turns sleeping with her at night. So every other night, Ruth did not sleep with me.

This had all the earmarks of generating a big strain on our marriage. You have to remember that Ruth and I were lovers. Ruth was not far away; she was in the same house. Her mother's bedroom was not isolated from the house; it was in the house, located next to the living room. So after everyone had gone to bed, whenever Ruth wanted me to visit her for a while at night in the living room, I did. It was kind of fun to quietly sneak down the stairs, tiptoe through the house to the living room, and have a tryst with my wife! Fortunately, our love did not fail us. Ruth and I were good at turning adversity into opportunity.

Chapter 33

Ann's Health

Ann Needed Me

In the long time period when Ruth stayed home to raise the children and Ann was working at the office without Ruth, Ann's health declined. She began complaining of pains in her stomach. After a long series of doctor's visits and tests, it was concluded that Ann had fibroids throughout her stomach. In those days, the recommended treatment was an extensive "exploratory" operation where they open up your belly with a large incision and searched for and removed the fibroids. After her operation, the two-week recovery time at home was the big problem.

In her recuperation, Ann was sleeping on the first floor with her mother because she couldn't yet climb the steps. Also, she couldn't get herself up out of bed to use the bathroom. Ruth didn't have the strength to help her up. Ann's husband, Jim, didn't have the ability to be coordinated enough to help her out of bed without causing her severe pain. So I was called to duty. I was able to get her up with minimal discomfort. After that, she didn't want anyone else to help her but me.

Ann Peach Hat

This meant that I would be needed at night. I volunteered to sleep on the nearby living room couch so I could hear her call me. As luck would have it, this was also in the worst part of her menstrual period. She needed to use the bathroom a lot! On the upside, all this reinforced the bond between Ann and me.

I must mention that this type of situation allowed me to gain advantage of a typical twin characteristic. They say that one twin can feel the pain or pleasure of the other twin. I learned through experience that Ruth appreciated and loved me more for helping Ann through an ordeal, or tough situation, than if, instead, I had helped her through it. This was not subtle; it was quite obvious. Essentially, for any specific endeavor, I received more appreciation and love from Ruth for helping Ann through it than I would have by helping Ruth through it. This is a result of twin love.

In the next few years, Ann was in the hospital twice. When she was at home recovering from having her hemorrhoids removed, I was called to duty again to help her in and out of bed. Likewise, when she was at home recovering from a double wrist carpal tunnel operation, I was her hands. More love from Ruth! More bonding with Ann!

Chapter 34

Our Second House

Ann's Bedroom Was a Romantic Heaven

Eight years after we moved into our nice double town house, much to our dismay, a large hospital was built on the empty lot across the street from us. It was a huge, overpowering thing and took several years to construct. As a result, our neighborhood gradually became essentially commercial, with all the disadvantages thereof. The hospital parking lot was not free. To avoid paying for parking, patient visitors filled our neighborhood streets with their cars. Parking space became a problem for us. For instance, when we returned from grocery shopping, there were no parking places available near our house. We had to carry our groceries from a distance.

Prior to that, the only people seen walking the streets of our residential neighborhood were those who lived in the area. Now, we had undesirable transient strangers wandering in our neighborhood, even in the middle of the night. In addition, the hospital was a twenty-four-hour-a-day facility. The noise from the hospital rooftop air conditioning units kept us awake at night. Noisy delivery and garbage trucks were coming and going at all hours of the day and night. Soot from the hospital chimney rained down on the neighborhood, filling our windowsills and outdoor furniture with a black layer.

We realized that our neighborhood was no longer a desirable area in which to live or raise children. We were very disheartened about this, and we began to look for a new place to live. We were searching for the equivalent of what we had presently, a five-bedroom house. In all the areas we wanted to live, we could not find a five-bedroom house for sale. A year passed, and we still couldn't find a house. Meanwhile, our neighborhood was getting even worse. There was now a lot of pressure and incentive for us to move.

In 1977, we started an extensive real estate search for an appropriate house in what we considered a suitable neighborhood in the suburbs. We finally found a large ranch house in a nice neighborhood on a two-acre lot with a large kitchen and three bedrooms. We had a contractor build an addition to the house with a large bedroom, bath, and family room, giving us a total of four bedrooms.

This ranch house was indeed magnificent, but it was seriously lacking in storage area. There was no basement. The basement was always where my stuff was located. We decided that the nice two-car garage would have to be used for storage instead of cars. We had a large walk-in clothes closet installed in the garage area and another shelved closet for general household storage.

Essentially, I had no room to use as a workshop and no room to store my stuff. For this reason, I didn't like the house. It was not a house for someone like me. I had to store my things in the attic. We all know that an attic is not a desirable storage area. It is dirty and very hot in the summer. In addition, there were field mice up there in the winter.

Ruth knew that I was unhappy, but she was just totally enamored with the house and the grounds. As a living space, it was great. I reasoned that I would rather see Ruth happy than make a big issue out of its disadvantages for me.

The nice large bedroom and bath in the new addition was for Ann and her husband. The three bedrooms and two baths in the bedroom wing of the main house were for Ruth and me and our children. Our family was finally together and separated from Ann and her husband. We all lived under the same roof and shared the other facilities of the house, but our personal living quarters were definitely separated. This fact contributed greatly to the successful upbringing of our children

Essentially, my mother-in-law didn't have a bedroom. We knew this and planned it that way. Sadly, she had regressed to the point where she didn't recognize any of her own possessions. So we all agreed that she really didn't need a room to call her own since she was now confined to a wheelchair. She was an invalid, requiring total care.

When we moved, we sold her bedroom furniture. Our options were to locate a hospital bed somewhere in the house, buy a sofa bed, or let her sleep in one of our beds. For obvious reasons, we knew that we needed to have her located in close proximity to a bathroom. So the choice was either my in-laws' bed and bedroom or ours. My brother-in-law, Jim, adamantly disapproved of using his bedroom. As usual, Ruth and I made the sacrifice and let my mother-in-law sleep in our bed. This meant that I had to sleep on the living room sofa on a rather permanent basis.

For the average couple, this kind of arrangement would surely cause serious marital problems. But Ruth and I survived. We did not let even this adversity interfere with our love life. Ruth and I had no problem in being together. Grandmother was almost totally deaf and couldn't see without her glasses. So when she slept in our bed, she was totally unaware of anything going on in the room. Everyone in the house knew that I would often go to sleep in our bedroom on the lounge chair, just to be in the same room with Ruth. Sometimes I would sleep half the night there. So my absence on the living room sofa was nothing unusual.

Instead of separating us, all this made Ruth and me closer than ever. We made love in our bedroom everywhere but on our bed! Our love life was certainly not dull or ho-hum! A regular sex life is mandatory to the success of any marriage. Ruth and I never had any problem with this. Our enduring marriage testifies to this. We always turned adversity into advantage.

Weekends were great for Ruth and me. We got a break from caring for Grandmother on Friday and Saturday nights. We had an agreement with Ann and her husband. For the weekend, Ann would sleep in our bed with her mother, while her husband slept on the living room sofa, and Ruth and I would sleep in their bedroom. Ann, of course, did not mind giving up her bedroom for the weekend because she was very grateful that Ruth and I relinquished our bed to her mother for the other five days of the week.

Ann's bedroom was located on the end of the wing of the house. For Ruth and me, Ann's bedroom was a romantic heaven. We loved our weekends of lovemaking in the quiet isolation of the bedroom in the wing. This room had two large windows with a view of the beautiful gardens of our property. The windows of our neighbors' homes were far away and situated so that they did not allow a view into our windows.

When Ann slept in the room, she closed the curtains at night, making it totally cold and dark inside. Whenever Ruth and I were there, we opened the curtains, letting in the soft light from the out-side that gently illuminated the room, giving it a warm, cozy atmo-sphere that was very romantic. There, in the near total darkness of the room, Ruth and I became two totally uninhibited lovers, engulfed in the joy of our union. Did we enjoy our weekends? We certainly did!

On weekend mornings, Ann always politely and naively asked us if we were able to sleep all right in her bed. Ruth and I would then give each other a quick glance, knowing that we indeed did not sleep very much in her bed. My standard answer to Ann was, "Oh sure, we slept just fine. We are just tired, that's all!"

This was the way we all lived for two years. In that time, Grandmother kept getting worse. Finally and sadly, she died on her birthday at age eighty-six of natural causes after a short stay in the hospital. Our daughter, Judy, who was eleven at that time, had a very large teddy bear–shaped birthday card for her grandmother. Circumstances did not allow her to give this card to her grandmother before she died. Judy was upset about this and decided to just tape the card to her bedroom door, in memory of her grandmother. This card has remained on the door for many years, even though Judy has grown up and moved away.

We all had a lot of adjustments to make with the passing of Ruth and Ann's mother. We had lost a member of our household.

If there was an upside to all this, it was that Ruth and I got our bed back. Since we moved into the house two years ago, we had never slept in it. We had to adjust to the fact that I no longer slept on the living room sofa and could now sleep with Ruth in our own bed again. For us, it was as if we just moved in! After the grief of the passing of her mother diminished, we were able to resume our normal love life in our "new" bedroom.

One day, Ruth, Ann, and I were shopping in a nearby department store, and we heard a dog barking. This was very unusual. We knew that dogs were not allowed in the store. We followed the sound to a corner of the store and were surprised to find that they had a small pet section. The barking dog was a frisky white miniature poodle puppy that jumped up and down when it saw Ruth and Ann. The twins were so attracted to this dog that they bought it! This was their first pet dog. They named it Daisy. For all their life, the twins wanted a pet dog. Now they had one. This was the first of a long series of pet dogs for the twins.

As time passed, more dogs came into our household. Here again, the twins were making up for lost time and kept adding dogs until they had seven, each of a different breed! Ruth and Ann assumed total responsibility for the dogs. They walked them, cleaned up after them, fed them, trimmed them, bathed them, and took them to the veterinarian. They were not a burden to anyone else in the household. They were, however, a financial burden!

The rear of our new house had a large awning-covered flagstone patio. We removed the awning in the fall and put it back up in the spring. The awning was forty-five feet long, and it took every member of our household to remove it and put it back up. This was a semiannual formidable task. We decided to have the patio enclosed with sliding glass doors and screens. Then we installed heat and air conditioning units, making it usable year round. This became everyone's favorite sunny room. We often had our evening supper on the patio. Naturally, we had an outdoor gas grill adjacent to the patio. Ruth and Ann would not go near flame or fire, so the responsibility for operation of the gas grill was given to me. I was often called on to cook the meat for our supper.

Chapter 35

Ruth's Health

A Good Doctor

Ruth's blood pressure was always in the normal range. After the birth of our second child, there was a slight rise in her blood pressure that caused the doctor to prescribe a minimal dosage of pills to lower it to normal. It seemed to be nothing to be alarmed about. Unfortunately, as the years went by, her pressure was slowly rising, causing her to need an increasingly higher dosage of medicine.

At that time, a specific type of over-the-counter painkiller tablets were available. They really worked well and had been universally in use since the 1940s. Our medicine cabinet was always well stocked with them. Ruth and Ann loved working in their flower gardens all day and were almost always outdoors, enjoying their hobby. Garden care and landscaping is a vigorous activity requiring extensive use of all the body muscles. The twins learned that these tablets worked quite well in reducing the pain of overworked muscles.

Quite simply, the medicine allowed them to get twice as much work done in a day. The recommended dosage was four tablets a day. Ruth and Ann worked from sunup until sundown, so in the long summer days, this could be twelve or more hours. Four tablets a day didn't keep their pain away, so they increased their dosage to six or often eight a day. This went on for several years.

Then, the Federal Drug Administration found that these tablets damaged the kidneys and removed it from the market. In retrospect, Ruth and Ann had damaged their kidneys. Kidney function and high blood pressure are closely related. Ann's kidneys weren't in as bad a shape as Ruth's since she had never been through childbirth. Ruth's kidneys started to fail, and her blood pressure went up. I took Ruth to a nephrologist, the proper doctor for this problem. After much testing and diagnosis, the doctor solemnly informed us that if Ruth didn't have one of her kidneys removed, she would die. This was devastating news! We had only been in our nice new home for a few years, and now this!

It seemed that I might lose my beloved wife. This was terribly upsetting to Ruth and me, and she cried a lot. This was a very serious situation, and I wanted a second opinion. My intuitive, negative feeling about this doctor was reinforced by his terrible bedside manner. For whatever reason, I couldn't find anyone to recommend another nephrologist. They seemed to be scarce. In desperation, I turned to the yellow pages of the phone book. There was only one nephrologist listed.

I called him and made an appointment for Ruth. He conducted an extensive testing of her condition. Several days later, he called on the phone to tell us that Ruth's condition was definitely not serious enough to require kidney removal. In addition, he had consulted with two other doctor friends of his, and they agreed with this diagnosis. He then informed me that he had a copy of all these records and wanted to deliver it personally to our house. I thanked him and told him that he didn't have to do that. He then informed me that it would be no trouble because, from the knowledge of our address, he lived in the house right behind us, and he would be there in a half hour!

This was how we met the doctor who lived behind us! We were so happy to get this news. Ruth cried. We considered that he had saved Ruth's life and were indebted to him. I considered him a good doctor. Naturally, he became Ruth and Ann's nephrologist.

Chapter 36

Raising the Children

Their Mother Loved Them Very Much

As the children grew up, Ruth and I continued to have a wonderful life together. It seemed impossible, but we loved each other even more with the passage of time. Ann continued to love our children almost as much as Ruth did. After all, they were her twin sister's children. We were very indebted to Ann for providing us with built-in babysitting and a caring love for our children. In that and many other respects, I loved Ann for who she was, my wife's twin sister. I always tried to be a good brother-in-law.

As each of our children approached the age of ten years, they became naturally more cognizant of and sensitive to their surroundings at home. Since they were not a twin and were still children, they had difficulty understanding adult twin stuff. It was all very strange and confusing to them. The children recognized that they had a problem in understanding adult twins, so they naturally looked to me for understanding and guidance whenever they had a problem. I was not a twin, and I better understood their problems.

Family

They wanted to know why their mother was so different from other mothers that they knew. I had to explain it all to them. They seemed to understand that twins are like one person who is split into two persons. Twins radiate sharing, loving, and togetherness. These qualities contribute to the unity of families.

There was one point that I always drilled into our children. I impressed on them that their mother loved them very, very much. The observation that their mom and dad also loved each other very, very much helped the children immensely.

Children tend to take many of the positive things in their life for granted. On the negative side, child psychologists tell you that the permanent presence of more than two adults in the child's home is detrimental to their successful upbringing. This is absolutely true for the average, nontwin person. The home with twins, mixed with average people in it, can be totally beneficial to all concerned as long as there is a compromise on the part of both of these types of people. My household was always a living testament to this.

Ruth had only one problem in raising the children, and that was the twin stuff. As a twin, Ruth did not, in any way, understand sibling rivalry. I was constantly reminding her that our children were not twins! She could not believe that it was natural for our children to fight with each other, even just a little bit, and wanted to punish them for doing so. When our children were just scrapping, it upset Ruth so much that she cried. She could not bear to see her children fight. I knew that this confounded the children, and I had the impossible task of trying to explain this whole thing to them while they were still too young to grasp it. Up until this point, I thought I had all the twin stuff under control.

I was fully aware that twins live in a different culture, and fighting with one another is a breach of their culture. It took all the power of the great love between Ruth and me to enable her to back off from this and let me handle the everyday minor scraps between a brother and sister.

On the positive side, Ruth, as a twin, was a great teacher of love, understanding, and kindness for our children. If ever you need a person to teach love and kindness, get a twin to do it. The children could always count on either their mother or father to help them through their everyday childhood problems.

Ruth and I repeatedly took our children to every amusement park and theme park within two hundred miles of our house. Most of the time, Ann went with us. This was good for Ann. We enjoyed seeing our children happy, so a great time was had by all. In addition, we made sure that all the annual holidays and birthdays were special for our children. For vacations, when the children were young, we always made sure our destination had something that Ruth and I liked and also had something that was appealing to the children.

Ruth and I always spent New Year's Eve at home with our young children. At midnight, the children were always asleep in bed. We would not have cared if they stayed up to see the New Year in, but they always grew tired and went to bed. At the stroke of twelve, Ruth and I would kiss each other and then run upstairs to our children's bedrooms to say a prayer for them and kiss them as they slept. Then, Ruth and I would kiss and hug each other for a while. This was where we wanted to be for New Year's Eve. No parents loved their children more than we did.

As our children grew up, I became more and more of a buffer between them and their mother. This was not in the sense that I was attempting to separate the children from Ruth. You have to understand that twins living under the same roof spend a lot of time with each other and spend a lot of time being concerned about each other. The average, nontwin mother does not do this. The average mother does not have another person in their house to distract them.

I am not saying that Ruth neglected her children at all, because she didn't. It is just that when Ruth was busy with Ann, the children couldn't get any one-on-one time alone with their mother. Ann did not understand why the children couldn't discuss everything and anything in front of her and her twin sister. This just doesn't work!

Alone is something that twins don't understand. So the children came to me instead with their problems. I made sure they understood what was going on. There were many times when the children had good one-on-one time with their mother. They loved their mother just as much, if not more, than a nontwin mother. Our children could see and feel the great love that their mother expressed toward them. A twin knows how to express love better than anyone else. The children couldn't help but notice this.

The subject of politics never came between Ruth and me. I didn't care whom she voted for or what political party she favored. Likewise, she didn't care how I voted. The subject of religion has caused a lot of stress and strife among married couples. Ruth and I were blessed by having the same preference in religion and church attendance. We have always been wandering Protestants, going from one church to the other. By that I mean that we might change churches once every five or ten years.

We deviated from this to establish stability for our children by remaining with the Lutheran Church for a twenty-year period, starting when they were old enough to attend Sunday school. For nearly all that period, Ruth and I sang in the church choir. This exemplary church activity on our part accentuated our involvement with the church, greatly benefited the children, and provided spiritual growth for our family.

As music lovers, Ruth and I always looked forward to our church choir activity. The Lutheran Church that we attended had a very large, forty-member choir. The choir director was exceptionally good. My voice was in the lower tenor range, and Ruth's was soprano. My ear was attuned to Ruth's voice, and I could always hear her singing in the soprano group. For me, her singing voice was like an angel. I became aware of this in my early days with her as we stood together and sang hymns in church. I don't see how anyone could not love Ruth.

With reference to choice of music, Ruth and I loved all popular music and dance music. We also enjoyed the semiclassical religious music of Christmas and Easter. In contrast, Ann preferred the semi-classical operettas. For all indoor household activities, Ruth had the radio tuned to the music stations. In those days, portable radios were bulky, heavy, and cumbersome. As a result, for all the many hours that Ruth and Ann spent outdoors in their flower gardens, there was no music. I am thankful that Ruth and Ann loved the quiet sunset and evening hours with no radio as we sat on the porch and just talked. I reflect on those times with warmth and fondness.

The deep love between Ruth and me seemed to be a foundation on which we could build anything or do most anything. We have been so fortunate to have this bond, this trust between us for all our life. We were both constantly learning to be a better person by being patient and giving attention and love to each other.

They say opposites attract. You could say that for Ruth and me. As a result of her personality and childhood experience, Ruth started out being very shy and timid. Being with me and facing life in general changed her a lot, for the better. In contrast to Ruth, I always had a great self-confidence and was ready for anything at any time. In this respect, she needed me, and I needed her to establish an emotional balance.

Very early in our relationship, I learned that Ruth loved to eat and lived to eat, preferring a solid, well-rounded meal. In contrast, I eat to live and prefer light, short, and quick meals. This never created a problem between us; I just ate less than she did.

I have always been the night owl, staying up late while Ruth was just the opposite. Ruth goes to bed feeling cold and wakes up feeling warm. I am just the opposite. This always causes an interesting exchange of blankets in the middle of the night!

We each had different hobbies and interests, over and above those that are common to the male or female gender in general. Ruth and her twin sister love to work in the outside garden. They each had a green thumb. Our property grounds looked beautiful and perfect all the time, thanks to Ruth and Ann. My interests and career were focused on electronics, physics, astronomy, and space exploration. My hobbies are amateur astronomy, amateur radio, and general photography. In addition, I am mechanically inclined and I have been quite successful over the years at repairing, fixing, or changing almost anything in the house.

Because I loved her, I got a lot of pleasure out of being with Ruth and helping her when she was working in her flower gardens. I liked being outdoors, close up to nature and breathing the fresh air. Ruth does not have a technical mind and could never get an in-depth understanding of my interests and my work. This did not bother her at all, and I didn't mind it. This did not interfere with our love in any way. We loved each other for who we were and what we were to each other. We were lovers! Nothing else mattered! Our love was great enough to cool the fires of any irritation that presented itself.

In spite of all our differences, my personality and Ruth's seem to blend perfectly. The commonality of our interests in family rearing, home decoration, music, entertainment, dancing, and traveling by car were quite enough to render our relationship as one of very deep love and joy.

From the first grade and up, I tutored my children and helped them get through school. This included college for my son, Tom. This effort took a great deal of my time in the evenings and on weekends. I never regretted one minute of time I spent in helping my children with their schoolwork. Ruth loved me even more for doing this.

It is interesting to note that at the elementary and middle school level, Ruth was a far better communicator with the teachers. I dealt with the teachers on a purely intellectual level, which always turned them off. Ruth, on the other hand, dealt with the teachers on a purely emotional level, which always made them feel comfortable. Everything was fine as long as I let Ruth communicate with the children's teachers. In retrospect, I think that I clashed with the teachers because my comments were almost always misinterpreted as criticism to their individual styles and approaches to teaching. I had far less difficulty communicating with the faculty of the upper grades in high school and the college level.

As we live our lives, we are continuously learning and experiencing. Our education never ceases. I am not ashamed to say that some things took me quite a while to learn. Most of my personal decisions were made using logic and intelligence, which follows my training and experience as an engineer. In contrast to this, many times I have observed Ruth making an emotional decision that defied logic and intelligence but was, in retrospect, absolutely correct. I stand in awe at this column of here

When I remind myself of that one day in May in 1947 that I found Ruth at the youth gathering, I remember that I was being driven by forces unknown to me, by emotion, to do things that were not logical but led me right to Ruth. This leads me to the conclusion that intelligence filtered through the heart produces wisdom.

People have often told me that my life was the typical American dream. However, in my opinion, my life has not been that of the typical American dream. Marrying a twin certainly did not make my experience "typical!" Those who think my experience is typical do not have a clue concerning what it is like to live in the world of twins.

Our children grew into well-rounded adults. We always loved our children deeply and stood by them and supported them whenever they needed it. The deep love between Ruth and me held us together and helped us weather the storms of our children's adolescent and young adult years. As any parent knows, there are many big storms to endure.

Unfortunately, it seems normal for young adults to assume that they know everything and are just as smart as can be. They don't see it, but they are lacking in experience and are unwilling to listen to the advice of anyone older and more experienced. In our youth, Ruth and I did not go through this phase. We always respected our elders. In this, we were very unusual and, in retrospect, blessed.

Ruth spent a lot of time alone with me and a lot of time alone with the children. All this gave her a great deal of experience in being a nontwin. This did not make her any less a twin, but it made her a twin with experience outside of the exclusive world of twins. This was a significant thing for her. As an identical twin, she was unusual in that she had no trouble in leaving the twin world and fully entering the nontwin world. In contrast, Ann never left the twin world. She lived in the nontwin world while constantly maintaining her twin identity.

Chapter 37

Ann's Life

She Tolerated Her Husband

When they first got married, Ann's husband, Jim, provided her with a companionship that was greater than that which Ruth and I could ever have provided. This was a good thing. We were more than fully occupied with our own lives and could not afford to give Ann the full companionship that she deserved and needed. Jim was never able to make the adjustment from single life to married life. And he didn't have a clue as to how to deal with twins. He was constantly disturbed and confused by their twin stuff. Also, he did not know how to deal with babies and young children. It seemed to me that he considered the children as competition to him. Which meant that his mental maturity was at their level, and he treated them as if they were undesirable competition.

Sadly, as the years went by, he became less and less of a companion for Ann and withdrew into himself. I tried to give him advice, but my discussions fell on deaf ears. They never had any children. Ruth and I never interfered with Ann and Jim's relationship or marriage.

Ann more or less tolerated her husband as he was contributing very little, other than money, to the upkeep and maintenance of the

household. As the years went by, he became more and more with-
drawn from his immediate surroundings at home.

Jim was insecure and not very intelligent and was accustomed to
telling lies, half-truths, and just plain fiction to impress those around
him. He was not really connected to the real world around him. Ann
didn't realize how extensive these characteristics were until she had
been married to him for several years.

Many times, we would find paper money lying on the driveway
next to his car. For whatever reason, he carried his money in his pants
pockets rather than in his wallet. When he got out of his car, apparently unknown to him, loose money would fall out of his pocket.

In an attempt to bolster his self-confidence and importance, he
claimed that he was good friends with important people. He claimed
first-name-basis acquaintance with a judge, three state policemen,
the vice governor of the state, and a county councilman. In addition,
he proudly claimed that "everybody knew him" at the local food market, drug store, bank, auto repair shop, and department store. He did
not realize how immature all this sounded to the average person.

In his immaturity, Jim had a childlike mind. He considered all
children as competition to him and behaved accordingly. He always
attempted to belittle my two children as they were growing up. We
were able to deal with this as my son, Tom, grew up. However, he
declared outright war against my daughter, Judy. He became obsessed
with the defamation of Judy.

Jim realized that his immaturity was always showing, and he
went to great lengths to shield this from those around him through
outright lies and exaggerations. This attribute was most difficult for
me during the time when my daughter, Judy, was growing up. He
was always accusing her of wrongdoing or misbehavior. Many times,
with the full knowledge of the truth, I defended Judy against his
accusations. Of course, Jim's family knew nothing of these problems
in our household. Often, Ann found it easier to accept him as an
adult and thereby incorrectly defended him. Later, she expressed
regret in doing that.

With all his idiosyncrasies, Jim was not malicious and not a bad person. He just couldn't find a place in society. He was sophomoric and expressed megalomania.

Then, there was the day that I discovered that he was an exhibitionist. It was five o'clock in the afternoon. I knew that he had just come home from work and was in his bedroom. I needed to ask him a question, so I went to his bedroom. To my astonishment, I found him lying in his bed, totally naked and masturbating while watching TV.

He seemed totally undisturbed that I had entered the room. He expressed no shame. This was not normal on his part. I told him that he shouldn't be doing that at this time of day. He simply replied, "Oh, I do this all of the time!" This was very bad. Obviously, Ann had never caught him doing this, as she was always busy in the kitchen at that time of day.

I hastened to Ruth and told her what I had discovered. I expressed to her that he was a menace to our children and us and that he shouldn't be living with us. Ruth was very distressed at this, but she proceeded to protect her sister by exclaiming, "I agree with you, but don't tell Ann about it! She has enough to worry about!"

I knew that this was not the correct thing to do, but I honored Ruth's request and didn't tell Ann. Our children disliked Jim and never went near him unless requested to do so by an adult. If it had been up to me, I would have thrown him out of the house immediately!

The only reason that Ann's marriage lasted was that she always had her twin sister as a companion in the house. She was able to get release from the frustrations of her marriage by concentrating on Ruth and me and the children.

It was Christmas Eve in 1983. The usual festivities of gift giving and a family Christmas dinner were planned for Christmas Day. Jim, as usual, had retired to his bedroom after supper. In typical fashion, Ann was doing her household chores so as to have the next day cleared of domestic duties. She had completed the ironing and was carrying the ironing board to its storage place in the garage. There were four downward steps leading to the garage. As she descended the stairs, she tripped and fell to the garage floor, with the ironing board on top of her. I was nearby and heard the crash. I rushed to her aid, helping her to her feet. She couldn't stand on her right foot. I helped her up the stairs and to a nearby kitchen chair.

I then called our neighbor doctor friend and told him what had happened. He rushed to our house and examined Ann's foot. He thought that she had broken her ankle. He was a senior member of his hospital, and he called and told them that he was bringing Ann in his car to the ER for an x-ray of her foot.

Ruth and I were busy with typical late Christmas Eve activity, and our two children were similarly occupied. Ann and Jim's bedroom was located at the outer end of our ranch house. It was a fact that you couldn't hear anything going on in the rest of the house from their bedroom. As a result, Jim had not heard any of the commotion with Ann's accident. It was after eleven o'clock at night, and we knew that he usually went to sleep at that time.

Ruth and I were very busy preparing for Christmas Day activities with Tom and Judy. As usual, Ruth and I would be up early the next day to get to church for choir rehearsal. We assumed that Jim would eventually come looking for Ann.

At midnight, Ann and the doctor returned. She had broken her ankle, and her right leg was in a cast up to her thigh. She had to use crutches to walk. She didn't want to go down the six stairs leading to that end of the house to get to her bedroom. She decided to sleep on the sofa in the living room instead. After making sure that Ann was comfortable on the sofa, we all retired for the night.

When we awoke on Christmas morning, we found Ann still on the sofa. She was very angry with Jim. He had not come to see what had happened to her. He spent all Christmas Eve night there in his bed without missing her and wondering where his wife was! Later in the morning, when he finally showed up, he was confused and couldn't believe that Ann had broken her ankle. Well, Ann was so angry that she told him to pack up and leave immediately. What a Christmas Day that was!

Ann started divorce proceedings immediately. They had been married for twenty-five years. The proceedings went on for years. In that time, I took Ann to see her lawyers and to attend court many times. The fact that Jim's name was on our house deed complicated matters considerably. When we bought the house, I recommended that Jim's name be excluded from the deed. I have never been an "I told you so" person, so I didn't remind Ann of this fact.

As part of the settlement, Ruth and I had to give Jim a large sum of money representing his one-fourth investment in our house. Ann had no money, so it was up to Ruth and me to come up with the money. I was happy when the divorce was finally completed. As fate or luck would have it, less than six months after the divorce, Jim died of a heart attack while at work at the young age of sixty. Ann did not attend his funeral.

As a result of Ann's separation from her husband, she became a very close friend of the unmarried doctor who lived in the house located directly behind ours. This was the best thing that ever happened to Ann. He was an affectionate, kind, and caring man and a good companion for Ann. The doctor and Ann obviously liked each other very much but never got married. Since his house was right behind ours, it was convenient for Ann to walk between houses. She spent some nights at his house and some nights at ours. Her daytime residence was always at our house. She cooked at and cleaned both houses. She had breakfast at his house and lunch and supper at our house.

The doctor almost always ate supper with us at our house, after which, he and Ann walked to his house for the night. He took Ann on vacation with him to exotic places in the Bahamas, Hawaii, and upscale destinations in the States. He owned a beachside condominium at nearby Ocean City, Maryland, where he spent a week for all the national holidays. This is where Ann spent the holidays with him. For the first time, Ann was leading a happy life. Of course, this made Ruth very happy.

Chapter 38

The Middle Years

I Really Didn't Retire

Whenever the chips were down, Ruth and I always stood by each other. And there we firmly stood, as a unit, all by ourselves, facing the world together. We did not need anyone else. This is the way it should be, and this is the way it is with true love between a couple. We never ran to anyone else with our problems, not even her twin sister. We faced life together and made decisions together.

Our children, Judy and Tom, managed to graduate from high school, survive their teenage years, and eventually grow into responsible adults. When Tom decided to go to college, I volunteered to tutor him through it.

As adults, our children were able to look back on their lives with firsthand appreciation for what they had as young people. They have asked us, "How in the world did you ever put up with us?" The answer is found in one word—*love.*

Through much time and effort, Ruth and Ann kept the grounds around our big ranch house ablaze with colorful flowers and shrubbery. It was the talk of the neighborhood. Ruth and Ann often

Family

acted as landscaping consultants for many of our neighbors. I was convinced that they could have easily been successful landscaping contractors. While they worked together on the gardens around our house, it seemed to me that because they were twins and thought and acted alike, they actually did the work of four people!

In that time period, I began working on a project at NASA that involved many field trips to NASA centers from coast to coast. Often, I was away for several weeks at a time. Ruth and I didn't like this, but it was very good for my career, and I was promoted to supervisor. For my entire career, these business/field trips were all full of adventure, both on the job and for the time that I was just a tourist. I have documented these adventures, and they make a separate story of their own.

Our large home with two and a half acres of ground with its large living room and large enclosed patio became the focal point for many social events and parties. There were church choir parties, birthday and anniversary celebrations, bridal showers, baby showers, family reunions, and retirement celebrations. Also, the major annual national holiday celebrations were held at our house.

All this naturally required the preparation of the proper food for these occasions. Ruth and Ann loved to cook, so this need was adequately met, to say the least. With two ladies cooking in my kitchen, I never had the opportunity, desire, or need to cook anything. Since I eat to live, I never had the desire to interfere with any kitchen cooking activities. The exception to this was my volunteering to wash the pots and pans and dishes. It was the least I could do since I didn't help with the cooking.

In contrast to this, I was in charge of cooking on our outdoor gas grill. The ladies would not work with fire or flame. They were always pleased with whatever meat I cooked. So I guess you could say that I did cook, but not in the kitchen!

Generally, Ruth and Ann did not follow or keep up with the advances in kitchen and household appliances. They continued washing the pots, pans, silverware, and dishes by hand at the sink even though there was a dishwasher in the kitchen. It took a little time for them to start using the dishwasher on a regular basis.

In addition, they did not want a push-button dial telephone in the house. They continued using the old rotating hand dial telephone. As they aged, they gradually and finally agreed to use the latest technology devices.

In 1982, Ruth and I celebrated our twenty-fifth wedding anniversary. In the afternoon, we were covertly asked to run an errand that would take two hours to complete. In the two hours of our absence from home, all the guests arrived at our house. When we returned and walked through the front door, our church choir director was playing the wedding march on our piano, and we found our big ranch house totally filled with relatives and friends that Tom, Judy, and Ann had secretly invited. We were expecting a few people but not the crowd that overflowed our house. A great time was had by all, and we received many beautiful gifts.

In 1989, at the relatively young age of sixty, I retired from my job with the federal government and went back to work at the same place as a contractor with NASA. So I really didn't retire.

In this period of time, I was once again working at NASA's nearby Goddard Space Flight Center. There was a dance club on base that had dancing lessons plus two hours of dancing every Wednesday starting at five o'clock in the afternoon. Every Wednesday, the doctor brought Ann and Ruth to NASA by car, where they joined me, and we had a pleasurable evening of dancing.

Other Great Vacations
Hawaii

Our Seating Arrangements Were Messed Up

In 1987, I decided to surprise Ruth with a trip to Hawaii for our thirtieth wedding anniversary in June. In March, I made all the airline and hotel reservations. In May, I surprised Ruth with the news. She couldn't believe that it was true and thought that I was just kidding. I convinced her that it was true and told her of the itinerary.

Our day of departure finally arrived. Our first stop was Phoenix, Arizona. I wanted Ruth to see the year-round beautiful flower gardens. She was not disappointed in what she saw. While we were there, I decided to take Ruth to see the Grand Canyon. When we arrived at the Canyon, I found that I couldn't keep her awake for longer than a few minutes. This was due to the high altitude of seven thousand feet. I didn't have this problem. At that time, I didn't realize that this was a precursor to future health problems for Ruth.

Next, we flew from Phoenix to San Francisco. After checking in to our motel, we drove down the famous very steep, winding road at Lombard Street at the time when the flower gardens were in bloom, which made a big impression on Ruth. Then, we went to see Fisherman's Wharf, Pier 39, and Golden Gate Park, all of which Ruth enjoyed immensely. The next day, we went for the famous cable car ride up steep inclines to the summit at Nob Hill. Then, we drove across the Golden Gate Bridge to Sausalito and on to Vallejo, both of which were nice, picturesque towns.

In the evening, we visited the famous Fairmont Hotel on Mason Street. We had dinner there at the fancy restaurant that had a large pool in the center. A full playing orchestra on a moving platform came from behind curtains at the side of the pool and came to a stop in the center of the pool, where it remained stationary and played ballroom-style dance music. A circular dance floor surrounded the pool, and that was where Ruth and I danced. That was definitely an evening to remember.

The next day, on our flight from San Francisco to Honolulu, we found that our seating arrangements were messed up, and we had separate seats. I complained to the stewardess, stating that were on our thirtieth wedding anniversary. Happily for us, she moved us up to two vacant seats in first class! We definitely enjoyed that trip.

The sun was shining brightly when we arrived at the airport in Honolulu. When I stepped out into the sunlight, my bald head immediately told me that the sunlight was hotter than anything I had ever experienced. This was because we were closer to the equator at 21.3 degrees north versus the 40 degrees north at home. I realized that I was going to wear a hat when outdoors!

To the delight of Ruth, beautiful tropical flowers were everywhere. We liked the banyan trees. We stayed at a modest hotel in the Ala Moana area. We were disappointed to find that the sand at Waikiki Beach was black and coarse and uncomfortable to our bare feet.

Since there was never any cold weather, we were amazed to find that all the hotels had no front doors. To accommodate this, the hotel entrances were well covered, and the front desk was set well back. Almost all restaurants had either a covered or uncovered outdoor dining area. Since there was a proliferation of beautiful tropical birds of all kinds, you found that they were very tame, and while you were eating, they also occupied your dining table and chairs! You had to *shoosh* them away while you ate.

On a serious note, we went to the Pearl Harbor Visitor Center and the Battleship Missouri Memorial. The Punchbowl National Cemetery was very beautiful and impressive.

We visited Waimanalo Beach, which was very beautiful, and visited the Polynesian Cultural Center. Nothing represents the Hawaiian Culture better than attending a luau, the traditional pig roast in the ground. There was a copious amount of Polynesian food and much native Polynesian dancing, including the hula. At the luau, Ruth and I felt as if we were experiencing in real life what we had seen many times in Hollywood movies.

We enjoyed attending the many and various night club shows. During one of the shows, we were surprised when the MC went into the audience, grabbed Ruth, and pulled her onstage to dance with the chorus line! You know, she did very well, and she didn't miss a step! She got a big round of applause from the audience. The MC congratulated her in doing so well and told her to come see him if she ever wanted a job dancing! This tells you something about Ruth's personality.

We had no trouble finding a place to eat. We found that fried chicken was on many of the menus, and this pleased Ruth. Of course, we also enjoyed the Polynesian food. I noticed that there were interstate highways, but none were connected to the mainland United States!

All too soon, it was time to go home, and we were waiting for our flight at the Honolulu Airport. Young identical twin girls, perhaps in their twenties, were sitting near us, so Ruth started a conversation with them. She informed them that she was an identical twin, and we were on our thirtieth wedding anniversary.

They were astonished that Ruth had found a nontwin like me that not only tolerated identical twins but also had been married for thirty years! They explained how much trouble they had in trying to find a nontwin guy that would tolerate the twin stuff! They said that Ruth was very fortunate to have found me and that I was a very unusual guy! Later, as a result of this conversation, I got a very nice kiss from Ruth! I must say that Ruth and I packed an awful lot of lovemaking into this trip!

Cancun

The Mayan Temples Were Fascinating

My daughter Judy's new friend Frank owned a timeshare at the Royal Caribbean Resort in Cancun, Mexico. In 1991, Frank and Judy generously invited some members of Frank's family, my son, Tom, and Ruth and me to join them when they went there on vacation. We all got our passports and happily joined them.

I was familiar with the genre of Mexico as a result of my extensive experience in the southwestern United States. Nothing surprised me, and I was right at home. The locals did everything that they could to please us. The resort was beautifully laid out, right on the ocean with a large swimming pool. It was a typical tropical paradise.

We rented a van and enjoyed sightseeing in Cancun and visiting various shopping centers and eating in Mexican restaurants. Then, we decided to be adventurous and travel down the coast, sightseeing and visiting the various ocean resorts long the way. As we traveled, we went by many small villages. They lived in virtual shacks. The lower standard of living was evident everywhere.

Our first stop was the Xel-Ha Resort. The setting was nice, but it was in the early stage of development with only a few buildings complete. Following that, we traveled to the Xcaret archeological site. The Mayan temple ruins there were fascinating to visit. I climbed to the top of one of the pyramids but found it very difficult to come down. It was scary!

Our last stop was at the Chemuyil Resort. It was more developed, and we enjoyed a nice supper there and then sat on the beach for a while. As the sun set, we began our long journey back to Cancun.

The food was not from the United States, and in about five days, I got sick and was out of circulation for a day. This did not spoil the trip for me. Ruth, of course, did not have this problem. In all, we had a very good time.

Bermuda Cruise

A Meclizine Shot

In early April of 1992, Ruth and I went with friends on a week-long trip to Bermuda on the *Westward*, a large Norwegian cruise ship, out of New York to celebrate our upcoming thirty-fifth wedding anniversary. Ruth and I had never been on a cruise before. I was impressed with the size of the ship. It was the largest ship at the dock. Upon leaving New York, it was interesting to have a close-up view of all the harbor landmarks, such as the Statue of Liberty and the Verrazano Narrows Bridge.

The two-day cruise to Bermuda was cold and cloudy. We couldn't use the outdoor deck area and pools at all. However, the indoor dancing, shows, movies, casino, entertainment, and food was good. I was interested in the ship control room and command center, and I went for a tour. For me, it was the most interesting place on the ship. Ruth did not go with me.

Our first stop in Bermuda was at the town of St. George. Bermuda is a series of islands. The Bermuda air was much warmer and pleasant and very clear with no pollution. The town was very pretty and quaint with the British heritage and flavor everywhere. We noticed that most homes and buildings had bright-white roofs. Pastel colors were dominant with shades of light blue, pink, or brown. The mailboxes were painted bright red and were cylindrical. We also noticed that all the roof downspouts emptied into a huge barrel instead of directly to the street. We saw the traditional British policeman dressed in their black shorts.

Our second stop was the town of Hamilton on another island. There, we went for a glass bottom boat ride and saw tropical fish that we had never seen before. We visited the Gibbs Hill Light House. We were surprised to find that Hamilton had a KFC (Kentucky Fried

Chicken)! We went to several night club shows that were different and enjoyable. Ruth and I both liked the steel bands music. The few days that we had in Bermuda were great. The weather was good, and we enjoyed the island sightseeing and the beauty of the tropical paradise.

The cruise back to New York in the Atlantic Ocean was miserable. There were huge, forty-foot waves and high winds in excess of forty miles per hour. Again, we were limited to indoor activities. The ship captain apologized to the passengers for keeping the ship tilted at twenty degrees all day long in order to keep on track to New York. With everything tilted, it was difficult to just walk anywhere. Eating was difficult and clumsy. The crew was busy just keeping the floors clean of spilled food.

In addition, the forty-foot waves caused the ship to rock up and down, fore and aft. All this was too much for me. I got really seasick. I stood in a long, miserable line waiting to get a meclizine shot at sickbay. The shot did the trick, but it took about an hour for me to feel better. I was happy that Ruth, with her cast-iron stomach, did not have any problem. I vowed to never again travel the North Atlantic Ocean by boat!

Chapter 40

Big Changes

Becoming Grandparents

It was a happy time in 1993 when our daughter, Judy, married Frank, the love of her life. She was married at a nearby Presbyterian Church, and I arranged for the wedding reception at a facility that offered both indoor and outdoor areas. The weather was kind to us, and we used the outdoor facility. I am biased, of course, but that was the best wedding and reception that I can remember.

My birthday was never celebrated on time because it was the day after Christmas. I shall never forget my sixty-fifth birthday celebration in early 1994. It was the one and only time in my life when my family was successful in arranging a surprise birthday party for me. In fact, it was the only big birthday party for me. They said that it was a very difficult thing to do. I am not easily tricked or deceived, and therein was their problem.

A large hall with a kitchen facility was rented. One hundred and fifty friends, neighbors, and relatives were invited and sworn to secrecy. Ruth and Ann provided all the food. Most of the food was prepared and cooked by them. They cooked all the food while I was away from the house at work. Many neighbors graciously agreed to store the cooked food in their refrigerators.

They were successful in making me believe that I was going to a party for a distant friend of mine. I was surprised and overwhelmed to find the hall filled with so many of my friends and relatives. The hall was festively decorated, and there was a DJ, music, and dancing. Thanks to the twins, I had a wonderful time.

The deep love between Ruth and I flourished through the autumn of our lives. We were so blessed to have each other. She was the love of my life, and I was the love of hers. Old friends and new friends kept reminding us that there was "something special between us."

One evening in April of 1996, the doctor did not show up on time for the usual supper that Ann prepared at our house. This was not unusual; a doctor's schedule is hardly ever regular. We waited for a while and then placed a telephone call to his house. The line was busy. Again, this was not unusual. An hour later, we became concerned and walked to his house to see what was happening. Ann, of course, had a key. We found him dead from a heart attack on his kitchen floor with the phone in his hand. This was a very traumatic experience for Ann. She had lost the love of her life. He was only sixty years old.

The doctor was very fond of Ann, and in his will, he left the largest part of his estate to her. She was now a rich lady! She paid off the remaining mortgage on our house and reimbursed Ruth and me for the money we had to pay to her ex-husband for his portion of our house.

In August of 1996, at sixty-seven years of age, I noticed that I would often break out in a cold sweat and become short of breath for no apparent reason. Also, physical exertion seemed to make me unnaturally tired. For my annual physical exam, my GP doctor said that my heart sounded okay and that my electrocardiogram also looked okay.

One day, as I was sitting at my computer at work, I became aware that my heart was not acting normally. I calmly asked the man sitting next to me to take me to the hospital. Upon arrival at the hospital, I was informed by a cardiologist that my heart rate was 180! It took a while for them to get me back to a normal heart rate. Further testing showed that all my heart arteries were 98 percent blocked and that I was scheduled for open heart surgery first thing in the morning! At this point, all my family was there at the hospital.

My five-bypass open-heart surgery went well, and my family visited me in the cardiac care unit. The following day, I was alert and sitting up in bed. Four days later, I was at home. I had never been to a cardiologist in my life. In hindsight, this was a big mistake.

My recovery from the open-heart surgery was not swift. It took many months for complete recovery. I was informed that the reason for my clogged arteries was high cholesterol as a result of improper eating habits. This made sense. I loved fast food and was constantly eating it! Needless to say, I stopped eating fast food and began a low-cholesterol and low-fat diet. I could now do physical labor without ill effect. I considered that my open-heart surgery was the best thing that could have happened to me!

In April 1997, my daughter, Judy, gave birth to her first child, a boy. Ruth and I were now proud grandparents. When he was a year old, Judy, of necessity, went back to work. Ruth was still working full-time, but Ann was not. Ann volunteered to provide daily babysitting at our house for her brand-new great nephew. Our kitchen and laundry room were very large and provided adequate space for him to roam and play. In addition, there were two adult dogs and two puppies in the kitchen with him. They were Ann's dogs. So my grandson grew up in our kitchen with dog playmates. This was an experience that my grandson enjoyed tremendously.

In May of 1997, as the fiftieth anniversary of our first date approached, I was inspired to treat this occasion with the same fanfare as a fiftieth wedding anniversary. I reserved a room at an upscale restaurant for the occasion and had fiftieth anniversary decorations. I had balloons, cards, and gifts for Ruth. Our immediate family was there, and all had a good time.

On a warm summer afternoon, Ann, Ruth, and I were walking the pleasant streets of our neighborhood with Judy and her family. We noticed that there were several homes for sale in the neighborhood. Ann commented that she would like to see the inside of the homes. When we rang the doorbell, the owners, with the knowledge that we were neighbors, gladly let us inspect their houses. When we returned home, Ann asked Judy and her husband which house they liked the most. They replied that it was the second house that they visited. Ann astonished us all by generously announcing that she would buy the house for them!

Judy and her husband stated that they could never repay her for the house because it was very expensive. Ann replied, "I don't care! I just want you to have it!" Two months later, Judy and her family happily moved in to their new house located just two blocks from our house. In fact, we could see her house from our rear windows, and she could see ours from her breakfast room.

Meanwhile, Ruth continued working as an office receptionist on a full-time basis. She rode to work with one of her lady office workers who generously provided to-and-from transportation.

As a result of declining health and aches and pains, Ruth and Ann's physical activity in tending the flower gardens began to taper off. This meant that I had to make time to do some of the outdoor work.

When in the house at night, Ruth began asking for brighter bulbs in our lamps, stating that she couldn't see very well. She had cataracts in her eyes that dimmed her vision. I had to convince her that we didn't have dim lights and that it was her vision. After removal of the cataracts in her right eye, she claimed that our kitchen lights were too bright! Shortly after removal of the cataracts in Ruth's eyes, Ann had her cataracts removed. What else would you expect from a twin?

In 1998, I retired from full-time work and began a twenty-hours-a-week schedule at NASA. This was satisfactory as I also had my retirement income. In my retirement, I became busier than I had ever been!

In 2002, as the forty-fifth anniversary of our wedding approached, I was inspired to plan a big surprise celebration in the same manner as a fiftieth. I invited everyone that we knew and hired an orchestra for dancing. Ruth was indeed surprised and pleased.

Ann developed a serious case of congestive heart failure. The excessive fluid in her legs and feet eventually caused her to be unable to walk. She became confined to a wheelchair. Judy's husband was a contractor and kindly built wooden ramps for our doorways for Ann to use. This did not stop Ann from cooking and house cleaning. I became an expert at lifting her wheelchair in and out of the trunk of my car.

Both Ruth and Ann's kidney function was slowly declining. The nephrologist had them on medication that decreased the rate of decline. This was good. However, it did not stop the decline.

Ruth's health declined to the point where she couldn't walk more than thirty feet or so without getting out of breath. We had no idea what was wrong. Finally, her doctor sent her for a lung function test and analysis. The results indicated that she had pulmonary embolism, a serious problem of blood clots in the lungs. This considerably reduced her overall lung area and explained why she was breathless and couldn't walk far.

She was hospitalized immediately. The doctor correctly suspected that her twin, Ann, had the same malady, and they both ended up in the hospital at the same time in the same room! The hospital staff had a tough time keeping their records straight. They both had the same birthday, so this was useless to tell them apart. In addition, they looked identical, and the staff had to ask their names to tell them apart. They were the talk of the hospital. The twins were pleased and amused with the notoriety that they received!

When Ruth came home from the hospital, she required oxygen. I rented a portable oxygen generator for her to use at home. Whenever she left the house, we used a small oxygen tank. Ann's condition did not require oxygen.

As Ruth's kidney function declined, she became subject to frequent urinary tract infections. The typical signs of this condition are incoherence or the lack of the ability to think or talk clearly and sensibly. This was easy for me to determine with Ruth. Whenever I noticed her in this condition, I told her that she had to go to the hospital right away, and I took her there. She was always in the hospital under heavy antibiotics for at least ten days or two weeks, during which time I stayed with her all day. I lost a lot of time from my job at NASA, and they very kindly allowed me to do this. In 2005, Ruth was in the hospital six times with this condition.

At this point in time, Ann could not propel herself up a ramp, and it was difficult for her to go down. Someone had to help her. That someone was always me. We tried letting Ann go down the ramp by herself, but it ended in a catastrophe one day when she rolled off the edge of the ramp and fell out of the wheelchair. It took a month for her bruises to go away.

Ruth didn't need a wheelchair, and she could get around in the house quite well with her walker. However, she didn't have the strength to help Ann on the ramp. So before I went to work, I took Ann down the ramp and left her in the kitchen.

In the years of the decline of Ruth's and Ann's health, it was obvious to me that I was needed to provide help to them in their daily life. They both slept in recliners in the same bedroom with me as I slept in the bed. I did not allow either one of them to get up in the middle of the night to use the bathroom without me helping them. I didn't want them to fall. Over their repeated objections, I kept Ruth's walker and Ann's wheelchair out of their reach as they slept. This forced them to wake me at night to use the bathroom. I didn't mind doing this because I could always go right back to sleep afterward.

Ruth had painful heel spurs. I removed a lot of the pain by rubbing her heels and feet every night. I carried the soiled clothes from the clothes hamper to the washing machine and the dried and ironed clothes to the bedroom. I set up the ironing board for them. I carried all the groceries from the car to the kitchen. I carried the trash to the garbage can. Whatever they couldn't do anymore, I did.

In early 2006, Ruth went to the intensive care unit at the hospital with pneumonia. I stayed with her every day she was there. She never came home. I was devastated at her death. I had lost the love of my life. I cried a lot. So did Ann. The passing of Ruth left a big void in my life. For Ann, her twin, her first love was gone. She had no children, no immediate family. Legally, she was all alone in the world. She had the love of her sister's children and me, her brother-in-law. I had earlier promised Ruth that, if she passed away, I would take care of Ann.

I was left with the singular care of Ann in her wheelchair. Taking care of Ann helped a little bit in missing Ruth. Ann became fully aware that I continued to take complete care of her even though Ruth was not around. This was the final step in my bonding with Ann. When I took her to the hospital for tests, the nurses would ask me to leave her room for a procedure but she exclaimed, "No! I want him to stay! He is my next of kin!"

Fortunately, I was able to go to work on a regular basis and take care of Ann. Before I left for work in the morning, I would see that she was secure in the big kitchen-laundry room in her wheelchair with all the supplies that she might need, including a change of clothes. Next to the kitchen, there was a powder room toilet for her to use. She was busy all day getting her meals, watching television, feeding and taking care of her two dogs, cooking supper for my son and me, and doing the laundry.

In the evenings and on weekends, Ann insisted on going outside in her wheelchair on the front walk with a small shovel and a trash bag to weed the flower beds for as far as her shovel would reach. Her desire to take care of her flowers was very strong.

Unfortunately, Ann's health continued to decline. Several months later, while she was in the intensive care unit at the hospital, Ann decided that she didn't want to live with all the tubes and apparatus to keep her alive. She had all her life support removed and called all of us to her bedside to say good-bye. One day later, she had gone to be with Ruth on the other side.

I was surprised to find that I cried at Ann's passing almost as much as I did with Ruth. I was left with the care of Ann and Ruth's canary and pet dogs, two white Westies. The canary was old and died about a month after Ann's passing. The dogs were only five years old and had a few good years left.

Chapter 41

Life without the Twins

The Phone Stopped Ringing

The year 2006 was a blur for me. I had lost Ruth, the love of my life. What I missed the most was the oceans of love that she had for me. I missed the casual love she expressed in her everyday activities and the deep love that we shared in our intimate moments together. In my opinion, my Ruth was the most beautiful, gracious, charming, loving, kindest, sweetest, and sexiest girl that God ever created. There is no way that anyone can be prepared for this great void in your life. In addition, I had the agony of Ann's passing to endure. In keeping with what Ruth always said, I indeed had "double trouble" all the way to the end.

I decided to stay in the big ranch house after Ruth and Ann passed away. At that time, life was very difficult for me. I had come full circle. Before I met Ruth and Ann, I was an only child, raised in an atmosphere of isolation in the big mansion where I grew up. Upon marrying Ruth, I was thrust into an environment of communal living that lasted for forty-eight years. Except for the fact that my son, Tom, who had never been married, was still living with me, I was once again single and relatively alone.

I was grateful to have my son with me. That helped a lot. However, we had never been alone together, and with our differing personalities, we had to learn to get along with each other. That adjustment took some time.

I was working two days a week at NASA, and my son worked full-time. My son got up much earlier than I and left for work before I got out of bed. Also, as a result of his long commute, he did not get home until very late. I went to bed earlier than my son, so I only spent about two to three hours with him per day, which included supper.

I couldn't put my life back together with the most important piece of it gone forever. I had trouble in finding my identity. I literally didn't know what or who I was supposed to be. I found myself crying a lot for no apparent reason. I was miserable without Ruth. However, I was not looking for another person to take her place. I did not want to get married again. Having lived with two ladies for most of my life, I confess that I missed the constant female companionship.

After Ruth passed away, the phone stopped ringing. None of our friends called me. No one came to see me. I felt cut off from the world I once knew. I couldn't believe that! Whenever Ruth and I heard of a friend that had lost a spouse, we expressed compassion and made a special effort to include them in our social lives. I couldn't help but think, *Hey, everybody! I'm still here!*

In all my life, I had never experienced the deep level of grief that engulfed me with the passing of Ruth. I had the irrational thought that I needed to go to Ruth's house on Longwood Street, where I first met her, and get her and bring her home. I found myself studying a map of the city to find the best route to her house. Then, I noticed that I was looking at the route from where I used to live in the city, not from where I now lived.

I realized that I was reminiscing to the pleasurable time when I first met her. It gave me some measure of solace to stare almost mindlessly at the map and let my mind relive those days when I was so happy when I drove to her house in my car. It took several weeks for this fantasy to go away.

For Ruth and me, music and dancing were a large part of our lives. After she passed away, I found that I couldn't listen to the nice music of our day and age without bursting into tears. However, I loved the music, and I missed listening to it. So I forced myself to listen to it. In the beginning, I could only stand a few minutes of listening before turning it off. Five minutes of listening turned into ten, ten into fifteen, and eventually, I could listen for hours.

Listening to *our* music gave me much pleasure. Often, when I heard danceable music, I would hold my arms as if I were dancing with Ruth and dance all around the room. In addition, I would sing the words to the tune. Music and dancing has always been an outlet of pleasure for me. Even now, many years after her passing, I can still see Ruth standing next to me as we sang a hymn in church, and I can still hear her sweet voice singing.

Whenever I attended a party or a social gathering, I found myself attracted to the female groups instead of the male groups. I actually related to the female topics of conversation better than I did the male. This was a result of my living with two females for most of my life. When I joined the female groups, I explained the reason to them. They understood and were amazed and pleased that I could join in their conversation no matter how personal the subject was!

I realized that I was lonely for female companionship in my age bracket, of course. To address this, I studied my name and phone number list, looking for widows. I was surprised to find that there were four such individuals. So I called each one and had a nice conversation with each. In my conversation, I stressed the fact that I just wanted to have lunch or dinner with them, nothing more. I stated that I didn't want to get married, and I wasn't looking for someone to live with me! Obviously, this made them feel comfortable about having a date with a widower like me.

Thus began my dinner dates with these ladies. My son and daughter seemed to be pleased that their dad had lady friends and was dating! My son claimed that I had more girlfriends than he! I also took my lady friends dancing but found that none of them danced as well as Ruth did.

My life without Ruth is a terrible thing to endure. After a few months, people kept telling me that I should "get over it and go on with my life." Sure, I am going on with my life, but I am not going to get over it anytime soon.

All my stuff was in the garage, shed, or attic. Otherwise, the house was filled with the belongings of Ruth and Ann. I really didn't know what was in all the furniture drawers, closets, and shelves in the house. So I proceeded to methodically go through everything in the house. This was a very emotional and tearful process for me.

I found that the twins had enough clothing for four or five people! It took me three months to go through it all and give it to charity. I kept a few articles of clothing that had sentimental meaning, such as the dress that Ruth wore to our daughter Judy's wedding. I also rounded up all the good diamond rings and jewelry and put them in a safe, secure place.

It took me a while to start fixing the house with things that I liked. For whatever strange reason, Ruth and Ann never liked photographs of people hanging on the wall. They liked curio shelves, wall plaques, and knickknacks for the walls. In like manner, all horizontal surfaces in the house were filled with French provincial statuary. They had family photos sitting only on tables. So I proceeded to remove the plaques from the walls and fill the walls with family photographs. I removed the statuary and knickknacks from the tables and replaced them with photographs.

The twins liked to fill every square inch of floor space in the house with furniture. There was just too much furniture. When an acquaintance of mine walked into our house for the first time, he looked around and said, "My god! There's enough furniture in here for three houses!" To remedy this, I called an auctioneer and had him remove about one-third of the furniture in the house. This was actually a relief for me. I could walk freely through the house without wandering between furniture!

An even bigger problem was the extensive outdoor flower gardens that the twins had made. I couldn't keep them weeded because I didn't have the energy or the time. So I contracted a landscaping company and had them remove all the outlying flower beds and fill the area with sod.

Next, I had to deal with the large, wide flower beds that surrounded the house. I removed some of them and had the rest reduced in size to twelve inches wide. Finally, I had flower beds that were somewhat manageable. With all that reduction, it was still too much for me to handle alone. I had to get landscapers to weed the remaining gardens and keep them neat.

In 2007, I decided to take a vacation with my son, Tom. He had never traveled west of the eastern US coast. I had spent much time in the southwestern United States and grew to like it. I wanted my son to experience the grandeur of the Rocky Mountains, so we went to Colorado Springs, Colorado, for two weeks. My son was duly impressed with the sights in Colorado and became aware of the different, nice culture of the people. Also, my son was a train enthusiast, both real-life sized and small, hobby sized. Therefore, we went on numerous old railroad train rides throughout Colorado.

In my career as a scientist, I worked on many different programs, and I kept and brought home all my files on each and placed them in the attic for future reference. I also had memorabilia from my family in the attic.

It was too hot in the summer in the attic, and it was very dirty. It was no place to keep things that you liked or wanted. I went up in the attic and tagged every box and item as either trash or keep. Then, I got a commercial company to remove all the trash and place all the keep items on my enclosed patio. This filled my patio! It took me a year of spare time to clear out my patio! I had now filled every closet and corner of the house with boxes. However, it gave me pleasure to know that none of my things were still in that darned attic!

Then came the garage and the garage attic. We had a two-car-size garage that was filled with everything but cars. This area was our only nonattic storage space. When we moved in, I built large storage closets in the garage. In addition, my electronic workbench, tools, and woodworking machines occupied the garage. There was very little walking space in there! I had a commercial contractor come and clean out the garage attic.

Expensive, long-term routine home maintenance issues began to surface. I was ashamed of the appearance of the windows of the house. They were sixty years old and needed to be replaced. The roof started to leak a little and needed new shingles. The toilets were also sixty years old and needed replacement. The front walk was deteriorating and needed replacement. Thousands upon thousands of dollars later, all this work was completed. When the windows were replaced, my heating bill went down one hundred dollars a month!

Chapter 42

Reflections

In Everyone's Life, There Are What Ifs

As I sat alone at my kitchen table, finishing my breakfast, I gazed out at the midsummer scenery through the large picture window in front of me. There was an acre of lush green grass spread out before me with large old silver maple trees lining the street, the major thoroughfare upon which I lived. The solid walls of the large ranch house muffled the roar of the many cars and trucks that went speeding by.

Through my window, a decade earlier, I would have been gazing at Ruth and Ann's many beautiful large flower beds, birdhouses, and birdfeeders that filled the property surrounding the house. All this was gone now, as I didn't have the energy, time, or money to keep them. The small flower beds that now surrounded the house are manageable.

My big ranch house was now very empty without Ruth and Ann. It served us so well in the years when the children grew to be teenagers and then adults. My memory is filled with the many happy social occasions that filled the calendar and our house with good cheer and good friends and relatives as the years went by

I was very lonely but certainly not idle. I missed Ruth's love and everything she did for me. It was evident that the interior of the house and outside grounds were no longer Ruth and Ann's. The property was mine, and I had altered it to suit my interests and desires.

In everyone's life, there are what ifs and turning points that shape our lives either for the better or the worse. The turning points in other people's lives can also be seen as directly affecting our life. I have earlier emphasized this in the prologue of this book and in chapter 9, "The Important People." It is not mentally healthy to dwell on the what ifs in our lives, but I find it interesting to consider the possibilities.

I proposed marriage to Ruth once, when she turned eighteen in 1950. She accepted it but postponed it. We discussed getting married three times after that. The next time was when she came to see me while I was in the army in Georgia in 1951. When I got out of the army in 1953, we again discussed it. The final time was our engagement in 1956 followed by marriage in 1957.

How different our lives would have been if we had gotten married in 1951 or 1953. Ruth was willing to get married and move away from her mother and sister in 1951. I know this for sure because, in her letters written to me while I was in the service, we were drawing our house room layout sketches. There were no rooms indicated for anyone but her and me and a nursery for our children. I still have these letters.

I predict that, if we were married earlier, we would have more children than two. I have no idea where we would have lived, but I assume it would have been in the local area. After our second child, Judy, was born, Ruth stated that she would like to have *more* children. This didn't happen.

When I look back at Ann's life, I remember her first job in the working world as the librarian at the Peabody Institute of Music at Mount Vernon Place in downtown Baltimore. She liked her job very much, and it seemed to suit her personality. She stayed there for two years or more. During that time, Ruth was lobbying Ann to quit her job and come work with her at the Traveler's Insurance Company, a job that definitely required an outgoing personality. As usual, Ann finally quit her job and went to work with Ruth.

It may be observed that this was a turning point, a crossroad in Ann's life. If she had stayed at her job at the library, her mental and physical health would have been considerably better, and it is likely that, in that environment, she might have met, fallen in love, and married some man that fit her personality. Thereby, her life would have been very much happier and healthier.

Unfortunately, staying with her twin caused Ann to have a significant on the job stress. The mental stress, the tension of trying to be something that she was not—namely, outgoing—caused her many health problems throughout her life. This is an example of the magnitude of love that she had for her twin. On one hand, she was happy being with her twin at the workplace. On the other hand, she was unhappy with her workplace duties and suffering thereby. What price being a twin!

If Ruth had been a nontwin and Ann was just her sister, it is likely that she would not have tried to get Ann to work at her office. It was "twin selfish" on Ruth's part to want her twin to come and work with her at her office. This twin selfishness is prominent and common in the lives of identical twins.

I am extremely grateful that, for my growing up, education, career, love life, marriage, and family experience, I seemed to have been in the right place at the right time doing the right thing. Otherwise, I would not have been able to do what I did in my life, namely, let Ruth and Ann live their life together in their twin world with me, a nontwin who largely understood them. Were it not for Ruth's great love, none of this would have been possible.

Obviously, in the divine plan of life, I was supposed to stay and take care of my family. I am still in good health and working half time at NASA. My family is taking care of me. They make sure that I don't get involved in any strenuous activities by doing them for me. I appreciate this a lot. I've come to realize that I still have oceans of love coming from my family.

Appendix A

About Identical Twins

Introduction

They Live in Their Own World of Togetherness

I am not a twin, but I was happily married to one for forty-eight years, and I had known her and her sister for fifty-eight years. I think that this qualifies me as something of an expert on the subject of adult twins. The fact that my wife was an identical twin was the determining factor for my life being different and very complicated. The answer to the question "What is an identical twin?" cannot be given in one sentence or phrase. Indeed, a dissertation on the subject is required. My description of the idiosyncrasies of identical twins has its origin in the long-term, direct, firsthand experience with my wife and her twin sister. In addition, I gained knowledge from communicating with the many other identical twins that have crossed my path, and I have read many books on the subject.

A large majority of the world population is not twins, triplets, or multiple birth individuals. The average person who spends a limited time socially or in an office environment with a twin or twins may think that they understand them, but they really don't. They think that they are really "neat" and "interesting" simply because they look alike and act alike. The reality of twins is far deeper than just heat and Interesting. Every aspect of the life of a twin has a meaning unto its own for the twin.

Most people think that twins, or identical twins specifically, are just two average people that happen to have a brother or sister that looks exactly like them, and they get along with each other pretty well most of the time. Well, that is not all there is to it. Twins get along more than just "pretty well."

The life of a twin is one of constantly being concerned about the well-being of the other twin. Remember, they are both thinking this way, not just one of them. Therefore, twins are constantly iterating about each other and are concerned about the other one. From the standpoint of twins, only their minds are normal; our minds are abnormal! Twins know and understand that they are quite different from the average person. On the other hand, the average person does not realize the great difference between themselves and twins.

Twins do not think of themselves as separate individuals. They consider themselves as a unit. They express no individuality. You have to remember that you are always dealing with the unit, not the individual. When they are living together, identical twins make all their personal decisions together, as a unit. They usually wear identical clothing. They are not doing this for the fun of it. They do this because it is what they, as a unit, want to do. They live in their own world of togetherness.

In my opinion, twins are the most marvelous people in the world. I do not feel that I made a mistake in marrying an identical twin. However, with reflection on my considerable experience and knowledge of twins, I can easily see why there would be those that considered such a move as a mistake. Identical twins are not "normal" people. They require serious adjustments and tolerance on the part of any involved nontwin. In fact, they may be considered as living in a separate culture of their own.

The "baggage" that came with Ruth, first as my girlfriend and later as my wife, was the fact that she was a twin. This turned out to be very heavy baggage. On a daily basis, I fought the battle and bridged the cultural gap between the twins and myself. In this connotation, battle does not infer physical or mental confrontation. Rather, it implies that there is a big difference in the way of life and thinking between twins and the average person. This wall was always there.

This situation is a two-way street. The twins had to do the same for all their life: fight the battle and bridge the cultural gap between themselves and the outside world that they lived in. This is a bigger battle for the twins than it was for me. I lived in and was a part of the average world. The twins lived in their own world surrounded by alien people that neither thought nor acted in the way that they did. They were really only comfortable when in contact with another set of twins. I have observed this interface with great interest. Happiness is the best word to describe the interface between sets of twins. Their eyes light up, and they smile from ear to ear as their conversation proceeds. I could read their minds: "Oh, wow! Finally, somebody who thinks and acts like us!"

For me, the price that I had to pay for this experience was well worth it, in spite of the fact that from my standpoint, my life has been anything but smooth and uneventful. I had to overcome many problems and issues that the average person might see as impossible. I essentially allowed the twins to be twins and happily live in their own isolated world of unity and togetherness. In doing this, I departed from the usual life of a nontwin individual to live with these twin ladies. I sacrificed a normal, usual life for one of living with twins.

All of us who are not a twin generally find it easy to relate to and get along with our fellow man (ladies included). Those of us singletons, as twins call us, should consider the plight of twins. As far as twins are concerned, we are the weird and unnatural ones. We think and act in a manner that is absolutely alien to theirs. Essentially, twins live in their own culture in another world that is only understood by twins. So here they are, living in this world filled with people that don't think or act the way that they do, and they are really only comfortable when in communication with either their own twin or another set of twins.

Of course, there are exceptions to every rule. There are twins that do not follow all their characteristics, I do not look on these individuals with any disdain. You are who you are!

The intrinsic characteristics of twins are interrelated. Each subject does not stand alone and describes an attribute that is related to or dependent on other attributes. I have attempted to avoid redundant phrases and sentences in describing these characteristics. I confess that the key word here is *attempted*.

Decisions

Twins do not make decisions in the same way as we, the average person. For twins, the decision-making process is solidly prioritized. First and foremost, they consider how a decision will affect their twin. Second, they consider how this decision will affect them as a unit called twins. Yes, twins are a unit—don't ever forget that! They never consider how a decision will affect them as a person. Individuality is missing here. Twins use this decision-making process for all decisions, even for such mundane things as deciding what to have for supper. This twin thought process causes twins to have problems when making serious decisions concerning crossroads in life, such as college, career, or marriage.

Isolation

Twins absolutely do not understand or comprehend separation, isolation, or independence. Twins see this in the same light as we see pain and sickness! In fact, twins recoil from and avoid isolation as if it were the plague. Unlike the average person, a twin does not need or even desire, extended time alone. To keep their sanity, the average person needs space or time alone. For us average people, this isolation is an absolute requirement for maintaining a healthy mind.

For the twin, either isolation or separation from their twin has the opposite effect and is not only undesirable but terrible. It is very upsetting for a twin to be alone, really alone. To help you understand this, consider the fact that twins have been together since conception. Nature has produced a very different set of individuals here. Mentally, they are not like us at all. Nature has bonded them in a way that seems unnatural to us. In contrast, twins see their bonding as natural. *Togetherness* is one of their attributes and is their natural way of life.

It is as unnatural and cruel to permanently separate twins as it is to separate a mother from her baby. In fact, the bond between twins is as strong as, if not greater than the bond between mother and child. Twins know and understand that they are quite different from us singletons. On the other hand, most of us singletons do not understand and do not have a clue as to the sheer magnitude of the difference! The differences between people in race, culture, religion, or creed are comparable to the differences between the average person and twins!

The average person is constantly at odds with and challenging the people around them and the world around them. The average person needs quality time alone. Sometimes, the average person needs to be alone and work alone. A twin would find being left alone for an extended period to be very traumatic. For them, this is both unnatural and undesirable. For the average person, having a sister that you can't stand to be in the same room with is normal. A twin finds this concept foreign and unbelievable. Twins are different, and we should learn to accept them and understand them for what they are, a culture onto themselves.

Social Behavior

If you are just casually acquainted with an identical twin, you may not notice anything unusual about that person. If they are office mates or colleagues at your place of business, it is likely that you will not be able to detect any abnormality. Generally, they appear to be very nice individuals with a pleasant personality. And they are. This is typical of the identical twin. However, if you become more closely or personally involved with a twin, you may begin to notice a few strange quirks in their behavior. Your observations are totally correct.

Since twins decide things as a unit, they decide together what they will do. This makes twin relationships or socializing with the average person very complex. For instance, if one twin is going to a baseball game with a nontwin person, the decision to engage in this activity was made by the unit, not by that individual twin. The twins decided in advance that this would be a good thing to do. If both of the twins, the unit, had decided that this was not a good thing to do, that individual twin would not go. The twin that went to the baseball game has deceived the average person into thinking that they individually decided to go. So we see that twins are constantly engaged in this twin deception process that is transparent to the average person.

Love

The love between identical twins is greater and deeper than the average love expressed between individuals in the nontwin world. Identical twins are born with an intrinsic, caring love for each other. Twin love is the love between individuals of the same gender that has absolutely no sexual connotation.

Twins are very happy people, and they are made of love. A twin understands and reflects love better than the average person. The love between identical twins is awe-inspiring. Twins have a 100 percent tolerance for each other. This is difficult to imagine. This does not exist between any other individuals except twins, or perhaps triplets. Even the best of married couples do not have this.

On the absolute scale, twin love is ever present and unalterable. Twins understand the real meaning of the word *love* better than anyone else. The average person may think that because they have been in love for a long time, they really understand the meaning of love. On the relative scale, yes, but on the absolute scale, including twins, no. I know from the direct experience of being happily married to a twin that twins express a love that far exceeds the conventional definition of the word. You have to experience this to realize it and understand it.

If someone is needed to teach the subject of love, a twin should do it. If the world were full of twins, it would be very different indeed. There would be no hatred, violence, or war.

Sharing

With twins, sharing goes along with love and communication. No one knows how to share better than a twin does. Sharing is and has been a major part of their lives. They began life by sharing the same womb. As babies and children, they shared every intimate detail of each other's lives. Sibling rivalry is unknown to them. As adults, this sharing continues uninterrupted. To the twin, it is natural and normal. The desire to share is a part of their love for each other. The decision-making process is also an integral part of the sharing process. They always share each other's personal possessions, no matter what that might be. Twins share a wardrobe, cosmetics, food, and other things that the average person does not wish to share with anyone.

Twins desire to share each other's pleasures. You can see that sharing each other's boyfriends or girlfriends creates problems of great magnitude for all concerned. The business of dividing goes along with sharing. A twin will go to great lengths to divide something, anything, equally with their twin. It is common for twins to share or have a common bank account between them. For the average, nontwin siblings this is unthinkable. No way! If a twin is responsible for cooking for a family and is in charge of filling your plates, you can bet that the quantity of food will be divided equally among the plates.

Communication

A twin needs some kind of regular contact or communication with his or her twin. Communication between twins provides them with a physical and mental high that cannot be attained from any other source. Healthy, happy twins are twins in communication.

On the subject of twin communication, I read somewhere about a male twin that married a female nontwin. After just a few weeks into their marriage, the wife began to see that her husband was becoming moody and depressed. He had talked on the phone to his twin brother but had not been to see him personally. Through casual circumstances, they visited her husband's twin. After that visit, the wife noticed a big change in her husband's mental attitude. He was the same happy person she knew. The wife then realized that her husband needed to see his twin. So she purposely and casually made certain that he regularly went off to visit his brother. Well, I could have told her that!

Marriage

I have talked with and read about many young adult twins concerning the problem of finding a suitable mate in a world filled with nontwins. This is a serious problem among twins.

The problems encountered in courtship between a twin and a nontwin are generally misunderstandings that result in the separation of the couple. Marriage, sharing, communication, and love go together. Marriage is a most difficult endeavor for a twin. The nontwin thinks that they are dealing with an individual when they are not. They are dealing with a unit called twins. A married twin has two loves in their life. First, the love for their twin, and second, the love for their spouse. Note that the first love is always for their twin. As long as the married twin is in communication with their twin, the love expressed by that twin is enhanced and magnified. There is no greater love than that expressed by a happily married twin. I consider myself very fortunate to be the recipient of such love for an extended period of time.

In the standard marriage vows there is generally some statement that each individual is taking the other as their "one and only love." If a twin makes that statement, they are essentially telling a white lie. Their one and only love is that for their twin. When they marry, their spouse is their *second* love. They never give up their first love. The nontwin has to understand that this is the way it is. Like it or not!

This is the problem in twin-non-twin marriages. The nontwin does not realize it, but they have actually married the unit. In my case, I had two wives with all the disadvantages thereof and none of the advantages. My wife was always telling me that I had double trouble!

Twin Children

We are all children at heart. A lot of my knowledge of adult twins can be directly related to twin children. I suppose that the parents of some twin children are a bit mystified by the other-than-normal behavior of their children. What the parents do not understand is that the twins understand each other perfectly. It is us that they don't understand!

Often, the parents of twin children will mistakenly plan separate activities for them as if they were just plain siblings. To best nurture and serve the twins, all activities should involve interaction between them, not separation and isolation. Twins are individual people, but they are not isolated individuals as we understand the word; they are twins, and they are a unit. Twins think alike, and when speaking, you often find that one finishes the other's sentence. This characteristic exists for some nontwin individuals that have been married for a very long time.

Twin children are experiencing all the characteristics that I have described but not as in depth. With time and experience, as they grow, all the twin characteristics become reinforced and honed to perfection.

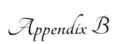

Return to the Mansion

I Just Stood There and Cried

The last time that my family and I visited my parents in the mansion downtown was in 1970. The children, Tom and Judy, were little and didn't really remember the place. Shortly after that, my father retired, and my parents moved into the house behind us. Unfortunately, my mother passed away in 1974, and my father sold the house and moved into an apartment downtown. A few years later, the church decided to move, and the mansion and property went up for sale. This was my last knowledge of the place.

In 2014, I began compiling notes summarizing the history of the various homes in which I had lived. With my curiosity piqued, I Googled the mansion address, and bingo, it had its own website! I was astonished at this and found that it had been purchased and refurbished by a large holding company along with eight other mansions in the downtown Baltimore Mount Vernon area.

With a phone number and e-mail address in hand and the information that this had been my home for twenty-two years, I began negotiating for a return visit to my old home. A few weeks later, I had arranged for a Saturday visit that included me, my son, Tom, my daughter, Judy, and my two grandsons. I loved the old mansion and was very happy to be able to visit it again. I knew that this visit would also explain a lot about me that my family didn't really know and understand.

On a warm summer Saturday morning, we met the two ladies who were our hosts in the park across the street, and we all approached the mansion. I noticed that the front doors were still the original from 1824. As I entered, I was engulfed with emotion. I was so happy to see it again and to see that everything was freshly painted and cleaned. It was so beautiful. I couldn't help myself. I just stood there and cried. Everyone comforted me. I gathered my composure, and as I looked around, I kept saying, "Oh, my! Oh, my!"

I took a video, and my son took photos as we walked from room to room and ascended the majestic stairway from floor to floor. I hadn't seen the place for thirty-six years, and my emotional high continued. It was exciting and interesting to my family as our hosts unlocked doors and led us through the hallways and rooms of the mansion. I explained what each room was originally as the mansion, what rooms the church used, and what each room was in the third- and fourth-floor apartment area where I lived.

Logically, the owners of the property had refurbished the electricity, plumbing, heating, and air conditioning, replaced the rear windows, and had installed all the amenities of the twenty-first century, such as Wi-Fi. With this, they were renting individual rooms or areas as office space. Evidence of this was everywhere as there were desks, chairs, tables, computers, and printers in many rooms.

As we descended the stairs, I slowly visited each room again, just to make it last. When we reached the first floor, I asked permission to visit the basement. With permission granted, my family followed me to the basement. The rooms had not been upgraded and were still typical basement. My family followed me to the room where there were large steel doors on the floor that covered the stairs leading to the dirt floor sub-basement. Unfortunately, some heavy equipment was stored on the doors, and we couldn't open them.

This area was used as a wine cellar in the old days. There was no electricity down there, and a flashlight was required. In all the times that I had been in the sub-basement, I never saw any rats, mice, insects, or seeping water.

With a bit of sadness on my part, the visit to the mansion drew to a close. I thanked our hosts for allowing us to visit and reluctantly went out through those majestic old front doors.

It was obvious to everyone that I knew a lot more than our hosts about the original purpose of the rooms and why they were arranged the way they were. As a result of my dissertation, our hosts claimed that they were now experts on the mansion!

About the Author

Born in Baltimore, Maryland, Gilbert Ruley Smith served in the military during the Korean War. He is a semiretired Physical Scientist / Engineer working part-time at NASA and is a Registered Professional Electrical Engineer. He is a member of the Optical Society of America. Part of his expertise is technical writing, and he is the author/coauthor of forty-three scientific and technical publications. He enjoys writing and finds it relaxing. This is his third book.

CPSIA information can be obtained
at www.ICGtesting.com
Printed in the USA
FSOW03n1301260917
39041FS